MURDER MOST WILDE

A RIGHT ROYAL COZY INVESTIGATION MYSTERY

HELEN GOLDEN

DREW BRADLEY PRESS

ALSO BY HELEN GOLDEN

A Right Royal Cozy Investigation Series

A Toast To Trouble (Novella)

Tick, Tock, Mystery Clock (Novella)

Spruced Up For Murder

For Richer, For Deader

Not Mushroom For Death

An Early Death (Prequel)

Deadly New Year (Novella)

A Dead Herring

I Spy With My Little Die

A Cocktail to Die For

Dying To Bake

A Death of Fresh Air

I Kill Always Love You

Murder Most Wilde

The Duchess of Stortford Mysteries (Coming soon…)

An Heir is Misplaced

A Husband is Hushed Up

ISBN (P) 978-1-915747-31-0

Edited by Marina Grout at Writing Evolution

Published by Drew Bradley Press

Cover design by Helen Drew-Bradley

First edition June 2025

To Lissie M

There is nothing on this earth more to be prized than true friendship
— Thomas Aquinas

We've shared deadlines, laughter, and more cups of tea than is probably healthy, and along the way we've built a friendship that's stood the test of time. Thank you for all your support.

NOTE FROM THE AUTHOR

I am a British author and this book has been written using British English. So if you are from somewhere other than the UK, you may find some words spelt differently to how you would spell them. In most cases this is British English, not a spelling mistake. We also have different punctuation rules in the UK.

However if you find any other errors, I would be grateful if you would please contact me helen@helengoldenauthor. co.uk and let me know so I can correct them. Thank you.

For your reference I have included a list of characters in the order they appear, and you can find this at the back of the book.

1

EARLY EVENING, THURSDAY 30 SEPTEMBER

Perry Juke's chest tightened as he stepped onto the stage of the Windstanton Theatre Royal. The smell of dust and old wood enveloped him, and a thrill of excitement shot down his spine. He looked out towards the red velvet seats, then up at the glittering chandelier. *This is it. I'm a real actor now.*

Emily Shaw, the stage manager, clapped her hands. "Alright everyone, listen up! This is our first walk-through in the actual theatre. With four weeks to go before we open, I expect you all to be off-script. No excuses!"

Noel Ashworth raised his hand, a sickly sweet smile on his face. "But, Em, my dear," he said in his best actor voice. "It's only been a month since the first read-through. And I have the most lines of anyone, you know."

Perry bit his tongue and stifled a huff. He was pretty sure he had just as many lines in his role as Algernon as Noel had in his as Jack, if not more. And anyway, Noel had only needed a small amount of prompting yesterday, so why was he pushing back on Em? *Should I say anything? No...* He didn't want to make waves. Especially as Noel seemed jumpier than usual today, his hand rummaging in his jacket pocket, presumably fidgeting with his ever-present vape machine. *The nerves must be getting to him too, even with all his experience.*

"I'm simply the messenger passing on Liv's instructions," Em said brusquely.

Noel turned to Perry and whispered, "And why isn't she here to tell us herself?"

Perry shrugged. This was the second time Olivia Belmont, the manager of the Theatre Royal by day and director of the Windstanton Players by night, had not been here to direct them in as many days. A short text from her an hour before rehearsals had simply stated that a family issue had come up and she would be late and that she would, "leave you all in Em's capable hands until I get there".

Em continued, "Kurt and Tom are on book and will prompt you if needed. But try not to need it, eh?" She fixed them with a steely look. "Now, this is the first time we're using all the props and doing blocking, so I'll be calling out the stage directions. Places everyone!"

As the cast scrambled into position, Perry's gaze drifted back to Noel. The actor's piercing blue eyes darted around the theatre as one hand ran through his dark wavy hair. *Has he lost more weight?* Noel's clothes seemed to be hanging off him these days. "Everything alright, Noel?" Perry asked quietly.

Noel's winning smile flashed, although it didn't quite reach his eyes. "Absolutely. Merely getting into character."

Perry nodded, and looking at the floor, he took a deep breath. *You can do this, Perry!* As he raised his head, a sudden movement in the backstage curtains on the other side drew his attention. Stella Vance, who played Gwendolen Fairfax, burst onto the stage, with her dark hair swinging and a look of confusion on her pasty face.

Is she okay? She looks a little sickly...

Em threw up her hands. "Stella, what are you doing here?"

Stella blinked, her forehead creased. "But I thought... Isn't this the full Act One rehearsal?" She glanced around as if seeking the other cast members she expected to be here.

Noel bounced forward, a smirk plastered on his face. "Stella, my dear, it was all very clear on the call sheet. We're doing the first part now—the scene before Gwendolen and Lady Bracknell arrive. Your bit won't start for another hour and a half," he said rapidly. His tone was light but with a snarky edge.

Red blotches appeared on Stella's cheeks. "I... I must have misread it. I'm sorry. I thought…" She trailed off as she met Noel's gaze.

Is she still *chasing after him?* Yesterday, Ralph Harvey, who was playing Lady Bracknell, had told Perry the whole sordid saga about Noel and Stella's recent dalliance—the older man always had the best gossip—until Noel had ended things shortly before they'd begun rehearsals. Seeing them together now, there was no denying the tension between them still.

Em sighed. "Okay, well, no harm done. Let's move on, shall we? Stella, we'll see you later."

Noel flashed Stella a dazzling smile. "Yes, I think it would be best if you left. No distractions, you know. I need to concentrate." He made a little shooing motion with his hand.

Stella's jaw tightened, and for a moment, Perry thought she might snap back. But she whirled around and stormed off, flicking the curtain behind her as she disappeared backstage.

Em cleared her throat. "Right. So in this scene, both

Algernon and Jack are revealing their double lives. But there's a key difference. Algernon revels in his deceit, while Jack is more sincere. A less skilled liar, if you like. Keep that in mind."

Noel raised a hand, his voice dripping with false sincerity. "Em, my dear, Liv already went over this with us. I think we've got it."

Rude! Perry gave Em an apologetic smile, then said, "I'm ready when you are."

Em gave him a grateful nod. "Fantastic. Places then. Kurt, you're up."

Kurt Grant, who played Lane, the butler, and who was Jack's understudy, took his position centre stage, holding a silver tray.

"Lane, you're preparing afternoon tea," Em called out. "Now Perry, make your entrance."

As Kurt's footsteps echoed on the hallowed wooden floor, Perry felt a sudden flutter of nerves. *No more cosy village hall; this is the real deal.* He squared his shoulders and strode onto the stage. "Have you got the cucumber sandwiches cut for Lady Bracknell, Lane?" he asked, the familiar dialogue flowing smoothly from his mouth.

As Kurt responded and the scene unfolded, Perry lost himself in the moment. He was no longer Perry Juke, the newbie actor. He was Algernon Moncrieff, the witty, devil-may-care bachelor based on Oscar Wilde himself. And he was absolutely loving it.

———

"Mr Ernest Worthing," Kurt announced in his best butler voice a short while later.

Perry grinned, his stomach fluttering. This was one of his

favourite parts—the verbal sparring between Algernon and Jack, who was pretending to be Ernest. Thankfully, it had been left very much as it was in the original script, having survived Liv's attempt to shorten the play to bring it down to a manageable one hour and thirty minutes, the maximum length she considered an amateur production should be.

Em's voice rang out, "Jack, enter now."

A grimace passed over Noel's face, then he lifted his chin and scurried to the centre of the stage, beaming. As they launched into their lines, Perry felt increasingly comfortable in his role as Algernon.

Liv's words from day one of rehearsals were still stuck in his head.

"Algernon's only passions are for food, drink, and his clothes, Perry," she'd said as the full cast had sat around the table in the village hall. "His life is one of deceit. He lives as an upper-class man without any means to support it. He lies about Bunbury, about the sandwiches, even about his name when he later pretends to be Ernest in the country. But he's not a wicked man, Perry. See him more as… er, morally flexible." Everyone around the table had laughed. "And, of course," she'd said with a satisfied smile as she'd looked around at them, "that's his purpose. To make us laugh."

But as Perry found his rhythm, Noel stumbled, his timing just a hair off. Kurt, who stood by the table, a copy of the script to hand, had to feed him lines more than once, earning an irritated glare from Noel each time.

After a particularly long pause, Em called for a break. "Let's take ten, everyone," she said, barely able to disguise the exasperation in her voice.

Fishing his vape pen from his pocket, Noel stalked offstage. *What's rattled him so badly?* Noel hadn't struck Perry as someone who would suffer from stage fright. Not after all these years of leading amateur productions. But there was no denying he was wound up as tightly as a Victorian corset today.

"Perry?" Em called from in front of the stage. He bounded over to her, always open to feedback that would help him improve. "You're doing a great job, you know," she said as Perry stopped at the edge of the stage. "Liv's right. You're a natural."

Oh my goodness! Perry beamed at the stage manager. "Thanks, Em. I have to confess, I'm really enjoying it."

Behind him, someone huffed. *Tom Hatlee!* Tom, who played Merriman, Jack's butler in the country, and who also doubled as Perry's understudy for the part of Algernon, stomped off the stage. A mutter of, "Natural my ar—" trailed after him as he disappeared behind the curtains leading backstage.

"Don't mind him," Em said with a sly smile. "Tom's a ham who wouldn't know talent if it came up and bit him!"

Perry turned and walked back into the middle of the stage just as Noel reappeared, a vape pen clutched in his hand, a determined set to his jaw. "Shall we continue?" he said as he stuffed the electronic cigarette into his pocket. "Don't want to fall behind schedule, do we?"

Em's face flushed a little, then she said loudly, "Right. Let's take it from Algernon's line about Cecily. Perry, ring the bell."

Kurt appeared in front of him, his back stiff in his role as butler.

"Bring me that cigarette case Mr Worthing left last time he was here, please, Lane," Perry said.

Em called out, "Algernon should take the case and keep it away from Jack's reach as you go through the next bit of dialogue."

Perry reached for the case Kurt presented on a silver tray, then playfully held it just out of Noel's reach as they bantered back and forth. For a moment, it felt like they'd found their rhythm. But then Noel went blank, his eyes darting to the wings, looking for Kurt. An uncomfortable silence stretched out. Finally, Kurt called out, "Give me my cigarette case first."

Noel repeated the line.

"Here it is," Perry said, handing over the case with a flourish. "Now about that explanation? And it better be believable."

Em's voice rang out, "Perry, take a seat. Noel, take out a cigarette, then offer one to Perry."

As Perry settled into the chair meant to represent a sofa, he eyed the prop cigarettes laid out as Noel held the case out. *I really hope they've sterilised them since the last time they were used.*

He gingerly took one as Noel began, "My dear fellow. My explanation is perfectly ordinary…"

Perry glanced at the prop in his hand. Even though he knew the fake cigarette only produced a harmless vapour, the thought of putting it in his mouth made his skin crawl. He glanced up at Noel, who had already placed his cigarette between his lips and taken a deep drag in between lines. *It's okay for him. He vapes all the time…* But still Perry hesitated, the prop cigarette poised between his fingers.

Noel suddenly coughed, waving his hand as if to clear the air. "That's strong," he said, frowning.

Kurt's voice piped up. "Old Mr Thomas Cardew—"

But Noel's face had gone flush, and he tugged at the neck of his T-shirt as if it were constricting him.

Well, that's it! If a seasoned vaper like Noel couldn't handle the prop cigarette, there was no way he was putting it in his mouth. *I could have a word with Liv again about whether we really need to use these horrid things at all.*

Em's concerned voice cut through Perry's thoughts. "Noel, are you alright?"

Perry's gaze snapped back to Noel, who was now visibly sweating, a confused expression on his face. Suddenly, he swayed, reaching out as if grasping for something to steady himself. The cigarette tumbled from his fingers and clattered to the floor as he clutched at his chest.

Perry's stomach plummeted to his toes. *Is he having a heart attack?*

He leaped from his chair, rushing towards his fellow actor. But before he could reach him, Noel's legs gave way, and he crumpled to the ground, gasping for air.

Thud!

His head hit the wooden stage as he took a final, shuddering breath.

A WEEK EARLIER. THURSDAY 23
SEPTEMBER

T*he Windstanton Echo* online article:

The Windstanton Players Prepare to Wow with Wilde

Windstanton's much-loved theatre group, the Windstanton Players, is set to delight audiences with their upcoming production of Oscar Wilde's classic comedy, The Importance of Being Earnest. *With rehearsals soon to move to the historic Windstanton Theatre Royal, excitement is building for what promises to be a sparkling evening of wit, charm, and theatrical flair.*

Olivia Belmont, the group's esteemed director and manager of the theatre, returns to the helm of this production. She's known for her ability to breathe life into well-loved classics by drawing out the essence of the work in a modern and authentic way. Belmont expressed her enthusiasm: "Wilde's writing is as fresh and funny today as it was when it debuted. We're working hard to make this a performance Windstanton won't forget."

The cast features a comforting array of familiar faces. Noel Ashworth steps into the role of Jack Worthing, the play's dashing protagonist. Known for his commanding stage presence, Ashworth has been a pillar of the troupe for years. Stella Vance brings her elegance and poise to the role of Gwendolen Fairfax, while the experienced Gina Travers takes on the part of Cecily Cardew. The ever-popular 'dame', Ralph Harvey, promises to steal scenes as Lady Bracknell, ensuring audiences are in for a comedic treat.

There are also two new faces. Amelia Trent has recently joined the Players and takes the role of Miss Prism. Trent is a TV and film extra, so is certain to bring a new perspective to the company. But the most surprising addition is Perry Juke, the business partner of the newly engaged Lady Beatrice, the Countess of Rossex.

Juke, who is married to Simon Lattimore, crime writer and co-owner of the popular new restaurant in Windstanton, SaltAir, is currently working with the King's niece on furbishing the purpose-built recovery complex for military personnel and veterans, Three Lakes, which is situated outside Fawstead. The facility is the passion project of ex-army officer, Lord Frederick Astley, who, like his sister Lady Beatrice, currently lives at nearby Francis Court estate, the home of their parents, Charles Astley, The Duke of Arnwall, and the King's sister, Her Royal Highness Princess Helen. The opening date of Three Lakes has not yet been confirmed, but it is expected to be after the royal wedding of Lord Fred to Ms Summer York on 20th November.

Making his debut with the Players, Juke takes on the role of Algernon Moncrieff. Although new to the world of amateur theatre, he is already being described by insiders as "a natural talent" and "a breath of fresh air".

Tickets are selling fast, with the public opening night scheduled for Wednesday 27th October and the final night for Saturday 30th, so be sure to book your seats soon at the theatre box office or online!

THE NEXT DAY. FRIDAY 24 SEPTEMBER

L ady Beatrice, the Countess of Rossex, couldn't help but grin as she read aloud from the *Windstanton Echo*. "…he is already being described by insiders as a natural talent…" She raised her eyebrows at her best friend, who was sitting over the other side of the staff room table at the Three Lakes rehabilitation centre. "I feel so honoured to be in the presence of such an acting genius," she said, raising her hand to her chest. "Is that why I've hardly seen you for the last few weeks? You actors don't want to mix with the likes of us—"

"Stop!" Perry cried, trying not to laugh. "I know you're jealous of my newfound fame. Can I help it if it turns out I'm the next Lawrence Olivier?" He slapped the back of his hand to his forehead and looked off to the side.

"It's true," Bea said, bowing her head in mock agreement. "We both know how much I love the attention. But I do have one concern." She furrowed her brows deliberately as she rose and stared at the door. She tutted. "I think we might need to get these doors made bigger. You know, to make sure we can fit your head through them!"

They both dissolved into laughter as Bea sat down again. She wiped her eyes. "Seriously," she said, reaching out and patting Perry's arm. "I'm so proud of you. You know that, don't you?"

Perry's blue eyes sparkled with delight as he took her hand and squeezed it. "Oh, hush," he said, letting her hand go and running his through his spiky blond hair. "I'm really loving it, Bea. Honestly. It's the most fun. I can't wait until we're in the actual theatre." He gave her a beaming smile.

Bea smiled back. She'd really missed spending time with him lately, but it was worth it to see him this happy. She scooped up her cup and took a swig of hot black coffee. "And you're still getting on with everyone?"

Perry's nod was a little stilted. "Mostly," he said, taking a sip of his drink.

She paused and tilted her head to one side. "That's not as enthusiastic as the last time we talked. What's up?"

Perry sighed theatrically. "Most of them are still lovely. It's just a couple…" He trailed off as he took another sip of coffee.

"Do tell," Bea said.

"Well, there's Noel Ashworth—"

Bea remembered the article she'd read. "He's the one playing Jack?"

Perry dipped his chin. "He's been with the Players for years and normally takes a lead role. He's a bit erratic. Charming one minute, then snarky the next. He's fine with me, quite pally, really. But with some of the others, he's… a bit of a bully, I suppose."

"Really? I'm surprised Olivia's not dropped him by now. I wouldn't have thought she would have time for anything like that." Bea had met Olivia Belmont during a local investigation they'd been involved in earlier in the summer, and she couldn't imagine the theatre manager taking any nonsense from anyone.

"But that's the thing. He makes these subtle digs and 'suggests' things all the time with this smile on his face that makes it look like he's being nice and helpful." Perry put down his cup. "Oh, and he's always calling everyone 'my dear', but it's said with a slight sneer."

"So you don't like him then?"

Perry spread his hands. "As I said, he's fine with me. And he's an excellent actor, that's clear. We have a lot of fun doing the banter Algy and Jack have. It's just there's this… er, tension when he's around. It's a shame…" He looked down at his cup and turned it around. "Then there's Tom."

Bea didn't recognise the name. He hadn't been mentioned in the news report.

"Tom Hatlee—he's playing Merriman. He's the butler when they're in the country, but he's also understudying my role. He seems to have it in for me."

"What do you mean, in for you?"

"He keeps giving me these looks. He has to act as my prompt, and the minute I pause, you know, for comic effect, he immediately jumps in and feeds me the lines. I think he's trying to make me look like I don't know what I'm doing."

Bea suppressed a smile. Perry could be a tad dramatic, and this didn't sound too serious to her. Maybe this Tom was a little overkeen in his role as prompt? "But why would he want to do that?"

Perry leaned towards her. "So according to Ralph—"

"Playing Lady Bracknell?"

Perry smiled. "You've remembered well. Yes, Ralph's huge fun, and he makes a really great dame. He knows everyone and everything, having been there since the beginning. He says Tom has had his nose put out of joint because

Liv brought me in to a lead role that Tom thinks should've been his."

"I suppose that would explain it then," Bea agreed.

"I know, and I felt a little bad about taking the role from him. I talked to Liv, but she said not to take any notice. She said he's nowhere near as good as he thinks he is. She gave him a significant part in their last production, and she said he was more hammy than a pack of bacon."

Bea snorted into her coffee.

Perry let his shoulders sag. "I'm hoping he'll get bored with it all soon."

"Try not to worry," she said, wiping her mouth with a piece of kitchen roll. "You're clearly the perfect man for the part. Don't let anyone make you doubt that."

Perry smiled. "Thanks, hun. I can't believe I've never thought to give acting a go until now."

Bea nodded. It really seemed as if Perry had found something he was truly meant to do. Her ribs squeezed tight as it suddenly hit her that she didn't quite feel that way about her life. Of course, she loved being a mother to Sam, and she was very happy doing interior design. She was proud of the refurbishing projects she'd worked on. She'd even admit to receiving a massive sense of achievement from being part of a team that had successfully caught a handful of killers over the last two years.

All of it had been immensely satisfying.

But none of it had felt like her *true* purpose.

Something niggled in the back of her memory, making her think she'd felt it fleetingly at some stage in her life. Earlier. *But when?* She couldn't put her finger on it, but she felt certain it had been before her husband James had died seventeen years ago…

"Bea?" Perry's voice dragged her from her thoughts. "Are you okay?"

She mentally shook herself. *Your life is great. Your son is thriving. You're engaged to a wonderful man. You have fabulous friends. You're working on a project here at Three Lakes that will change lives.* She was so lucky. She smiled at Perry. "I'm absolutely tickety-boo."

"Good," Perry said, but his smile faltered as his blue eyes clouded over with concern. "I wish I could say the same about Simon."

Bea's eyes widened, and she leaned forward, her red hair falling over her shoulders. "What's wrong with Simon?" Perry's husband was the most stable and content of all of them. She felt a little breathless suddenly. *Isn't he?*

"He's stretching himself too thin since we got back from holiday." Perry blew out a breath, running a hand across his chin. "Between being at the restaurant on weekends and trying to hit his writing deadlines, he's barely got time to breathe."

Bea had thought Simon, winner three years ago of the TV show *Celebrity Elite Chef*, had been taking on a lot when he and Ryan Hawley, the fine dining chef and TV's *Bake Off Wars* judge, had purchased Clary House in Windstanton earlier this year. Both of them had poured their heart and soul into the downstairs restaurant, SaltAir, and despite the discovery of the skeleton of the previous chef in the wall of its dining room, all of their hard work had paid off, and SaltAir had opened on time in July to much acclaim. It had been busy all summer, and the monthly supper club, SaltAir Fine, held in the more formal supper room on the first floor, kept selling out within minutes of the dates being announced each month.

But Simon also had a very successful career as the author

of the best-selling Detective Inspector Billy Pike crime series, drawing on his experience as an ex-detective at Fenshire Police.

No wonder he's feeling overwhelmed.

"And now his agent's planning this massive book tour for next year—Europe and the States. It's celebrating his tenth book. Can you believe it?" Perry continued, beaming with pride before his expression sobered again. "But he's not sure how to fit it all in. And then there's Isla."

Simon's nineteen-year-old daughter had recently started university in Spain.

Bea smiled. "How's she settling in?"

"It's only been fresher's stuff so far, but she loves it. She's desperate for us to visit and see where she lives. But with my rehearsals and Simon's schedule…" Perry trailed off, looking dejected.

Bea's mind raced, seeking a solution. "What days are you rehearsing at the moment?"

"Wednesday through to Saturday. Why?"

"And Supper club isn't this Sunday at Clary House, is it?"

Perry shook his head. "No, it's the second Sunday of the month."

Suddenly, her green eyes lit up. "I can cover everything here for a few days. Why don't you and Simon fly to Barcelona on Sunday morning and come back on Tuesday?"

"What, this Sunday?"

"Yes. Before your rehearsal schedule gets even crazier."

Perry's face brightened. "I suppose we could do. Are you sure you don't mind holding down the fort here?"

"Of course not! Go and see Isla. It will be good for all of you."

"I think you're right," Perry said, grabbing his phone and typing. "I'll see what Simon says right now."

Bea watched his fingers fly across his phone screen as she took a sip from her coffee cup, a contented smile on her face.

Perry finished, then placed his phone on the table in front of him. He leaned back in his chair, a mischievous glint in his blue eyes. "So, anyway, enough about my drama. How are you and Rich coping with all the press attention? The news outlets still seem to be pretty obsessed with the two of you."

"Tell me about it," Bea replied. "There are still paparazzi camped outside Francis Court. We're having to leave via the trades entrance. We always knew it was going to happen as soon as we announced our engagement…" Her smile faltered a touch. She hesitated.

"But?" Perry prompted.

"It's Rich. As you would expect, he seems to be taking it all in his stride, but I'm worried about how it's affecting his job. He says people are treating him differently now. He's working more and more from The Dower House and letting Fred rope him into stuff here at Three Lakes."

"Which he's enjoying, isn't he?" Perry interjected.

"Yes, but… I can't help feeling like I've ruined his career." Bea's throat tightened, her eyes stinging. *Get a grip, Bea!*

Perry grabbed her hand. "Honestly, Bea, I get the impression he's never really enjoyed this new job as much as he did when he worked for PaIRS."

"Exactly! But he can't go back to royal protection now we're together, so basically being with me has taken away the job he loved."

"And he knew what he was doing when he left there for City Police. He chose you, Bea, and I don't believe he regrets it for one minute."

Bea gave a wobbly smile. "I hope you're right, Perry. I simply want him to be happy."

"He *is* happy, you daft bat. He's got you!" Perry squeezed her hand. "Talk to him, okay? Don't bottle it all up."

Perry's right. Rich had chosen her. He'd chosen this life. All she could do was love him and trust that together they could face whatever challenges lay ahead.

Perry reclaimed his hand and picked up his coffee once more, eyeing Bea over the rim of his mug. "And how's Sam coping with everything?"

Bea smiled at the mention of her son. "Oh, you know Sam. Rugby and food. That's all he cares about these days. He and Archie are loving the informality of sixth form." She chuckled. "And get this—they've made Archie a prefect."

"No!" Perry's eyes widened in mock horror. "That's unexpected."

Bea nodded in agreement. Sam's best friend, Archie Tellis, was chaos personified. "Indeed," she said, imagining the mischief the two boys were likely getting up to. "I'm grateful the press seems to have left Sam alone for now. Wilton College has been very supportive." Sam's boarding school in Derbyshire had several high-profile parents and took security seriously.

Perry nodded, his expression turning sly. "And what about the wedding? Any progress on that front?"

Bea groaned, burying her face in her hands. "Don't even start. Ma's already talking about dates and plans. I'd hoped she'd leave it until after Fred's wedding in November, but apparently, that's too much to ask."

"Of course it is!" Perry laughed, his eyes twinkling. "Come on, Bea. You had to know she'd be wanting to get going. Two royal weddings in less than a year. She must be fit to burst."

"I know, I know," Bea said, lifting her head. "It's just... Rich and I don't want some grand royal affair. We want something simple, intimate. But I don't know if we'll be able to persuade her."

Perry pulled a face. "I hate to break it to you, but you don't stand a chance!"

Bea inhaled deeply. "I know." She'd hoped that her brother's wedding would be enough to satisfy her mother. And it wasn't as if this was her first wedding either. She and her late husband, James, had had the big royal wedding in London when they'd married eighteen years ago—horses, carriages, parading around the streets, even commemorative merchandise. It didn't seem appropriate to do that all again.

But when she'd pointed that out to her mother, Princess Helen had strongly disagreed. "The public looks to the royal family as a symbol of continuity and tradition, especially in uncertain times, darling. A royal wedding reassures them that the monarchy is strong and steadfast. So it's not only about you, Beatrice. It will bring joy to people across the country. It's a moment where everyone feels connected to something bigger than themselves. A national celebration. A historic moment. You can't deny them that." *What can I say to that?*

"Right, I suppose we should get on," Perry said, necking the last of his coffee. Bea gave a brief grunt of agreement and did the same. As they stood to leave, he glanced around the room, then out of the large window, a satisfied smile on his face. "This place is really shaping up, isn't it?"

Bea followed his gaze, looking at one of the three lakes, all of which had cabins spotted around their edges in amongst the trees. Pride swelled in her chest, seeing Fred's vision come to life. "It really is. Oh, and I heard the new centre's CEO will be appointed soon."

"Oh, yeah?" Perry raised an eyebrow. "Any idea who it is?"

"It's all being kept quiet at the moment. I think they want

to make a big announcement. All I know is that Fred, Rich, and some of the Care for Heroes board members finished the interviews at the end of last week and have made a selection. Speaking of which…" Bea checked her watch. "We should get going. We're meeting Fred and someone from the charity to look at the newly fitted-out cabin in ten minutes."

Perry's eyes lit up. "Brilliant! If it's up to scratch, does that mean we'll get given the green light on the rest?"

"That's the plan." Bea grinned, excitement bubbling up inside her as they left the staff canteen and made their way through reception and outside. She didn't know why she'd had a wobble earlier. *This is what I do. This is what I love.* Turning blank walls into something warm and inviting, creating spaces where people felt comfort, safety, and hope— it mattered. The cabins, this centre—it wasn't merely decoration. It was a way to help people heal, to give them a place where they could start over. How could she think this wasn't enough? It was everything she wanted: creativity, purpose, and joy. She was being silly. *This is enough, isn't it?*

4

FIVE DAYS LATER. WEDNESDAY 29 SEPTEMBER

P erry glanced at his watch again. Where in the world was Noel? He and Kurt, as Algernon and Lane, had just wrapped up their lines for the first scene of Act One, and now the entire rehearsal had stalled, waiting for their leading man.

Olivia Belmont paced across the creaky wooden floorboards of Windsham Village Hall, her petite frame casting a long shadow in the late afternoon sun that was streaming through the dusty windows. Her blue eyes flashed behind her glasses as she checked her watch for the umpteenth time. "This is ridiculous," Liv muttered, running a hand through her loose brown hair. "We can't waste time like this." She stopped and turned to face Perry and Kurt, her hands on her hips. "Alright, if Noel doesn't show up in the next five minutes, we're moving on without him. Kurt, you'll step in as Jack. I'll be Lane. We need to get on." Her tone brooked no argument.

Perry blinked slowly, trying to ignore the knot of anxiety forming in his stomach. He'd spent weeks perfecting his lines, even having practiced them while he'd been away with Simon in Barcelona. He'd fitted them in between being shown around by an excited Isla. But now they were home again, it was back to business. With opening night looming in four weeks, every minute of rehearsal time was precious.

He looked across at Kurt. His eyes were widening behind his glasses. A mix of surprise and excitement flashed across his face. "Of course, I'd be happy to help, Liv," Kurt said eagerly.

Perry raised an eyebrow. He'd always seen the man as quiet and reserved, more suited to his role as the bumbling Canon Chasuble or the serene butler Lane than the dashing Jack Worthing. Could the quiet, fidgety Kurt really pull off the confident, charismatic Jack? He suppressed a smile. *What if Kurt turns out to be brilliant and steals the show?* He caught Kurt's eye and gave him an encouraging nod.

Perry studied Liv as she resumed her pacing. Her mouth was tight, and her shoulders were rigid under her beige cardigan. Poor Liv. She was so eager to keep everything running smoothly. *I hope Noel has a good excuse to keep us all waiting like this.*

Liv clapped her hands together. "Alright, places, you two. Let's take it from where we left off."

Kurt nodded, squaring his shoulders. For a moment, Perry held his breath, wondering if they were about to witness an unexpected transformation.

"Mr Ernest Worthing," Liv announced in her best butler's voice.

"How are you, my dear Ernest? What brings you up to town?" Perry asked in Algernon's slightly bored voice.

Kurt stepped forward. "Oh, purely pleasure, dear boy. Why else would one be here?"

Perry's excitement quickly deflated like a punctured balloon. While Kurt recited his lines flawlessly, not a single hesitation or glance at the script, his delivery was as flat as

23

fizzy water that had been left to stand overnight. He'd none of the sparkle and energy that Noel brought to the role.

The scene limped on, but Perry's mind was already leaping ahead to tomorrow's rehearsal—their first in the hallowed arena of the Windstanton Theatre Royal. A flutter of excitement rose in his stomach. *My first time actually on the stage...*

As Kurt began the lines where he exclaimed Jack's love for Gwendolen, the door banged open with a resounding crash. Noel burst into the hall, his dark hair wild and his blue eyes fever-bright. *What on earth?* Perry blinked, taken aback by the manic energy radiating off the actor.

"Liv, my dear!" Noel cried, his words tumbling out in a breathless rush. "I'm so terribly sorry for being late. It wasn't my fault, I was—"

But Liv cut him off with a sharp gesture, her jaw tight. She took him firmly by the elbow and steered him away from the stage, murmuring something Perry couldn't quite catch.

Perry turned to Kurt, who stood frozen, the script dangling, forgotten in his hand. "What's going on, do you think?" Perry asked, his voice low.

Kurt didn't meet his gaze, his hazel eyes fixed on Noel's retreating back. Then he gave a quick shake of his head. "No idea," he mumbled as he withdrew his mobile phone from his pocket and began to scroll. Perry wished Ralph Harvey was here. He would've been more than happy to speculate with Perry.

After a long moment, Liv returned with Noel in tow. He seemed to have regained some of his composure, though his smile still held a brittle edge. He left Liv and walked towards him and Kurt. "Perry," Noel said, clapping him on the shoulder. "Terribly sorry for the delay. Shall we pick up where you left off?"

Kurt cleared his throat. "Noel, are you sure you're alright?" he asked, his eyebrows drawing together.

Noel waved away his concern with a dismissive laugh. "I'm fine, Kurt. Thanks for filling in, but I think I can take it from here. Back to prompting for you, eh?"

Perry winced at the sting in Noel's words. He caught Kurt's eye and offered a small, grateful smile. "Thanks, Kurt. I appreciate you stepping up to help me."

Kurt ducked his head, his cheeks flushing pink. "It was nothing," he muttered as he backed away.

Liv clapped her hands. "Places, please. We'll go from Jack's entrance as Ernest."

As they took their positions, Perry couldn't help but wonder what drama was unfolding behind the scenes of their little production…

5

THIRTY MINUTES LATER,
WEDNESDAY 29 SEPTEMBER

D *ing!*
     "Ah! That must be Aunt Augusta. Only relatives
or creditors ring in such a dramatic manner. Now, if I get her
out of the way for ten minutes so that you can propose to
Gwendolen, can I dine with you tonight at Willis'?" A cough
caught Perry's attention, and his eyes darted to his right,
where Tom Hatlee lounged against the wall, script in hand.

What? Did I get the lines wrong? Perry was fairly sure
he'd stuck exactly to Liv's script. His understudy looked up,
his slicked-back platinum-blond hair gleaming under the
harsh fluorescent lights, a stark contrast to his bright orange
glasses. His eyes locked with Perry. Then he gave a smug
smile and returned his gaze to the script. *You*—Perry took a
deep breath. *I'm sorry you were overlooked for the part, but I
won't let you bully me out of it!* He returned his focus to Noel,
who was playing Jack, who in turn was pretending to be
Ernest.

"I suppose so…" Noel replied hesitantly, then took a drag
of his fake cigarette. A small cloud of smoke erupted from the
prop.

Perry glanced down at the fake cigarette in his own hand. He suppressed a shiver as he tried to ignore the thought of how many other mouths it had been in over the years. When he'd raised his concerns with Liv a few weeks ago, she'd insisted they needed them for authenticity but had reassured him that the props were sterilised after each performance. *But even so…*

Opposite him, Noel seemed to enjoy it. *Why is he actually puffing on it?* They were only doing run-throughs… *Focus, Perry!* "Yes, but you must be serious about it, old boy. I hate it when people are not serious about a meal. It's so shallow of them."

Kurt walked into Perry's line of sight. "Lady Bracknell and Miss Fairfax, sir."

"And we'll stop there," Liv cried out.

A booming voice filled the hall as Ralph Harvey made his grand entrance. "My darlings, are we ready to create some theatrical magic?" Ralph, who preferred to be referred to as Rafe, resplendent in a paisley waistcoat that clashed magnificently with his polka-dot bow tie, walked over to join them. His white hair stood up in tufts, as if he'd stuck his finger in an electrical socket, and his blue eyes twinkled with mischief.

Perry couldn't help grinning. Ralph had that effect on people—his joyful energy was infectious, lifting the entire cast's spirits.

Behind Ralph was Stella Vance. She headed in their direction, her dark waves bouncing with each step. She was normally the picture of glamour, even in rehearsal attire, but today she looked wiped out. As she approached them, Perry couldn't help noticing the way her eyes immediately darted to Noel. *Are the rumours that they're an item true?*

Liv clapped her hands. "Alright, let's take it from Lane announcing Aunt Agatha and Gwendolen, shall we?"

Kurt repeated his line, and Perry walked forward to greet them.

"Good afternoon, dear Algernon. I hope you're behaving?" Ralph asked in a voice that was pure pantomime dame —loud, crisp, and dripping with over-the-top elegance. He drew out every word just enough to make it funny. It was so exaggerated, Perry had to suppress a laugh. But there was no question—it worked perfectly for Lady Bracknell.

Perry responded, and they continued their exchange. He felt reinvigorated as they bantered back and forward. At one point, from the corner of his eye, Perry spotted Tom leaning forward, his lips moving silently as he mimed Algernon's lines, his gaze fixed on Perry as if willing him to misstep. Perry drew himself up straighter and carried on. *This role is mine, and if you want it, you'll have to prise it from my cold, dead, beautifully manicured hands!*

"Excellent, you two," Liv called as they reached the point where Lady Bracknell and Algernon left the scene. "Alright, Noel and Stella, the stage is yours."

Perry and Ralph moved off the area marked as the stage and stopped a little way behind Liv to watch. As Noel and Stella began their scene as Jack and Gwendolen, Perry felt a growing discomfort. Noel was really hamming it up, his declarations of love growing more grandiose with each line.

"I adore you, Gwendolen," Noel proclaimed, grasping Stella's hands. "My love burns with the intensity of a thousand suns!"

Perry leaned over to Ralph. "That's not in the script, is it?" he whispered.

Ralph stroked his moustache, his eyes gleaming. "Oh, but it's so deliciously dramatic, don't you think?"

Onstage, there was a mesmerised quality to Stella's expression, like Mowgli caught in the coils of Kaa in

Disney's *The Jungle Book*. She was drinking in every word, every touch from Noel as confusion flickered across her face.

"You are the visible personification of absolute perfection," Noel continued, his fingertips grazing Stella's shiny cheek with calculated tenderness.

Perry shifted uncomfortably. "Is it me, or does this feel… excruciatingly awkward?"

Ralph jerked his head towards the back of the hall, a conspiratorial grin spreading across his features. Perry's stomach fluttered as he followed the actor to a quiet corner. "What's going on?"

Ralph raised his hand to his chest. "You know me, I'm not one to gossip."

"Who are you kidding, Rafe?" Perry asked the older man with a sly grin. "Come on, spill the beans."

"Oh, darling, it's positively scandalous," the thespian whispered, fanning himself dramatically. "Our lovebirds had quite the torrid affair this summer."

So the rumours were *true…* "So what happened?"

"Noel wanted to keep it quiet, but Stella, bless her heart, wanted to shout it from the rooftops. She was positively smitten."

Perry frowned. "I take it things didn't end well then?"

"The wrap party for *Noises Off* was the last act of their little drama," Ralph continued. "Noel, three sheets to the wind, announced to everyone that Stella was—and I quote—'clingy, whiny, and a dreadful kisser'. Can you imagine?"

Perry winced. "That seems unnecessarily cruel."

Ralph nodded solemnly. "She still harbours quite the resentment, as one might imagine. But it seems she's under his spell despite it all."

Perry glanced over at Stella, noting the way her eyes

followed Noel's every move. *She's got it bad, but he's only playing with her, by the look of things.*

Ralph leaned closer, his voice dropping to a conspiratorial whisper. "Between you and me, I think she still loves him and wants him back."

Before Perry could respond, Liv's voice cut through the hall. "Alright, everyone. Five-minute break."

As Perry and Ralph joined the others, Noel stepped back, flashing a roguish grin at Stella. "I think that went great. Don't you agree, my dear?"

Stella nodded mutely, a fragile smile gracing her lips. She seemed to be emerging from a dream, blinking as if she'd suddenly been thrust into harsh daylight.

Noel laughed before pulling out his vape and heading for the door.

Perry and Ralph exchanged a concerned glance, then made their way over to her. Up close, she looked shell-shocked, her usually vibrant face pale and drawn. She reached out and steadied herself on the back of a chair.

"Here, love." Ralph pressed a water bottle into her hands.

Stella accepted it gratefully, taking a long swig. Colour returned to her cheeks.

Liv approached, a broad smile on her face. "Great work, Stella! You nailed those lines."

Stella gave a weak smile. "Thanks, Liv," she muttered. Then, to Perry's dismay, she turned and headed in the same direction Noel had gone.

No, don't do it! Don't give him the satisfaction... He watched helplessly as she disappeared from view. *Some people are determined to learn the hard way…*

6

AN HOUR LATER, WEDNESDAY 29 SEPTEMBER

Perry stood off to the side, grinning as Ralph, as Lady Bracknell, delivered his final despotic line in Act One.

"...I and Lord Bracknell would never dream of allowing our only daughter—a girl brought up with the utmost care—to marry a cloakroom and have a relationship with a parcel!" Ralph swept his head back and clutched his chest at the horrifying thought. "Good morning, Mr Worthing!" Swinging around, he staggered dramatically out of the area marked on the floor to represent the stage.

Perry resisted the urge to clap. He'd done that the first time he'd seen Ralph rehearse and realised it would look a bit too fan-girly to do it again.

"And cut!" Liv's voice rang out, breaking the spell. "Fantastic work, both of you." She smiled at Noel, who was still standing in the middle of the designated stage, bouncing from one foot to the other, a grin on his face, then at Ralph, who had stopped to her right. "That was fantastic."

Ralph bowed with a flourish. "Always a pleasure, dear girl."

"Rafe, you're done for the day. Thanks for coming in. See you tomorrow. The rest of you—" She was interrupted by the ringing of her mobile phone. "Sorry," she mumbled as she stepped away to take the call.

Noel clicked the silver prop cigarette case open and shut before announcing, "Well, I'm going out for a vape while we wait." He sauntered past Stella, who, along with Kurt, were standing to the side. As Noel passed, he grinned at her. She crossed her arms and pouted.

She's clearly still not happy with how things are between them. A hand clapped Perry on the shoulder. It was Ralph, grinning impishly. "Wonderful work earlier, dear boy. I'll see you on the morrow!" He winked and headed for the door, nearly colliding with a brooding Tom, who was skulking in the doorway. Tom sloped off towards the wall to the left of the stage area, his eyes fixed on Perry as he stopped and retrieved his script from a chair.

Liv ended her call, a slight frown creasing her brow. "Em?" she called out. "Emily, are you here?"

Emily Shaw strode into the hall from one of the open doors along the right-hand wall, a smudge of blue paint on her cheek. Tall and broad-shouldered, with short black hair tucked under a baseball cap, she had a no-nonsense air about her. "What's up, Liv?" the stage manager asked, her rough hands fidgeting with a pair of pliers.

Perry strained to hear as Liv pulled Em aside. "I need to pop out for about thirty minutes. Could you take over directing while I'm gone?"

Em's eyes widened. "But Liv… Colin and I still have a ton of props and scenery to get ready for tomorrow's move to the theatre. I don't know if I can—"

"I know, I know," Liv said, her blue eyes pleading. "I wouldn't ask if it wasn't important. I won't be long, I promise. Here's my script. We're in Act One, and Lady Bracknell has just left." She pressed the well-thumbed pages into Em's reluctant hands.

Em pinched the bridge of her nose, her shoulders slumping. "Alright, but hurry back."

Liv turned to address the room. "Everyone, I have to step out for a bit. Em's taking over. Please give her your full support." With a nod, she grabbed her handbag and hurried out.

What's up with her?

The door opened, and Noel sauntered back in, a curious expression on his handsome face. "What's going on? I just saw Liv leaving."

Em cleared her throat. "She'll be back soon. In the meantime, I'm stepping in to direct." She thrust her pliers into a pocket in her cargo pants and unfolded the script in her hand.

Noel raised an eyebrow at Kurt and Stella. "So isn't this an interesting turn of events?" he murmured, his voice dripping with sarcasm. "Are you sure you're happy with this, Em?" he asked in mock concern. "We can always wait if you'd rather?"

Em stiffened, her knuckles turning white as she gripped the script. But just as quickly, she composed herself. "I'll be fine, thank you, Noel. Right, let's pick up from where you were. Noel, you're onstage, please. Perry, you're ready to come in."

As Perry moved to his mark, he couldn't help but feel a prickle of unease. With Liv gone and Em reluctantly at the helm, the rehearsal's delicate balance seemed to be teetering on a knife's edge. He glanced at Noel, who was fiddling with his prop cigarette case, a devilish gleam in his eye. *This could all go horribly wrong...*

At that moment, Colin Myatt, the lighting technician and

Em's stagehand, appeared, his lanky frame clad in paint-splattered overalls, a brush clutched in his hand. His messy auburn hair stuck out at odd angles, and he blinked in surprise at the scene before him.

"What's going on?" he asked, his eyes darting nervously around the room.

Em rubbed at her temples. "Liv had to step out for a bit. She's asked me to direct until she gets back."

Colin frowned. "But we still have painting to do, and I need to check the lights are all ready for—"

Noel, however, was less amused. He flashed a dazzling smile that didn't reach his eyes. "Colin, my dear, we really need to get on. At this rate, Liv will be back before we've said a word."

Colin seemed to shrink under Noel's gaze, his shoulders hunching. "Right, right. Okay. I'll just... get back to painting then." He backed away, but Em stopped him with a gentle hand on his arm. She leaned in close, whispering something Perry couldn't quite catch. Colin nodded, his expression troubled, before slipping out of the room.

Em returned to her spot, squaring her shoulders. "Noel, whenever you're ready."

Noel smirked, his voice low but still audible to Perry and Em. "About bloody time."

As Noel launched into his lines, Em mimicked the sound of the wedding march. Perry watched unsettled as Noel strode to the imaginary door so he was standing only a short way away from Em. "For goodness' sake, don't play that ghastly tune, Algy. What an idiot you are!" His face contorted with fury as he shouted. It felt personal, almost too real. Em flinched as if she'd been struck.

Perry winced. Noel's intensity seemed excessive even for

the scene. But as he entered, falling into the familiar rhythm of banter with Noel's Jack, the other actor relaxed, and the tension eased.

They traded witty lines, the dialogue flowing quickly and smoothly until Noel stumbled, forgetting his words. Kurt called out the missing line. "…half an hour after they've met, they will be calling each other sister."

Noel recovered, flashing a brief, tight smile as he repeated the line.

"Women only do that when they've called each other a lot of other things first." Perry paused, letting the moment hang for comedic effect. His mouth opened to continue—

"What shall we do after dinner?" Tom's voice rang out from over by the wall.

Perry froze. He was certain, absolutely certain, that wasn't the next line. Anger and confusion warred within him as he turned to face Tom. "I'm sorry, but I don't believe that's the correct line," Perry said, his voice calm despite the frustration simmering beneath the surface. "It's, 'Now, if we want to get a good table at Willis', we really must go. It's nearly seven.'"

Em's eyebrows rose, her expression grim. "You're right, Perry. Tom, you're ahead of yourself in the script."

Tom held up his hands in mock surrender, a smirk spreading across his face. "Sorry. My bad. Got a bit carried away there."

But as Tom met Perry's gaze, there was a glint of something darker in his eyes, a challenge or perhaps a threat. Perry's stomach churned. *Is Tom trying to sabotage my performance to make me look incompetent in front of the others?*

As the scene resumed, Perry tried to push the troubling

thoughts aside, focusing on saying his lines. But the unease lingered, a shadow at the edge of his consciousness.

How badly did Tom want this role? *And how far will he go to get it?*

7

LATER, WEDNESDAY 29 SEPTEMBER

"That's nonsense, Algy. You never talk anything but nonsense." Noel gave an exaggerated eyebrow lift as he looked at Perry and took a puff of his fake cigarette.

Yuk! Perry still couldn't bring himself to put one of those props anywhere near his lips.

"Nobody ever does," he replied with a sly grin.

Noel's face contorted into an indignant scowl, then he stormed off the makeshift stage, leaving Perry alone in the spotlight. Perry picked up a prop cigarette from the box on the table and mimed lighting it. That was as much as he was prepared to do at the moment unless Liv said anything. He gave an overdone inspection of his imaginary shirt cuff, then produced a self-satisfied smile. He rather enjoyed playing the rakish gentleman.

"Cut!" Liv's voice rang out through the village hall. She'd reappeared ten minutes ago, looking somewhat flustered as she'd taken over from a relieved-looking Em. "Thanks, Noel and Perry. That was excellent."

Perry preened inwardly at the praise. He'd worked hard on his timing, and it seemed to be paying off.

Liv adjusted her glasses, her petite frame commanding attention despite her size. "Everyone, take a break before we start Act Two. We'll push through for another hour, then call it a day."

Perry ambled over to his bag and took a swig from his water bottle. Noel joined him, leaning against the wall with a dull thud. The handsome actor ran a slightly trembling hand through his dark, wavy hair. "I think you're doing a smashing job, you know," he said, his charm cranked up to eleven. "You've really picked up the part of Algernon super quick."

Perry beamed, though a small part of him wondered if Noel's praise was entirely sincere. "Thanks, Noel. You're not too shabby yourself."

Noel chuckled, flipping the silver prop cigarette case over with his fingers. "Oh, I've had plenty of practice playing the reprobate." He clicked the case open and shut as he laughed deeply.

There's something calculating in those piercing blue eyes, a hint of ruthlessness behind that winning smile, Perry thought as he grinned in return. *I'm glad he's on my side!*

Liv's voice cut through the chatter as she addressed the cast milling about during the break. "Stella, you're free to go. Noel, you can head out too if you'd like. We probably won't get to your scenes in Act Two tonight."

Stella, standing to Liv's right, hesitated, her gaze fixed on Noel. The air between them crackled with unspoken tension.

Noel flashed a dazzling smile. "I think I'll stay for a while, Liv, just in case. You never know when you might need a dashing gentleman to save the day."

Stella's face fell, a flicker of hurt crossing her features before she turned and stalked out. Perry winced inwardly. *She really should give up now…*

"Okay, thanks, Noel," Liv said. She turned to Perry.

"Perry, are you alright to stick around? We may get to the scene where Algernon arrives at Jack's country estate."

"Absolutely," Perry replied. Even when he wasn't onstage, he loved being around the others, looking for tricks and tips that could improve his performance.

"Great. The rest of you, we'll begin in five." Liv headed to the back of the hall, pulled out a pen, and began scribbling on her script.

Tom sidled past Perry and Noel. He shot Perry an inscrutable look before disappearing through the door beyond them. Perry stifled a sigh and looked around to see Kurt hovering at the edge of the tape on the floor that marked out the stage. His script in hand, the poor man was practically vibrating with anticipation for his turn as Canon Chasuble.

The door to Perry's right swung open, and Gina Bernet walked in, her eyes glued to her phone. Her long brown hair was hanging in a braid down one shoulder, and she shuffled across the stage. *She looks a bit worn out already*, Perry thought as she pasted on a warm smile and joined Kurt. The two began chatting quietly, their heads bent together.

Em entered the room in Gina's wake and made a beeline for Liv. They conferred for a moment before the stage manager headed to the back of the hall and rummaged through a stack of scenery flats.

The door burst open again, and Amelia Trent swept in. Her petite frame was clad in a vintage-inspired dress, the bold pattern perfectly complementing her pixie-style haircut. She practically skipped towards Perry and Noel, her green eyes sparkling with excitement.

"Hey, you two!" she said, her smile dazzling. "How's it been tonight? Absolute carnage, I hope?"

Perry grinned. "Oh, you know, the usual—"

"Disaster," Noel cut in, a faint tinge of sarcasm in his

voice. "We're all waiting with bated breath for your arrival to show us how it's done, Millie, dear."

Millie's smile faltered for a split second before she recovered, tossing her head. "Let's see if those acting classes I've been taking are paying off then."

Before Noel could retort, Liv clapped her hands. "Alright, everyone, let's take our places, please. Act Two from the top!"

Millie shot Perry a conspiratorial wink as she dropped her bag on the floor. "That's my cue." She sashayed over to the marked-out stage, where Gina slowly joined her. Millie attempted to engage Gina in conversation, her animated gestures contrasting with Gina's reserved demeanour, but Gina only responded with short, clipped answers, her eyes darting to her script. Millie caught Perry's eye and pulled a comical face. He couldn't help but smile. There was something about Millie's irrepressible spirit that drew him in. Like him, she was new to the theatre group, navigating the complex web of relationships and egos. It was good to have another person going through the same thing.

As Em exited with a piece of scenery, Liv called for quiet on the set. Noel leaned in close to Perry. "I need a bit of fresh air. Back in a few."

Perry glanced at the door, wondering what sort of 'fresh air' Noel was indulging in. *Is it more than a nicotine fix he needs?* There were whispers that Noel was taking something. *What was it they were saying? Uppers?* It would certainly explain the almost-manic energy Noel had sometimes. *But then, it's just talk...*

He turned his attention to the stage, where Millie, as Miss Prism, launched into her lines with gusto. Millie was a natural. Her delivery was flawless, her timing impeccable. She moved across the stage with purpose, inhabiting her character completely. In contrast, Gina stumbled over her lines, constantly referring to her script. Her movements were stiff and her expression unsure. Perry felt a pang of sympathy for her. *She doesn't look like she wants to be here.*

Liv called for a break as she rubbed her temples. She pulled Gina aside, their whispered conversation growing heated.

"I know my lines," Gina insisted, her hissing voice carrying across the hall. "I simply need a little prompting, that's all."

Liv sighed. "Fine. Then we'll have someone prompt you. But put that script down and give me some energy. You need to put in the work, Gina. We open in less than a month."

Gina sulkily handed over her papers as Liv scanned the hall. At that moment, Noel sauntered back in, a faint whiff of vapour clinging to his T-shirt. Liv waved Gina's script at him. "I can't see Tom. Would you mind prompting for us, Noel?"

His eyes gleamed with satisfaction. "Of course. I'd be happy to help, my dear." Noel took his place, script in hand.

Kurt entered the stage area, taking a deep breath before beginning his line as Dr Chasuble. "And how are we this morning, Miss Prism?" He paused, glancing at Millie with his head tilted slightly to one side.

Noel jumped in. "You are, I trust, well—"

"I knew that," Kurt snapped, his face flushing. "I was pausing for Millie's reaction."

Noel raised an eyebrow. "There's no reaction needed. You're only saying good morning. You need to speed things along."

Perry flinched. *That was harsh.*

Kurt looked to Liv for support, but she wasn't looking at him. "Let's get on with it, shall we?" she said briskly.

As the scene progressed, Kurt's confidence seemed to

crumble. He stumbled over his lines, relying on Noel's prompts more and more. Gina, too, faltered, her eyes darting to Noel with increasing frequency.

Perry's heart went out to them. He'd had his fair share of losing-it moments during the early days of rehearsing.

Tom reappeared, hovering beside Liv as Millie and Kurt made their exit, and he got ready to enter as Merriman, the butler.

Gina stood alone onstage, panic etched across her face as she grasped for her next line.

The silence stretched on, broken by an impatient sigh coming from Noel. Then his smooth voice cut through the awkward atmosphere. "My dear, I believe you're supposed to say—"

"I think that's enough for today, everyone," Liv said, holding up her hand. Next to her, Tom's face fell, disappointment etched in every line.

Gina rushed over to Liv, apologies tumbling from her lips. "I'm so sorry, Liv. I've just been so busy with organising the wedding… I promise I'll work on my lines as soon as I get home."

Liv nodded, her expression softening as she turned to the rest of the group. "Overall, I think we're shaping up nicely. But some of us" —her gaze lingered on Gina and Noel— "need to get our lines nailed down."

Gina flushed, but Noel ignored the dig, seemingly unconcerned. Perry narrowed his eyes. How could Noel be so cavalier about the whole thing?

"And remember, starting tomorrow, we'll be rehearsing in the theatre itself. We've only got four weeks until opening night," Liv continued.

Perry's mouth went dry. *Four weeks!*

Her tone grew more serious. "Once we're in the theatre,

things get real, so try not to let nerves get the better of you. You'll all be fine."

Perry swallowed. *Oh my goodness!*

"Thank you for all your hard work this evening, and I'll see you all in the Theatre Royal tomorrow. Good night."

As everyone dispersed and Perry gathered his things, excitement buzzed through his veins. Tomorrow, he would finally set foot on a real stage. *I can't wait!* It was a dream come true.

8

THE NEXT EVENING. JUST AFTER NOEL HAD COLLAPSED, THURSDAY 30 SEPTEMBER

*O**h my giddy aunt!*** Perry's heart hammered against his ribs as he raced towards Noel's crumpled form.

Crunch!

His polished boot crushed something beneath it, but Perry barely registered it. His mind was laser-focused on Noel as his eyes locked on to the unmoving form of his fellow actor.

Em beat him there by a hair's breadth, dropping to her knees beside Noel's body. "Noel! Can you hear me?" Her normally unflappable voice pitched with urgency.

Perry joined her on the floor. Noel lay still, his skin a sickly pale sheen of sweat. Perry's stomach twisted. *This is bad. Really bad.*

"Call an ambulance! Now!" Em barked over her shoulder, her steely gaze resting on Kurt, who stood rooted to the spot, gaping at them, his face pale and blank as if his mind had short-circuited.

Perry clenched his fists. "Kurt! Call for help! Ring an ambulance!"

Kurt blinked at him dumbly. Perry wanted to shake him. *Of all the times to go into shock!* He patted his pockets out of habit and groaned. No phone. *Brilliant!* "Do something, man!" he bellowed, his frustration bubbling over.

That seemed to jolt Kurt into action. He fumbled for his phone. His movements were jerky as he turned away, muttering into the receiver.

Beside Perry, Em was trying to reposition Noel's limp body. "We need to get him in the recovery position. Perry, help me."

He hesitated. His instinct told him it was already too late. He'd seen his fair share of corpses over the last few years. The grey tinge to Noel's skin, the slackness in his face... Perry swallowed hard. But he bit back his doubts. If there was any chance Noel could be saved, then they had to try. Together, he and Em rolled Noel onto his side. His head lolled unnaturally, his skin waxy and slick with sweat. She pressed a trembling finger to Noel's throat. The pause that followed seemed to last forever.

Her face twisted. "I can't feel..." she whispered, her composure cracking as she rolled Noel onto his back. "Colin! Get the defibrillator!"

Without hesitation, she clasped her hands and began chest compressions—firm, fast, steady. "If it is a heart attack, we might still have a chance, right?" Her eyes met Perry's. He gave her what he hoped was a reassuring smile as he heard footsteps bolting in the direction of the wings.

He crouched nearby, his heart thudding in his throat, watching her hands rise and fall in rhythm. *If Colin doesn't come back quickly... What do I have to do? Think!* He'd practised CPR before, years ago—but had never used it in real life. What was the song you have to give compressions to? He remembered and began reciting the words of the children's song "Nelly the Elephant" under his breath, mentally preparing himself to take over from Em.

"Come on, Noel," Em muttered, breathless with effort. "Come on…"

Footsteps thundered back into the room. Perry stood and shuffled back to make space, his foot landing on something small and hard. Noel's fake cigarette, its casing broken. Without thinking, he scooped up the pieces and tucked them into his pocket.

Colin skidded to a halt beside him, his eyes wide, the defibrillator clutched to his chest. "I've never used one of these before!" he gasped, thrusting the machine at Perry. "I'll take over CPR."

Perry caught the unit, nodded, and shuffled into place beside Noel as Colin dropped to his knees opposite Em and immediately took over compressions.

Perry suppressed a sigh of relief as he flipped the lid up. *At least the machine will talk me through what to do…*

He powered it on. The device came to life with a mechanical voice. After telling him to call for help, it continued, "Apply pads to patient's bare chest."

He knelt closer and helped Em tear open Noel's shirt. The skin was clammy beneath the pads, the adhesive slow to stick. Still, they got them in place as shown in the illustration.

Perry knelt back as the voice instructed, "Analysing heart rhythm. Do not touch the patient."

Colin stopped, and everyone froze.

"Shock not advised. Begin CPR."

Em gave a curt nod, and Colin resumed compressions, singing what sounded to Perry like "Staying Alive" by the Bee Gees under his breath.

Perry swallowed hard. *No shock?* That must mean there was no shockable rhythm…

A sharp scream startled him. His head jerked up to see

Stella standing frozen half-way along the stage, her eyes wide with horror, one hand clamped over her mouth.

"Tom!" Em shouted, her voice snapping like a whip. "Get Stella out of here!"

Tom remained rooted in place, gawking at Noel's lifeless form. Em shot Perry a pleading look. "We've got this, Perry. Can you…?"

He nodded and rose. "Come on, Stella," he said softly, going over to her. Her gaze didn't waver from Noel, her limbs rigid. He put an arm around her shoulders, but she didn't budge.

"Is he…?" she whispered.

"They're doing everything they can," Perry told her, though the words felt hollow.

Just then, Millie appeared, looking flushed. "Can I help?" she asked as her eyes settled on the morbid tableau taking place before her.

Perry blinked, surprised to see her. *She isn't due until later.* Then again, maybe she'd mixed up the schedule like Stella had.

"Noel's been taken… er, ill," he blurted. "Please, Millie, take her somewhere. Get her a cup of tea. Plenty of sugar. She needs to sit down."

Understanding dawned in Millie's eyes, and she murmured her agreement, her face solemn. She gently pulled Stella towards the curtain, whispering reassurances.

Perry's gaze darted back to Noel. *Should I take photos of the scene?* He shook his head. *No. That's ridiculous.* This was almost certainly a heart attack, not something nefarious. Noel was very young to have a cardiac arrest, but if drugs were involved… He let the thought trail off as the distant wail of sirens reached his ears.

The paramedics arrived moments later, their movements

swift and professional. Perry stepped back further, letting them pass. Em and Colin were nudged aside, their faces etched with worry. "What happened?" the lead medic demanded, kneeling beside Noel.

"He collapsed mid-scene. No pulse. He's not breathing. We've been doing CPR, but..." Her voice trailed off as the paramedics set to work, their movements precise and urgent.

Perry watched, transfixed, as they checked for vitals, prepped IVs, and continued doing CPR—using a mask with a bag attached, presumably to get air into him. Their voices were low and urgent, but he could see from their body language that it wasn't going well.

Minutes ticked by, each second an eternity. Perry's gaze flicked to Em and Colin, their faces etched with a growing realisation. Em's hands were clasped, her knuckles white. Colin chewed his bottom lip, his arms dangling uselessly by his sides.

They know, Perry thought. Just like he did. His heart constricted, a hollow ache spreading through his chest.

Twenty minutes later, the clearly exhausted lead medic sat back on his heels, his shoulders slumping. The other one glanced at Em and shook his head. "I'm sorry," he said, his voice gentle but firm. "There's nothing more we can do."

A heavy silence settled over the stage, broken only by the crackle of the paramedic's radio.

Perry's heart constricted, a hollow ache spreading through his chest. He looked at Noel, now still and quiet, and felt the weight of finality settle over him.

Noel Ashworth, the charismatic star of the Windstanton Players, was dead.

9

FORTY MINUTES LATER, THURSDAY
30 SEPTEMBER

Perry leaned against the cold brick wall outside the Windstanton Theatre Royal. His phone was pressed to his ear, and he kept his voice low. Every now and again, he glanced nervously at the entrance. After they'd been shooed off the stage by the local police and herded into the Green Room, they'd been told to stay there until the investigating officer arrived. But the reception had been dreadful, and he'd wanted to ring Bea. No one had been outside the room to stop him, so he'd risked it and slipped out. "He simply collapsed, Bea. Right there onstage. One minute he was fine, and the next—"

Bea's voice on the other end was tinged with concern. "And you're thinking it was a heart attack?"

Perry exhaled, his breath forming misty clouds in the chilly evening air. "It seems the most likely explanation."

"But he wasn't very old, was he?"

Noel had been younger than him. He swallowed. "No. But there were rumours, you know, about him taking something."

"What something?"

"Speed maybe? I don't know that much about these things, but he'd certainly been very high-energy recently. Could be it all caught up with him perhaps?"

"Indeed. Although, with your track record, we can't rule out the possibility that it's mur—"

"Stop!" Perry cut her off. "You see murder everywhere these days... I'm sure it's simply the tragic death of someone who died far too young." *I'm right, aren't I?* There was nothing to indicate foul play...

There was a pause, then Bea puffed out her breath. "You're right. Sorry. So who's there from Fenshire Police? Anyone we know?"

Perry glanced around the empty street. "That's the weird thing. No one's shown up yet except two local PCs and a doctor. We're all waiting in the Green Room."

"You sound like you're outside."

How does she know?

"Yeah, well, I snuck out to call you. They—" A police car appeared around the corner. Perry dived into the shadows. Behind the patrol car was a sleek dark-coloured BMW.

"Bea, they're here. I've got to go," Perry said hurriedly.

"Alright. Text me when you're done."

"Will do." Perry ended the call, and pulse thrumming, he dashed back inside as the cars pulled up to the curb.

A few minutes later, he paused outside the Green Room. He took a calming breath and opened the door. Inside the dimly lit space, with its mismatched chairs scattered around and a sagging sofa pushed against one wall, the air was thick with tension. Hunched in a corner, Kurt was nervously polishing his glasses, while Stella, perched on the sofa, was clutching a mug of tea with shaking hands, her face pale and drawn. Next to her, Millie was chewing her lip as she glanced up at the door. Em stood by the counter. In front of her was a kettle long past its prime, sitting next to a cluster of chipped mugs. She was stirring a cup of tea, her eyes unfocussed. Tom lounged in an armchair, his long legs crossed, sipping from a mug with an air of affected nonchalance, and Colin sat ramrod straight on a wooden dining chair, his face a complete blank.

As Perry sank into an armchair, Millie rose from the sofa and came to sit beside him. "Do you know what happens now?" she asked in a quiet voice.

"I think the police detectives have arrived. They'll probably want to talk to us, either now or tomorrow, so they can piece together what happened."

Tom snorted, uncrossing his legs and sitting up straight. "Listen to you. Regular little expert on police procedure, aren't you, Perry?"

Ignoring the jibe, Perry leaned in to Millie and said, just loud enough for Tom to hear, "My husband, Simon, was a detective with Fenshire CID."

Tom's smirk faded, and he took a sullen sip of his drink.

Silence fell over the room again, awkward and heavy. Perry stared at the scuffed carpet. *I hope Bea's initial concerns aren't founded...*

Ten minutes later, the door swung open and a familiar figure, with broad shoulders and a thickset frame, stepped in. Detective Inspector Mike Ainsley's dark-grey hair was cropped close to his skull, and his blue eyes were sharp and assessing as they swept the room. His rumpled suit and weary face suggested that it had already been a long day for him.

A surge of relief passed through Perry's body. He and Bea had worked with Mike on a handful of local cases, and he knew the DI to be a good man and a thorough investigator.

Mike's gaze landed on Perry, and he gave a brief nod of acknowledgment before addressing the room at large. "Folks,

I'm Detective Inspector Ainsley from Fenshire Police. I know it's been a rough evening, so I'll try to get you finished up here as soon as I can. Forensics are on the way, but it's going to take some time to process the scene. It's getting late, so I'm going to have my officers take a quick statement from each of you. We'll likely have more questions tomorrow, but for now, this will let us get the basics down and get you home faster."

A collective murmur rippled through the group. Mike continued, "I'm going to ask that you all stay put in here for now. Someone will be in shortly to get started." His gaze swung back to Perry. "Mr Juke, can I have a word?"

"Of course," Perry replied, a thrill of excitement running through him as he stood and followed Mike out of the room. *Is he going to let me in on things?*

They made their way through the theatre to the stage. As they stopped, Perry's stomach dropped. The scene was eerily empty—only two uniformed officers and Noel's sheet-covered form. No bustling forensics team. No flashing cameras.

Mike stopped and turned to Perry with a tired smile. "Good to see you, Perry," he said, holding out his hand.

"Likewise," Perry replied, shaking the inspector's hand. The bags under Mike's eyes were more pronounced up close.

"I wish it were under better circumstances."

"Me too." Perry glanced around again. "Where's everyone? I thought it would be teeming with people by now."

Mike gave a dry laugh, scrubbing a hand over his face. "We're short-staffed at the moment. Big undercover operation going on in King's Town. Most of my manpower has been reassigned."

He jerked a thumb over his shoulder. "I've got one DC to take statements, and I've posted a couple of extra uniforms outside the theatre, but that's about all I can spare right now."

Perry blinked in surprise. "That's… er, not ideal."

"Tell me about it," Mike grumbled. "I'm holding down the fort, but it's a bit like trying to bail out the Titanic with a teaspoon."

Perry could feel the man's frustration. "I'm so sorry. I—"

The doors at the back of the theatre opened, and Liv Belmont strode in, her petite frame radiating annoyance. A uniformed officer trailed behind her.

"This lady insisted—" the officer began, addressing Mike. Perry winced. *Liv won't enjoy being addressed as 'this lady'.*

"This lady," Liv snapped, her blue eyes flashing behind her glasses, "is the Theatre Royal's manager and director of this production." She clattered up the wooden stairs that led to the stage and approached Perry and Mike as the uniformed police officer retreated, clearly deciding that she was the inspector's problem now.

Perry stepped forward, eager to defuse the tension. "Mike, this is Olivia Belmont. Liv, this is Detective Inspector Mike Ainsley from Fenshire CID."

But Liv wasn't looking at them. Her gaze was fixed on the white sheet in the middle of the stage. Her face drained of colour, and she stumbled a little. "Oh my god," she whispered, her voice trembling. "What... what happened?"

Perry hesitated, glancing over at Mike. The inspector dipped his head. "I'm so sorry, Liv. Noel collapsed during rehearsal. He…well, he's dead."

"Dead?" Liv repeated, her voice now much quieter.

"After a valiant effort from both your team here and the paramedics to revive him, the doctor proclaimed him dead a short while ago, I'm afraid," Mike replied.

Liv's eyes met Perry's. At his sober nod, she pressed a

hand to her mouth, her eyes welling with tears. "But how? He was fine yesterday!"

Mike cleared his throat. "I'm sorry for your loss, Ms Belmont. Were you aware of any medical issues Mr Ashworth might have had? Any history of health problems?"

Liv shook her head vehemently. "No, nothing that I'm aware of. He was always so vital, so full of energy. I can't believe this is happening."

Perry squeezed her arm in sympathy, his own heart aching at the shock and grief etched on her face.

"Is there an office or a room we could use to interview the cast and crew?" Mike asked. "We'll need to take statements from everyone before we can release them."

Liv blinked, visibly pulling herself together. "Yes, of course. You can use my office. It's down the hall." She gestured towards the exit to the right of the auditorium. "Second on the right."

"Thank you," Mike said, giving her a brief smile. "If you wouldn't mind waiting with the others in the Green Room? I'll have someone in to speak with you all shortly. And if you can reassure them we're doing everything we can…"

"Of course." Liv took a deep, shuddering breath, then squared her shoulders. "Leave it with me, inspector." With a final, woeful glance at the white mound on the stage, she turned and headed down the stairs.

"Look, Perry, I could use your help. You've got a good eye and know all the people here. Can you talk me through what happened, please?"

A good eye, eh? He swelled with pride. *I can't wait until I tell Bea what Mike said…* "Of course. Whatever you need."

"Tell me everything from when you all arrived."

Recounting every detail of the fateful rehearsal as best he could, Perry was just wrapping up when a trio of forensic technicians arrived, their black cases in tow. They fanned out across the stage with practiced efficiency, cameras flashing and gloved hands gently probing.

Perry swallowed hard and looked away. "There have been rumours," he told Mike, "that Noel was using. Something to keep him going, give him an edge. I don't know what exactly. Maybe speed?"

One of Mike's eyebrows arched. "Drugs? And you're sure about this?"

Perry gave a helpless smile. "I can't say for certain. But he's been erratic lately. Moody, you know. Snapping at people for no reason."

"That could explain a lot," Mike murmured, nodding. "Cardiac arrest induced by drugs."

Perry's phone rang in his pocket. He took it out and switched it off. "Sorry about that. I—" As he shoved it back in his pocket, his finger touched something sharp. *The cigarette!* He fished around carefully and withdrew the prop. "Oh, there's this." He opened his hand to show Mike the contents. "It's the fake cigarette prop that Noel was using before... well, you know. I trod on it, rushing over when he collapsed. I picked it up later without thinking when we had to make room for the defibrillator. Sorry."

Mike dug into his pocket for an evidence bag. "No worries. We'll have it checked just in case."

Perry dropped the fake cigarette into the bag, an unpleasant thought invading his mind. *What if it isn't merely a prop? What if the last thing Noel did...*

A chill ran through him. He pushed the thought away. *It's probably nothing. Isn't it?*

10

BRUNCH THE NEXT DAY. FRIDAY 1 OCTOBER

S unlight streamed through the tall windows of the Morning Room at The Dower House, casting a warm glow on the antique mahogany table, spread with breakfast items, and illuminating the vase of fresh deep-pink Chrysan-themums in the middle of it. Bea sipped her coffee, watching Daisy, her white West Highland terrier, circle the table with hopeful eyes. *You can hope all you want, young lady!*

Across from her, Richard Fitzwilliam buttered a slice of toast, his brow furrowed as he listened intently to Perry's animated recount of last night's events at the theatre. Next to Perry, his husband, Simon, was finishing his full English breakfast. As Simon lifted a piece of bacon to his mouth, Daisy slid under the table and appeared next to him, her liquid eyes pleading. He took a bite, then plucked the remaining bit of the rasher off his fork. Before Bea could say, "No!" he dropped it into the little dog's mouth. Bea's eyes widened. *Simon!* He looked up at her and winked.

She couldn't help but smile. It seemed like ages since she'd had her two best friends in her home for a meal like this. They'd all been so busy since getting back from their holiday in Portugal at the beginning of last month. Simon had thrown himself back into overseeing SaltAir, the restaurant he co-owned with Ryan Hawley, so he could return the favour and let Ryan and his girlfriend, Fay, have a break. At the same time, Perry had started rehearsing for the play, and that had taken up most of his evenings and weekends.

Not that Bea and Rich had been sitting around twiddling their thumbs either. After Rich had proposed in Portugal, he'd arranged to talk to her father, the Duke of Arnwall, on their return from holiday. Once the formality of getting the duke's blessing had been completed, there was the rest of their families to tell. This included Rich's mother, Dawn, who was delighted; Rich's sister, Elise, who said, "About time!"; and Bea's uncle and aunt, the king and queen, who were equally pleased about the arrangement, offering any one of the royal palaces for the wedding should Bea and Rich be so inclined. And on top of all of that, Sam, Bea's son, had had to be kitted out for sixth form at his boarding school, including a new set of cricket whites and a complete rugby kit since he'd grown out of the ones he'd had the previous term.

"I mean, poor Mike looked almost ready to keel over," Perry said to Rich, gesturing animatedly with a fork in one hand, a piece of sausage dangling off it. Daisy poked her head out from under the table and watched the morsel of food moving around, her eyes fixed on the prize.

Bea's throat ached. She felt for DI Mike Ainsley. She'd known him for quite a long time, ever since he'd been the self-defence instructor on a kidnapping prevention course she and her sister, Lady Sarah, had completed four years ago. Not long after that, he'd moved to Fenshire CID. He'd been investigating a couple of cases she had also (rather reluctantly) got involved in locally, and he'd never made her or the others feel like they'd been stepping on his toes. *I'm glad he's looking into Noel's death, but I also hope he gets a break soon.*

"The police seem completely snowed under with this big operation in King's Town," Perry continued. "They've barely got enough people to deal with a parking violation, Mike said, let alone a sudden death." He chomped on the sausage. Daisy moved away and curled up in her bed by the fireplace with a huff.

"How very inconsiderate of Noel to die when he did," Bea said, smiling wryly.

The corners of Rich's mouth twitched as Perry let out an undignified snort. "Quite right," he said with a straight face. "The man always had a flair for the dramatic."

Rich picked up his last piece of toast. "Did Mike say if they have any idea what happened? An accident or…?"

"I think an accident, but I suppose they'll have to consider all the options at this stage?" Perry replied, looking to his husband for confirmation.

Simon nodded. "I had a brief call with Steve earlier. He says it's madness at the moment with this special operation going on. Things are taking longer than normal." Detective Inspector Steve Cox of Fenshire CID, nicknamed CID Steve by Perry, had joined Fenshire Police with Simon when they'd both been nineteen. They'd moved to CID together, and even though Simon had left the force seven years ago, the two had remained close friends. Although Steve worked mainly on fraud and cybercrime cases, he'd proven in the past to be a valuable source of information for them. And, of course, it had worked both ways, with them often sharing with him information that they'd found out through less official sources.

Rich leaned forward as he wiped his mouth with his

napkin. "So did *he* say if they've been able to confirm the cause of death yet?"

Simon shook his head. "Nope. I also sent a message to Roisin, but she said they're backed up after a multiple shooting in Fenswich last night." Roisin, Simon's ex-flatmate from his early days in the force, worked in Forensics at Fenshire Police headquarters and was also a useful channel of knowledge. "She says they won't get around to Noel until much later today or even tomorrow." He paused and took a sip of his tea. "She did mention that the on-site report records that they found some drugs in Noel's coat pocket."

Rich's eyes widened. "Drugs? What sort of drugs?"

"She didn't know," Simon replied. "But it supports the theory that it could've been an accidental overdose that caused a heart attack."

A heavy silence fell over the room as they digested this new information. Bea studied Simon's face, noting the dark circles under his eyes and the weariness etched into his features. Hadn't Perry told her he was worried that Simon was overdoing it? "Simon, are you okay? You look exhausted."

Perry jumped in before Simon could respond. "No, he's not okay. He was at the restaurant until one this morning and then got up to write at six-thirty."

Simon shot Perry an exasperated look. "I told you, I've got a deadline to get my book to my editor. A few hours of missed sleep won't kill me."

But lots might!

Rich frowned, concern clear in his voice. "Are you sure you're not doing too much, mate?"

Simon's jaw tightened. "I need to pull my weight at the restaurant," he said firmly. Then, as if eager to change the subject, he said to Rich, "Anyway, have things calmed down at work for you?"

Rich exhaled slowly, rubbing his hand over his face. "Actually, they want me to go to a conference in Berlin next week. They've asked me to give the keynote speech."

Simon's eyebrows shot up. "The keynote? That's quite an honour, isn't it?"

"It's unprecedented for someone of my rank," Rich said, his tone laced with suspicion. "So I have to assume they're using me for publicity. And I hate being a pawn in someone's game."

The hair lifted on the back of Bea's neck. She and Rich had already discussed this, and she couldn't shake the worry that he was growing increasingly unhappy at work. The publicity department of City Police had been clamouring for him to attend more events than ever, and she could see it was wearing on him. Last night, after he'd told her about the Berlin event, he'd complained, "I was on camera loads of times when I was involved in Royal Protection, but no one was interested then. Now, just because we're getting married, they want to thrust me in front of the camera all the time."

Bea knew he hadn't meant to make her feel bad, and she didn't think he was having second thoughts about their engagement, but she couldn't help feeling guilty that the situation was causing him such discomfort. *How will he feel about attending official royal family events with me in the future?* Would he resent being put on display? She reached under the table and gave his hand a reassuring squeeze. He squeezed it back, then turned to Perry, clearly eager to shift the focus away from himself. "So what happens now with your rehearsals?"

Perry leaned back in his chair, a wry smile playing on his lips. "Obviously, the theatre's closed at the moment, so Liv is trying to get the village hall at Windsham back. She's very much 'the show must go on' type. She's called a meeting for tonight," he continued, his face now etched with worry. "The venue is yet to be confirmed."

Is he concerned that with the lead actor gone and the theatre closed, the future of the play hangs in the balance?

Rich seemed to think the same. "So what's going to happen to the show now that Noel's dead? He was one of the key players, wasn't he?"

Perry's voice faltered a tad. "Ah, yes. That's the million-dollar question, isn't it? Noel was our leading man. He's going to be almost impossible to replace at such short notice."

Bea's stomach dropped. Perry had worked so hard, only to have his efforts derailed by a tragedy beyond his control. *It's not fair!* "Well, hopefully, Liv will come up with a solution," she said softly.

"I guess I'll find out tonight," Perry said as he reached over and took a croissant from a plate in the middle of the table.

Bea crossed her fingers behind her back, willing Liv, wherever she was right now, to make it work so that her best friend's dream of being an actor didn't die along with Noel Ashworth.

11

THAT EVENING, FRIDAY 1 OCTOBER

Perry surveyed the Windsham Village Hall. The wood-panelled walls bore faded posters from local events, and the ceiling lights cast a harsh glare over the mismatched chairs that were arranged in a loose semicircle. A nervous energy buzzed through the air like static electricity. It was strange to be back again so soon. *It's a far cry from the grand stage of the Windstanton Theatre Royal,* Perry thought as he stood near the refreshment table, a cup of lukewarm coffee in his hand.

Clusters of cast members chatted in low voices. Snippets of conversations floated around him. "I wonder how Stella is doing?"; "Noel's family must be devastated."; "I can't believe we're back here so soon after…"

Perry scanned the room. Em and Colin stood by the far wall, their discussion punctuated by frequent glances in the direction of the door, while Gina and Millie huddled at the end of the refreshment table, whispering among themselves, anticipation radiating off them.

The questions continued in hushed voices "Will we be cancelled?"; "Who can take on the role of Jack?"; "Do you think Liv will postpone it?" Uncertainty clung to the air as they all speculated.

Ralph appeared by his side and patted Perry's arm sympathetically. "Buck up, dear boy. At least you're not poor Stella playing Gwendolen." He tipped his head at Kurt and Tom. "Can you imagine the stage kisses?"

Perry shuddered. "Where is Stella, by the way?"

Ralph shrugged. "No idea." He leaned in and whispered, "I suspect she's not up to it, don't you?" He raised an eyebrow, then grabbed a biscuit and began nibbling on it. "So what do we think? Will they cancel the whole thing, or are we soldiering on?"

"I don't know. Will the show be cancelled as a mark of respect? Is there a precedence for this?" Perry asked the more experienced actor.

"It's a first for me, dear boy. But" —Ralph pursed his lips — "I expect it will be a case of 'the show must go on'."

Millie, who had wandered over with a fresh cup of tea, chimed in. "Liv will have to recast Jack if we do."

Across the room, Kurt was hunched over a script, his glasses slipping down his nose as he mouthed lines to himself. *Does he think he'll get the part?* Perry's heart dropped at the thought. He'd seen Noel's understudy in action. *He simply doesn't have the personality to pull it off.* His gaze shifted to his left, to the only other contender for the role—Tom. He was currently hovering near the piano, his arms crossed tightly over his chest. He looked up and caught Perry's eye, a smirk crossing his face. Perry looked away. *I'm doomed whichever one of them gets the role!*

Ralph snorted. "If Kurt gets Jack's role, it'll positively kill the play!"

Perry grimaced. "It's hard to picture Kurt pulling it off." He sighed. "But what choice does Liv have?"

Millie tilted her head thoughtfully. "What about Tom? I know he's your understudy, Perry, but Liv could shuffle things around."

"I doubt it," Ralph said dryly. "She's not exactly a fan of Tom's... let's say... er, interpretive style."

"Hammy, is how she described it to me." Millie covered her mouth to stifle a giggle.

Despite himself, Perry smiled.

But his amusement faded quickly. The truth was that he didn't want Kurt *or* Tom playing Jack.

The heavy double doors banged open, and conversations sputtered out. Liv swept into the room, her heels clicking against the hardwood floor. Behind her walked a young man who drew every eye in the room. He was tall and broad-shouldered but lean, with thick, dark-brown hair that framed his strikingly handsome face.

Perry blinked, and beside him, Ralph let out a low whistle. "Well, hello, good-looking," the older man said under his breath, leaning towards Perry.

Perry didn't answer. The man was almost unfairly attractive. His olive skin and sharp jawline gave him a timeless, classic appeal—like a movie star from another era. Across the room, Em smoothed her hair, and Gina straightened her posture. Next to him, Millie fidgeted with the hem of her sweater as she took in a deep breath.

The new arrival gave a polite nod to the group, his hazel eyes flicking around the room, warm and curious, as if he were sizing everyone up but without appearing rude.

Liv clapped her hands for attention. "Everyone, thank you for coming on short notice," she began. "I know this has been an incredibly difficult time, and our thoughts are, of course, with Noel's loved ones." Her gaze swept the room, her expression solemn. "But I appreciate your commitment to the production."

Perry leaned forward, his pulse quickening. Was she going to cancel the show? *Please not after all our hard work.* His vision of making his acting debut to an enthralled audience was fading…

"Because of the ongoing investigation, the theatre will remain closed for a few more days." Liv paused, letting the news sink in. Murmurs rippled through the group. "But fear not! We shall convene our rehearsals here at the village hall until we move back."

Around him, the cast seemed to collectively exhale as Perry's legs went weak. They were saved! His shoulders slumped as his vision returned: he was standing on the stage, bowing low as the audience jumped to their feet, their clapping and whistles overpowering his senses. *Hold on!* His chest tightened as reality swiped away his daydream. Was that even a possibility with Kurt or Tom playing the part of Jack?

Liv continued, "Hopefully, it will only be for a short while, and I promise you we'll still have plenty of time to get comfortable onstage before opening night."

A ripple of relief spread through the room, and faint smiles appeared.

Liv gestured to the man beside her. "I'm thrilled to introduce our newest cast member. This is Gabriel Rossi. Gabe is in the area for a while and will join us for the duration."

There were murmurs of surprise and curiosity as Gabe offered a small, disarming smile at the group. "It's a pleasure to meet you all," he said, his voice smooth and confident.

Ralph leaned closer to Perry and whispered, "Where on earth did she pluck him from? A modelling agency?"

Perry chuckled softly, but he couldn't help agreeing.

Gabe's presence was striking, and it was clear he'd already made an impression. Gina was biting her lip, and even Millie looked like she was barely keeping herself together.

Liv carried on, "Gabe has been in several successful university drama productions in Nottingham."

Perry nodded appreciatively. *Sounds promising...*

"In fact, one of Gabe's previous roles was in *The Importance of Being Earnest*."

He exchanged a loaded glance with Ralph. *Is this going where I think this is going?* Ralph gave him a sly smile.

A beat of silence fell, then slowly realisation dawned on the group. Perry's gaze was automatically drawn to Kurt and Tom. Kurt's jaw tightened as he folded his arms across his chest. Tom shifted uncomfortably, his mouth opening as if he wanted to object, but then he closed it again.

"And that leads me nicely into the other matter we need to address. Recasting Jack."

Perry held his breath.

"I'm pleased to say that Gabe will be taking over Noel's role."

Perry couldn't help the grin that tugged at his lips. In a matter of minutes, all their assumptions and expectations had been tipped on their heads. *No Kurt. No Tom.* But someone who at least looked the part and knew the play. Gabe could be the answer to his dreams. Literally.

The reactions around the room were mixed. Em and Colin clapped politely, and an excited-looking Gina joined in, along with a beaming Millie.

Ralph arched an eyebrow at Perry. "Bet Kurt and Tom are thrilled," he hissed, a look of mischief on his face.

They clearly weren't. Kurt looked like he'd smelt curdled milk. Tom, meanwhile, had turned a deep shade of red, his fists clenched at his sides. It was hard to tell which one was angrier, but it was clear both of their egos had taken a significant hit.

Liv glanced at her watch. "Right, I think we'll call it a day for now. Rehearsals will start again tomorrow at two sharp."

Ralph raised a hand. "Before we go, Liv, my dear, any news on Noel's death?"

The room went still.

Liv shook her head, her lips pressed into a thin line. "I'm afraid not, Rafe. But I'm sure they're doing everything they can to get to the bottom of it."

Ralph turned to Perry, his bushy eyebrows knitted together. "Bit odd, isn't it? If it was a straightforward heart attack, you'd think they'd have confirmed it by now," he whispered.

He has a point. Initially, all that had been said in the local news was that a man had collapsed and died at the theatre. Later this afternoon, that had been updated to name Noel and confirm it had happened during rehearsals. But still no cause of death had been reported. Was that suspicious? But then Perry remembered what Roisin had told Simon. He shrugged. "I expect they're very busy with that shooting in Fenswich yesterday."

"Mm-hmm, I suppose so," Ralph replied.

Liv's voice cut through their whispered exchange. "Get some rest, everyone. We've got a lot of work ahead of us, but I truly believe Noel would want the show to go on."

Really? Perry barely suppressed a snort. What Noel would've *really* wanted was to be alive. Oh, and also…. probably *not* to have been replaced so easily by some Adonis-like newcomer!

12

THE NEXT MORNING. SATURDAY 2 OCTOBER

The Garden Room at The Dower House was bathed in warm autumn sunlight. Bea and Rich, with Daisy squeezed in between them, were settled into a plush sofa overlooking the garden. On her knee, Bea was balancing her tablet. Sam's face filled the screen, his reddish-brown hair damp and sticking up at odd angles.

"Rugby practice starts in twenty minutes," he said breathlessly, adjusting his shirt.

"How's it going?" Rich asked.

"Coach is shaking it all up today. He wants to try me as outside centre rather than my usual position of left wing."

While Rich and Sam discussed the merits of the position change, Bea's heart sank. *Does that mean he'll be in the scrum?* She knew nothing about rugby positions. All she cared about was that her son didn't get hurt. And as much as Sam, Rich, Simon, and her brother, Fred, had all tried to explain to her that Sam was no more likely to get injured in the scrum than he was outside of it, she'd been to watch Sam play, and she knew she didn't want him to be part of the mauling that was common in the scrum.

She glanced at Rich. He subtly shook his head. She let out her breath. *Thank goodness.* "Oh, really? That's nice, darling."

"You've no idea what I'm talking about, do you, Mum?"

Bea tried to look affronted, but when both Sam and Rich burst out laughing, she couldn't help but grin back. "No. Not a clue."

"That's okay. Anyway, never mind that. Archie says someone died during rehearsals in the play Perry's in. Is that true?" His brown eyes sparkled with excitement.

Bea exchanged a glance with Rich. Leave it to Archie, Sam's best friend, to know about it already. He could rival Perry when it came to being in the know. "Yes, someone collapsed during rehearsals," Bea said carefully. "But it's nothing to worry about. It was a suspected heart attack."

Sam's expression dropped into one of disappointment. "Oh. So... you won't be investigating another murder then?"

Bea shook her head slowly. "No, darling. No murders here, I'm afraid."

Sam sighed dramatically. "Boring!"

Beside her, Rich snorted with laughter, then turned it into a cough.

Gently slapping Rich on his knee and whispering, "Behave," she raised an eyebrow at her son. "Sam. Please remember someone died. It's not boring; it's tragic."

"Sorry, Mum," came the contrite reply from her son.

"Sorry, Mum," Rich whispered next to her. She fought a chuckle.

"But what about Perry?" Sam asked. "Will they have to cancel the play now?"

"Actually, they've found someone to play the role," Bea said, recalling the brief text message from Perry last night.

. . .

Perry: *We have a new Jack from outside the existing cast. Noses well and truly put out of joint here! Tell you all about it tomorrow.*

"So it will all carry on as planned," she continued.

"Cool," Sam said, then glanced off-screen. "Uh-oh, got to run. Coach is calling us."

"Have a good practice, Sam," Rich chimed in. "And don't forget to stretch!"

Sam rolled his eyes. "Yes, Rich." He flashed a cheeky grin, then waved. "Bye, Mum! Bye, Rich! Love you!"

"Bye, darling. Love you too." Bea blew him a kiss as the screen went black. She swallowed as she closed the cover and placed the tablet on the coffee table. It was always hard to say goodbye to her son, especially when she knew he wasn't coming home for a while. She wished he would come home every weekend. But with rugby practice on Saturdays and all the studying they were expected to complete for sixth form, it wasn't practical. Sam didn't seem to mind—he had his friends, and very few of them went home during term-time. But sometimes Bea simply wanted to hug her son, who was growing up so fast.

Rich's phone beeped with an incoming text message, redirecting Bea's attention away from how much she missed Sam. Rich's face lit up as he read the message. "Well, would you look at that?" he said, a grin spreading across his face. "Berlin's off. The conference venue's been flooded."

Bea raised an eyebrow. "And this makes you happy because…?"

"Because, my darling," Rich replied, his eyes twinkling, "I didn't want to go." He leaned across the snoozing Daisy and gave Bea a kiss on the side of her head.

She couldn't help but smile at seeing him so happy.

"In fact," he continued, "I think I'll take the week off."

Really? Something about Rich's eagerness to avoid work niggled at her. The concern that he was unhappy about his job resurfaced. "Rich, we only got back from holiday a month ago."

Rich waved a hand dismissively. "Oh, it's fine. I was meant to be out of the office all week anyway, and Fred's asked me if I can help him with some stuff on the Three Lakes project. Now I can say yes!"

The enthusiasm in his voice was unmistakable, and Bea felt a pang of unease. He seemed more excited about her brother's rehabilitation centre project than anything related to his own job lately.

Did he want to leave? *But what will he do?* Could he consult or move to a different role? She opened her mouth to broach the subject, but before she could say anything, her phone lit up with an incoming call.

She glanced at the screen, surprised to see DI Mike Ainsley's name flashing up at her. Casting Rich a curious look, she mouthed, "Mike Ainsley," to him, then she answered the call. "Mike. This is an unexpected pleasure."

"Lady Beatrice, I hope I'm not interrupting?" Mike's deep voice rumbled through the speaker.

"Not at all. What can I do for you?" Bea asked, her curiosity piqued.

"I was wondering if we could talk?"

Bea looked at Rich and pulled a face. "Of course. Is everything alright?"

"I'd rather discuss it in person. I'm in King's Town at the moment, but I'm heading to Windstanton shortly. Can I swing by Francis Court? It's on my way."

Discuss it in person? Why? "Indeed. Come directly to

The Dower House. I'll let security know to expect you." Bea's mind raced with possibilities.

"Great. I'll be there in about forty minutes," Mike replied. "Is Mr Juke with you?"

"Er, no. It's just me and Rich."

Mike sounded relieved. "Good to know Fitzwilliam is there. Would you mind asking Perry to join us? It would be helpful for me if I could talk to him too."

Talk to Perry? She caught Rich's eye. He gave her a small, one-sided smile. "Of course. I'll text him now."

"Thank you, my lady. I'll explain everything when I get there. Until then."

The line went dead, leaving Bea staring at her phone in bewilderment. She turned to Rich, who looked equally perplexed.

"What do you think that's all about?" she asked him as she sent a quick message to Perry, asking him to come over.

"I can only assume it's something to do with Noel Ashworth's death."

Of course! Perry had said Mike was the investigating officer. But that still didn't explain why he needed to talk to *her*. But Perry on the other hand… Her stomach dropped. *Unless…* "You don't think Perry's in some kind of danger, do you?"

Rich shook his head. "I wouldn't have thought so. It might be that Mike wants to talk to him away from the rest of the cast?"

Maybe. But it all seemed odd. She couldn't shake the feeling that whatever Mike had to tell them, it wasn't going to be good news.

———

"So what's the emergency?" Perry asked as he entered the Garden Room. Daisy ran to meet him, her tail wagging furiously. "Your message was cryptic," he continued as he ruffled Daisy's head, then scooped her up and carried her to the empty armchair by the side of the sofa, where he sat down, holding her on his lap. He gently rubbed circles on the little terrier's back as Bea told him about the call from Mike. Perry's eyes widened as she ended with, "He should be here in about ten minutes."

Perry shrugged. "Well, okay. I suppose it must be something to do with Noel's death."

"That's what we thought," Rich confirmed.

Daisy jumped down from Perry's knees and came to join Bea and Rich on the sofa. She circled twice and settled down between them.

"While we wait, let me tell you about last night at the theatre," Perry said, his eyes shining. He told them about Liv giving them all a pep talk and then Gabe being introduced as the new Jack. "Kurt, who is understudying the role, was fuming. His name was being bandied around by the rest of the cast as the obvious replacement," Perry told them. "And then there's Tom, who's my understudy. He thinks he's the next best thing since Anthony Hopkins and was clearly assuming he had a chance at the part."

"And what's he like, this Gabe?" Bea asked.

"Oh, you know. Tall. Athletic. Cheekbones to die for. Young."

Bea smirked. *Not that you noticed, obviously!*

"I want to hate him." Perry pulled a face. "But actually, he seemed quite nice and unassuming. Oh, and all the women simply melted, so that should make for some fun." He grinned. "I think Gabriel Rossi is really going to liven things up a bit."

Rossi? Bea tilted her head. "Did you say Rossi?"

Perry nodded.

"Any relation to Marco Rossi, Liv's boyfriend?" Bea pressed. "You know, the food critic? We met him when we were trying to find out who killed our Clary House chef earlier this year."

Perry's jaw dropped. "I… I hadn't even thought of that! How did I miss that connection?" He picked up his phone. "I'll text Ralph—he'll be able to find out."

As Perry tapped at his phone, Fraser, Bea's butler cum handyman cum driver, appeared at the door. "Detective Inspector Ainsley, my lady," he announced formally.

Mike stepped into the room, his thick-set frame filling the doorway. His jacket was rumpled, and his normally clean-shaven face was covered in day-old stubble. His eyes carried the weight of exhaustion. He gave a polite nod. "Morning, everyone."

They rose. Bea moved forward. "Coffee, Mike?"

"That would be great, thanks."

Bea dipped her chin at Fraser, and he left to make the arrangements.

Rich held out his hand. "Good to see you, Ainsley."

"You too, Fitzwilliam," Mike said. "How's life in City Police?"

Rich grimaced. "Oh, you know. A lot of meetings that could be emails, mainly."

Bea gestured to an empty chair. "Please have a seat, Mike."

The detective lowered himself into the chair, his expression unreadable. Bea tried to gauge his mood as he continued to chat with Rich. There was apprehension in his eyes and tension in his jaw. *Something is definitely up.*

Fraser delivered a fresh pot of coffee and left. Bea poured Mike's drink and handed it to him.

Mike took a sip of coffee before setting the mug down carefully. "Thanks for seeing me," he said. "I'm afraid I have some rather unfortunate news." He paused, his gaze sweeping over them.

Bea felt her stomach tighten. She leaned forward, her eyes fixed on his face.

"Noel Ashworth's death is now being treated as a suspected murder."

The room fell silent. Bea's throat ached. She'd known it would be something like that. Why else would Mike be here? Hearing the words though, words she'd heard an awful lot in the last few years, made her stomach sink to her feet. They never failed to shock even if they were expected. She glanced at Perry, who let out a sharp gasp.

Rich leaned forward, his eyes narrowing. "Murder? Are you sure?"

"Suspected murder," Mike corrected. "We found an extremely high dosage of nicotine in Noel's body. Far too much to be explained by his vaping habit or the drugs he had on him."

So the rumours Perry had heard had been true. Noel had been taking something.

Perry ran his fingers through his spiky blond hair as he blinked slowly. Mike looked at him and continued, "The broken fake cigarette you gave us contained a high concentration of nicotine in the cartridge. Only your fingerprints and Noel's were found on it, which makes us think someone wiped it clean before Noel handled it."

Perry paled. "You don't think I—"

"No," Mike said quickly. "We're not pointing fingers at

you, Perry. But we need to consider whether Noel was targeted or if it was more… er, random and meant to disrupt the play."

Disrupt the play? So anyone could have been the target?

Bea started as Perry made a choking sound, his eyes wide with horror. "You mean *I* could have died?"

A sudden coldness hit her core. *Could someone have tried to kill Perry?*

Mike held up a hand. "It's unclear at the moment, which is why I could do with your help, Perry. Walk me through exactly how that prop cigarette is used in the play. Every detail could be crucial."

As Perry launched into an account of the prop cigarette's role in the first act, his voice shaking slightly, they all listened intently. He explained how Noel always took a cigarette out of the case first before offering it to Perry.

"Did Noel always take the first one in the case?" Mike asked.

"As far as I remember." Perry's brow creased as he looked away. "Er, yes. I'm fairly sure that whenever he offered it to me, there was always a gap on the right—so his left."

Bea's mind raced. "So if Noel always took the same one, then someone could have targeted him specifically?"

Mike spread his hands. "If that is the case, then yes, it's possible, even likely, that Noel was the target."

Bea felt a little lightheaded. She took in a deep breath and slowly let it out. *Thank goodness.* She smiled at Perry, but he seemed less than happy.

"But you can't rule out that it was aimed at me?" he asked, his voice wobbling.

"Is there any reason why someone would want to kill you?"

"I don't think so…" Perry's voice trailed off as he rubbed his chin. "I don't really know anyone there that well."

"Then I think it's unlikely you were the target."

Perry's shoulders slumped as he leaned back in his chair.

"Mike. The drugs found on Noel—did they contain nicotine too?" Rich asked.

"They did," Mike confirmed. "But the levels in his system suggest he didn't overdose on them. They also had caffeine and some other stimulants in them, and he only showed small traces of them. The nicotine from the fake cigarette, on the other hand, was enough to kill him with just one puff."

The room fell silent as they absorbed the information.

"Do you know who might have done it?" Bea asked finally.

Mike hesitated. "Not yet. And that's partly why I'm here." He leaned forward, his tone softening. His eyes met hers. "This is highly unusual and completely unofficial, of course, but I need your help, my lady. I'm being told there are no extra resources that can be allocated to this case for at least three or four days. Everyone is tied up. I don't want the case to get cold, but I can't do it on my own with only a couple of local uniform PCs. We worked nicely together on the New Year's Eve case, didn't we?"

Bea blinked, taken aback. "You want me to help you investigate Noel's murder?"

"Not investigate it. That's my job." He cleared his throat. "But to sit in on the interviews with me. I know it's rather irregular," Mike said quickly. "But your insights were invaluable last time. And frankly, I trust your judgment." His gaze held hers, steady and sincere. "Will you consider it?"

Bea hesitated, her mind whirling. Did she really want to embroil herself in another murder case? The sensible part of her told her she had too much to do with the Three Lakes project and her upcoming wedding. But another part, the part that had come alive during previous investigations, was already intrigued, the familiar thrill of the puzzle sparking to life. *What shall I do?*

13

A FEW MINUTES LATER, SATURDAY 2 OCTOBER

B ea took a deep breath; a fleeting trace of orange zest and clove coming from the large vase of roses on the table by her side filled her nostrils. She glanced over Daisy, at Rich, meeting his steady hazel gaze. He gave her an encouraging smile. That was all she needed. She straightened her back and turned to Mike Ainsley, who was waiting patiently for her answer.

"Yes," she said, her voice steady. "I'll help you with the interviews, Mike."

A flicker of relief crossed his tired face. "Thank you, my lady. That's great."

A spark of energy that she hadn't felt in weeks pulsed through her. Then a worrying thought crossed her mind. *Am I getting addicted to the excitement of a murder investigation?* Over the last few years, she'd found herself entangled in murder cases on a much more frequent basis than most people. Was she getting a taste for it? She wrinkled her nose. *That isn't a good thing, is it?* She would talk to Rich about it later, but in the meantime, she'd agreed to help Mike, so she would. And anyway, she was only sitting in on a few inter-views. That wasn't the same as finding a killer, was it?

She glanced at Perry, expecting to see him equally enthused, but he was uncharacteristically quiet. His lips were stuck out a fraction and his chin turned down. *Oh my good-ness, is he pouting?* Bea suppressed a smile as she realised what was wrong. *Aw, Perry! I bet he feels left out, having not been asked by Mike to take part directly in the investigation too.*

Just as that thought crossed her mind, Mike turned to Perry. "Perry, I have a special task for you too if you're willing."

Perry's head snapped up, his eyes widening as a look of glee lit up his face. "Me?"

Mike tried to hide a smile as he dipped his head. "You're in the perfect position to keep your ears open when you're with the cast."

A slow grin spread across Perry's face. "Like an inside man?"

Now Mike couldn't contain his smile. "Er, sure, why not? People talk when they're nervous, and you might hear some-thing useful." He raised an eyebrow.

Perry's eyes lit up with excitement. He turned to Bea, practically bouncing in his seat. "Oh, this is brilliant! I can pretend to be as worried as everyone else. That'll get them talking!"

Bea and Rich exchanged grins. She was glad Perry had a role to play, and it was clear he was relishing the idea of being on the inside during the investigation.

Mike shifted his attention to Rich. "I was pleased to see you earlier, Fitzwilliam," he said, his tone sincere. "I know you're a busy man and can't get involved officially, but if there's anything you can do unofficially, it would mean a lot."

Rich leaned back on the sofa, a wry smile tugging at his lips. "It so happens I'm on leave next week, so I have some free time on my hands. Do you have anything I can be looking at?"

"I hoped you'd say that." Mike smiled and reached into his leather satchel. He pulled out a manilla envelope. "I've brought the autopsy and crime scene reports, along with the initial statements from everyone at the theatre on the night of Noel's death. I'd be grateful for any insights."

Rich took the envelope and slipped the papers out. As he flicked through them, his expression shifted into a focused intensity. Bea's heart fluttered. Already he looked more engaged than he had been when talking about the conference in Berlin.

Mike stood and stretched, looking marginally less weary than he had when he'd arrived. Daisy's eyes sprang open, and she jumped off the sofa. "Thank you all again. I'm incredibly grateful for your help," he said, glancing around at them, then reaching out, he patted Daisy on the head. "Lady Beatrice, I'll be interviewing at Windsham Village Hall. The cast is rehearsing there while the theatre's out of action. I've told Olivia Belmont that I'll explain everything to them before we start. Could you meet me there at one-fifty?"

Bea called Daisy back to her. "Of course. I'll be there."

As the door closed behind Mike, Perry let out a dramatic gasp. "Well, isn't that a turn up for the books? I feel like Austin Powers!"

"Johnny English, more like," Rich teased.

Bea snorted, then tried to cover it up with a cough. Daisy jumped up onto the sofa and tried to lick her face.

"Don't ruin this for me, Rich," Perry said with mock indignation. "I'm practically a spy."

Bea, gently pushing Daisy out of her face, exchanged an

amused glance with Rich, then said, "Okay, Agent Juke, don't get so carried away that you forget your acting responsibilities. You still need to rehearse, remember? The show must go on and all that."

"Of course." He pulled out his phone. "I need to tell Simon. He's going to love this," he said, holding up a finger for silence as the call connected.

"Simon!" Perry cried the moment the line picked up. "You'll never believe it. Mike Ainsley wants me to go undercover."

Bea raised her hand to her mouth to stifle another snort.

"What?" She heard Simon's muffled response through the phone, though she couldn't make out any more words.

"Turns out Noel Ashworth was murdered, so Mike wants me to spy on the other members of the cast," Perry babbled. "He said I should act as worried as everyone else, as if I'm a suspect, you know, and see if it gets them talking."

There was a pause as Simon responded and then Perry's eyes widened. "You already know he was murdered?" He paused. "Ah, of course, Roisin."

Perry nodded as he listened to Simon on the other end. "Brilliant," he said. "See you soon."

"Simon's on his way over. He says Roisin told him it's suspected murder. Oh, and he's bringing lunch."

Perfect. Her, Rich, Perry, and Simon eating and discussing possible suspects. *It all feels reassuringly familiar....*

14

FORTY MINUTES LATER, SATURDAY 2 OCTOBER

B ea savoured the last spoonful of Simon's homemade roasted tomato soup, the rich flavour lingering on her tongue. She glanced around the Morning Room of The Dower House. This was her favourite room at this time of day. Sunlight streamed through the bay windows, casting a soft glow on the antique oak table where they sat, while Daisy snoozed contentedly in her plush dog bed on the window seat overlooking the garden. Bea reluctantly set down her spoon. "Simon, you've outdone yourself. That was delicious. I might have to steal you away from Perry to be our personal chef."

Perry gasped in mock horror. "Er, think again, O royal one! I married him for his cooking skills."

Simon chuckled, his beard twitching with amusement. "And there was me thinking it was for my charming person-ality and rugged good looks."

"That too, love," Perry replied, patting his husband's hand affectionately.

Rich pushed his bowl to the side and leaned back in his chair. "Very tasty. Thanks, Si."

The door swung open, and Fraser entered, moving with his usual quiet efficiency as he began clearing the dishes. Behind him came Mrs Fraser, the housekeeper and cook, carrying a tray laden with a silver coffee pot, fine china cups, and a small plate of homemade fudge.

"I thought you all might like a little something sweet with your coffee," she said warmly as she set the tray down. She turned to Perry and handed him a small package wrapped in parchment. "And this is for you, Mr Juke. I hear you've got a busy afternoon of rehearsals. This will keep your energy up."

Perry accepted the package with an exaggerated bow. "Mrs Fraser, you're an angel."

Bea and Rich exchanged an amused look as the house-keeper beamed. "It's only fudge," she said modestly, though it was clear she appreciated the compliment. Fraser collected the last of the plates, then tipped his chin politely as he left the room with his wife in tow.

Rich reached for a file on the sideboard and brought it back to the table. "Alright," he said, opening it. "Let's start by putting together a list of suspects. It might change after Mike interviews everyone again, but it's a good place to begin."

Simon pulled his laptop from its bag and set it on the table, opening it with a decisive *click*. "I'll make the notes. Perry, why don't you walk us through the cast and their roles? Rich can match them to their statements as we go."

"Er, first, can you give us a summary of what the autopsy said? I think I'll find it useful before the interviews," Bea said, pouring herself and Rich a black coffee each.

Rich skimmed the top page of the file. "Not much more than Mike told us from what I can see. Cause of death was acute nicotine poisoning. The amount in Noel's system was far beyond what you'd expect from his vaping habit or the stimulants he had on him. The fake cigarette cartridge contained a high concentration of nicotine, more than enough to kill someone fairly fast."

Perry rubbed his chin thoughtfully. "The fake cigarette was fine the night before during rehearsals," he said. "Noel used it, and nothing happened. So someone must have tampered with it sometime after that."

"Okay," Rich said, picking up his coffee cup. "Over to you, Perry. Tell us what you know about the cast and crew of the Windstanton Players."

Perry grinned. "I'll start with Ralph Harvey, who plays Lady Bracknell. He likes to be called Rafe when he's at the theatre. He's the comic relief both on- and offstage. He loves a bit of drama—he's a total gossip and has no filter. If there's a whisper of scandal, he's already spreading it. He's also one of those actors who can't resist turning every line into a moment. He's camp as anything, and he's got a good heart. You can't help but like him even when he's being nosy." Perry chuckled. "If I were a betting man, I'd say Ralph's probably cooked up three different theories about Noel's death already."

Rich flipped through the statements in the file. "I don't have a statement for him. But there's a note here that says members of the cast who weren't present when the police arrived on the scene haven't been interviewed yet." He looked up at Perry. "So I assume you can confirm Ralph wasn't there?"

Perry nodded. "Lady Bracknell wasn't due onstage until later on in Act One."

So can we rule out Ralph Harvey as a suspect straight away?

"Then we have Kurt Grant," Perry said, his tone flattening. "He's an interesting one. He's playing Canon Chasuble and Lane, plus he's the understudy for Jack. He's the type who takes himself seriously—always banging on about his passion for theatre. The problem is, his delivery is terribly flat, and he doesn't have much range. He's also a bit... er, intense. Keeps to himself most of the time."

"Okay. I have him here. His statement says he arrived at about five-twenty. He says he got there early because he wanted to get comfortable with the blocking on the new stage before you started?"

Bea's eyes narrowed. *What does that mean?*

"Blocking is basically where we all stand, interact, and enter and exit." Perry explained. "We'd been practicing in the hall with the stage marked out with tape on the floor, but it's very different when you're actually on the stage and there are no marks."

"Okay, thanks." Rich continued to read Kurt's statement.

"Oh, there's one thing about Kurt you should know. He, playing Lane, is the one who brings out the silver case that contains the fake cigarettes," Perry told them.

Bea gasped. "So he delivered the poisoned prop?"

"It would appear so."

"Roughly what time was that?" Simon asked.

Perry tapped his chin. "Just around six-forty, I guess."

"So the tampering with the prop must have happened before then," Simon said, nodding and typing it into his laptop.

"Okay, who's next, Perry?" Rich prompted.

"Tom Hatlee. He's playing Merriman, who is a butler in Act Two, and he's also understudying for Algernon," Perry continued. "About my age, he's been with the Windstanton Players for quite a few years now. He's a decent enough actor, but he's got this... overly dramatic style Liv calls 'hammy'." Perry smirked. "He's not thrilled I got the role of Algernon. I've caught him giving me dirty looks during rehearsals, and he's made a few snarky comments. Honestly, I think he's bitter about being passed over for leads in the past."

"Got him," Rich said. "He arrived at five thirty-five, according to his statement. He says he was in the wings, prompting during the rehearsal."

"That's a lie! He never had to prompt me once!" Perry said indignantly.

Bea smirked.

Perry continued, "Stella Vance plays Gwendolen. She's elegant and polished—she practically glides across the stage. She always knows her lines, and she's always on time. But offstage, she's a bit... tightly wound. She and Noel were having an affair, by all accounts, but he ended it recently. She's still pining for him." Perry hesitated, then said sadly, "Poor Stella, she must be gutted."

Rich flicked the last statement over. "She's here at the end." He read the contents, then grimaced. "It says they couldn't get a statement as the witness was too distraught."

If she was still in love with Noel, then witnessing his death must have been traumatic for her.

"I'm not surprised," Perry said. "Only one thing. Stella wasn't really supposed to be there. Like Ralph, she wasn't needed for the first part of Act One, so we were all surprised when she appeared from the wings as we were about to start."

Interesting... "Did she have an explanation?" Simon asked, looking up from his screen.

"Some misunderstanding from the call sheet, I think."

Simon dipped his chin and made a note on his laptop.

Perry took a sip of his coffee. "Then there's Millie Trent. She's playing Miss Prism, and she's understudying for both Cecily and Gwendolen. She's new to the group—came in after the main roles were already cast. It's clear she's talented and has got big ambitions, although she can be awkward sometimes. But she's got bags of potential."

"Millie's statement says she arrived at six-thirty and then watched the rehearsal from the back of the auditorium," Rich said.

Perry shrugged. "It's too dark to see the seat from the stage without all the lights on. We haven't got to the lighting set-up yet." He continued, "Gina Bernet plays Cecily, and she's... well, she's a bit of a mystery to me." Perry picked up his coffee and took a gulp, then carried on, "She's quiet, very focused. Doesn't say much unless it's directly about the play. She's an excellent actress—natural, believable—but I feel she's not exactly passionate about the role. It seems like she's going through the motions. I'm not sure why."

"Gina Bernet?" Rich rummaged through the statements. "No, she's not here."

"Ah, Cecily isn't in Act One at all. Gina wouldn't have been on the call sheet for Thursday."

So we can rule her out too perhaps?

"Then finally we have the behind-the-scenes people. Emily Shaw is the stage manager. She's a force of nature," Perry said, admiration in his voice. "She's been with the Windstanton Players forever and knows the ins and outs of every production. If Liv can't be there, Em steps in as director. She's no-nonsense, super organised, and doesn't tolerate any diva behaviour. I actually think she's the glue that holds the whole thing together."

"Okay. Emily Shaw. She says she arrived with Colin Myatt at the theatre at about ten to five. They had all the props from the rehearsal hall with them," Rich said.

"That makes sense," Perry replied. "Colin Myatt is the lighting guy, but also Em's right-hand man backstage. He's the one who keeps everything running smoothly—always knows where everything is and what's supposed to happen next. He's friendly enough, but he's got a sharp tongue when things aren't going right. I've not seen it yet, but Ralph says he's got a slow-burning temper. The still waters run deep type. I think he cares more about the production as a whole than the cast as individuals."

"Anyone else?"

"Yes. Finally, we have Liv, our director. She's got a reputation for being tough but fair," Perry said. "She's incredibly passionate about theatre and puts everything she has into every production. And she doesn't mince words—if she thinks you're not performing as you should, she'll tell you to your face. But she also knows how to get the best out of people. I think she's under a lot of pressure right now with everything that's happened, but she's handling it fine."

"I have no statement from her." Rich put the papers to one side.

"No. She wasn't there when it happened. She'd texted us earlier to say she would be late, so Em was standing in for her. Liv arrived just after Mike did."

We can rule out Liv too then.

Perry looked around the table. "That's everyone."

"Thanks, Perry, that was really helpful," Rich said, taking a sip of coffee.

"Yes," Simon added. "We now have a provisional list of suspects. Next we need to work out when the fake cigarette was tampered with." He turned to Perry. "You said it was fine the night before, right?"

Perry nodded. "We used them the previous night at the village hall."

"So at the moment, our window is from when rehearsals ended on Wednesday night and when it was given to Noel at…?" He looked to Perry.

"Around six-forty."

"At the theatre, don't forget," Rich added. "They must have been moved to the theatre at some stage."

Bea suppressed a sigh. *Oh, I spoke too soon...* "So right now we can't even rule out the three members of the cast who weren't there the night Noel died as they could've tampered with it the night before at the village hall?" Bea asked.

Perry frowned. "I suppose so. Although the village hall is locked after we leave, so it would have had to be done before we left—"

"Or it's someone who has a key…" Rich added.

"Well, now that Mike knows the cigarette was the murder weapon, I think it will be the focus of his interviews with everyone," Simon said.

Bea tapped her fingers against the table. *Would it be easy to tamper with the fake cigarette?* "What exactly would someone have to do to tamper with the prop?"

Rich leaned back, considering. "They'd need access to the cartridge, and they'd have to inject or otherwise introduce the nicotine. I'll look through the reports and see if there's anything specific about that."

"I'll stay and help," Simon offered, his fingers still flying over his keyboard. "But you two should get going, or you'll be late."

Bea glanced at the clock and stood. "You're right. I'll ask Fraser to bring the car around."

When she returned a few minutes later, she found Perry receiving a last-minute briefing from his husband. "Remember, Perry, be your usual charming self. Get them chatting, but don't push too hard. Let them open up naturally in their own time."

Perry gave a mock salute. "I'll be the very picture of subtlety."

Simon raised an eyebrow, glancing at Bea. They exchanged a knowing look. Perry was many things, but subtle was not one of them.

Daisy trotted over to her, wagging her tail expectantly. Bea crouched down and scratched the little dog's ears. "Sorry, Daisy, but I think it's best you stay here with Rich and Simon." Daisy tilted her head to one side.

"Come on, Daisy. You can help me read the rest of these reports," Rich said, moving over to the window seat. Daisy jumped up and settled next to him in her bed. Bea blew Rich a kiss and mouthed, "Thank you."

She and Perry made their way to the door, with Perry practically bouncing with anticipation. Bea smiled. She, too, felt a sense of excitement bubbling within her. *I'm about to get my first look at the suspects…*

15

AN HOUR LATER, SATURDAY 2 OCTOBER

The storeroom in Windsham Village Hall was stuffy despite the open window. The space was cluttered with stacks of old chairs, folded trestle tables, and cardboard boxes labelled in faded marker. A faint musty smell lingered in the air, and a single overhead light hung from the ceiling, casting a dim light over the room.

A small table had been set up in the middle of the space, with three chairs. Bea sat in one of them, a little off to the side, her legs crossed.

A digital recorder rested on the table, its red light blinking, capturing everything.

Perry sat in the chair opposite Mike, his arms crossed, his usual energy somewhat muted as he recounted the events leading up to Noel's death. Mike had explained to Perry when they'd started that they'd be going over things Perry had already told Mike unofficially to get it recorded and into a statement.

"…and that's when I stepped on it," Perry said, shifting a touch in his seat. "The fake cigarette. I barely even noticed it at the time, but when I looked down, I saw it was broken. I picked it up and shoved it in my pocket without thinking."

"And how was Noel in the days leading up to his death? Did he seem worried about anything? Did he mention being in any kind of trouble?"

Perry considered the question, rubbing the back of his neck. "I mean, I've only known him for four weeks, so I can't really say what he was like before, but… let's just say he was unpredictable," he said. "He'd be charming one minute and then suddenly snide the next. He made a lot of sharp remarks, but they were presented as him being helpful. It was a skill, really—he could insult you in a way that made you think he was doing you a favour."

"Were his comments directed at anyone in particular?"

Perry shook his head. "Noel was always perfectly pleasant to me. He respected Liv, and he seemed to like Ralph well enough, but everyone else had been on the receiving end of one of his digs at some point."

"What about his relationship with Stella?" Mike prodded.

Perry's eyes darted to Bea. She gave him a reassuring smile. As much as Perry liked to gossip, she knew it was different when it was going down on record.

"Ah, rumour has it they were an item, but Noel ended things over the summer. If that's true, then I would say that Stella... She's not over it."

"How so?" Mike asked.

"He toyed with her," Perry said, his voice tinged with distaste. "During romantic scenes between them as Jack and Gwendolen, he'd lay it on thick. He'd really lean into it— longer eye contact, lingering touches, more intensity than was necessary. He even added his own dialogue to ramp it up. And then, as soon as the scene was over, he'd walk away, looking smug while she stood there clearly upset, as if for a minute she'd actually believed it all."

Bea felt a pang of sympathy for Stella, mixed with a growing dislike for the deceased.

Mike rubbed his chin, then switched topics. "Tell me about the fake cigarettes."

Perry made a face. "I hate them," he admitted. "I avoid putting them in my mouth during rehearsals if I can. But Noel always did. I think he liked the habit—he vaped you know—and they gave him an excuse to do it indoors and onstage."

Mike asked more about how the cigarettes were used in the scene, and Perry repeated what he'd told them earlier. But this time, when Mike asked if Noel always took the first one from the same spot in the case, Perry seemed a little less sure of himself.

"I… Yeah, I think so. Front left, usually." Perry hesitated, his brows knitted together. "But I can't swear to it."

Bea felt a slight chill at the implication. If they were certain that Noel always took the first cigarette from the case, it would mean the murderer had deliberately targeted him. But if there was any chance that he hadn't, then there was another question to be asked—who had been the intended victim?

"And finally," Mike said, "what time did you arrive at the theatre on Thursday night?"

One side of Perry's mouth pulled down. "Er, I arrived when Noel did. I think we were the last to get there." He squinted slightly. "Yes. Kurt, Tom, Em, and Colin were already there, so it would've been a few minutes before six. That was our call time."

Mike thanked Perry and asked him to send in Liv if she was free. As Perry got up, Bea noticed his usual enthusiasm was subdued. Her stomach clenched as she watched her best friend leave the room. *Is he worried he could've been the target? Surely, that's unlikely...* She tried to reassure herself. Perry had only known the cast for a month. Why would anyone want to harm him?

As the door clicked shut, Bea turned to Mike. "It's crucial, isn't it?" she asked. "That we find out if Noel took the first cigarette every time?"

Mike nodded. "It would help determine whether this was planned or a reckless act to cause chaos."

"Or Perry was the target?"

He gave her a short smile. "He's only known the cast for four weeks. Would someone really want to kill him after such a short time?"

Bea frowned, a thought creeping into her mind. "Unless there's some connection that we're not aware of. After all, he was born in this area..."

Mike dipped his chin. "That's a good point. I'll get on it." He picked up his phone and sent a text.

There was a knock on the door. "Come," Mike called out.

Olivia Belmont entered. She was immaculately put together, her tailored black trousers and fitted green jumper giving her an air of quiet authority. Her deep-brown hair was pulled back into a sleek bun, and her expression was composed, but there was some tension in her posture as she took the seat opposite Mike.

"Ms Belmont," Mike greeted. "Thank you for coming in."

"Please call me Liv." Her smile was warm, if a little strained. Her sharp blue eyes flicked briefly to Bea, to her left, then back to Mike.

"You already know Lady Beatrice, I believe. She's here as an observer."

"Of course," Liv said, giving a small smile in Bea's direction. "It's good to see you again, my lady."

Bea smiled in return. *Well, that was easy.* She'd been curious about how Mike would explain her presence at the interviews and whether anyone would push back. But if they were all like Liv, who seemed to accept her presence as if it was the most natural thing in the world to have a member of the royal family present during a police interview, then it would be fine. *Ah... But of course.* Liv had been a suspect in the death of the skeleton found at SaltAir. Bea and Perry had unofficially interviewed Liv during that time. So maybe that was why it wasn't such a surprise to the theatre manager. *But what about everyone else here? How will they take it?*

Liv settled into her chair, but there was a wariness to her. For the first time, Bea noticed the shadows beneath Liv's striking blue eyes. *The shock of Noel's death must be taking its toll.*

Bea's mind flashed back to Mike's announcement when they'd first arrived. The cast's faces had been a tableau of disbelief and horror when Mike had dropped the bombshell that the police suspected Noel had been murdered. All except Perry, who'd gasped dramatically, his hand fluttering to his chest. It had been all Bea had been able to do to stop herself from rolling her eyes at his over-the-top reaction.

Mike cleared his throat and switched on the recorder. "This interview is being recorded for transcription purposes. Can you confirm your full name and role in the Windstanton Players, please?"

"Olivia Belmont," she said smoothly. "I'm the director of the Windstanton Players and theatre manager at The Theatre Royal."

"How well did you know Noel Ashworth?"

Liv's expression barely shifted. "He'd been with the Players for about seven years. He was our leading man for the past four. A good, solid actor."

"Did he get on with everyone?"

Liv hesitated. "I always got on fine with him."

Interesting... she didn't answer the question.

"And the others?"

There was a slight pause. "I'd heard that some found him... er, a little difficult. But no one ever came to me with concerns, I might add."

Mike's brows drew together. "What do you mean by difficult?"

Liv's lips pressed together. "Noel had ideas. He wasn't afraid to voice them. He could be... er, somewhat blunt sometimes. But then he had more experience than most. He was just trying to be helpful." She made a noncommittal noise. "Not everyone is open to constructive criticism."

"Can you think of anyone who might have wished to harm Noel?" Mike asked. "Any disputes, grudges?"

"Not that I know of," she said, tucking a stray hair behind her ear. "I'm still finding it hard to believe that Noel was... murdered." The word seemed to catch in her throat. "It doesn't seem real..." She trailed off.

Mike let the silence stretch, then asked, "Had his behaviour changed recently?"

"Not that I noticed," Liv said. "He always gave his all in rehearsals."

Bea was watching closely. She saw the slight tension in Liv's shoulders, the flicker of reluctance in her gaze. *She did notice a change, but for some reason, she's reluctant to admit it...*

Mike leaned forward. "Were you aware of his relationship with Stella Vance?"

Liv didn't even blink. "I don't involve myself in the cast's personal lives, inspector." Her tone was neutral, a touch too casual. *She knew!*

"Who has keys to the theatre and this hall?"

"Em, Colin, and I all have keys for the theatre," she said. "The cleaners and the café manager also have access. For here, I was only given one key, so Em or Colin holds it, depending on who's locking up."

"Thank you. So on Thursday evening, you didn't arrive for rehearsals until about seven-forty, is that correct?"

Liv nodded. "I had warned everyone that I would be a little late arriving, and Em would be directing in my absence."

"And that was the first time you were at the theatre that day?"

Liv hesitated. "Well, no. I work there, so obviously I was there most of the day."

Bea's heart sped up. Colin's statement had said that he and Em had arrived at the theatre, bringing the props over from the Windsham Village Hall not long before five. So could Liv have tampered with the props earlier before she'd left work? *We should ask—*

"And what time did you leave work that day?" *Exactly!*

"Er, about four-thirty, I believe."

Rats! So it couldn't have been Liv, after all...

"So where were you when the rehearsal was taking place?" Mike continued.

Liv hesitated. "I wasn't there."

Mike didn't react. "I know you weren't. But I need to know where you were so it can be confirmed."

Liv looked away for a moment, her jaw tightening.

"This is a murder inquiry, Ms Belmont," Mike pressed gently.

Liv's jaw clenched. She glanced away, a faint flush creeping up her neck.

What's she hiding?

Finally, she spoke, each word pulled reluctantly from her lips. "I was on my way back from Nottingham with my partner. We were picking up... er, a relative of his."

Mike noted it down. "Thank you. That will be confirmed." Mike smiled. "I appreciate your cooperation. You're free to go now. Would you please send in Emily Shaw?"

Bea watched as Liv stood, her expression unreadable.

After she'd left, Bea turned to Mike. "I get the feeling she's hiding something."

Mike exhaled. "Me too. I wonder if she's protecting someone. The question is... who?"

16

SHORTLY AFTER, SATURDAY 2 OCTOBER

Bea watched as Emily Shaw strode into the cramped storeroom, her utility vest jangling with an impressive array of tools. The woman's short black hair was tucked under a well-worn baseball cap, and her sharp eyes darted around the room, taking in every detail. There was a flicker of hesitation in her stance as she glanced at Bea, as though unsure what to make of her presence.

Mike gestured for her to sit. "Thanks for your time, Ms Shaw. So you know, this interview will be recorded for transcription purposes."

Em gave a curt nod, shifting in her chair as she adjusted the sleeve of her boiler suit.

Mike cleared his throat and gestured towards Bea. "This is Lady Beatrice. She's assisting with our investigation."

Em's brows lifted slightly, and Bea caught the moment of confusion in her expression. But she didn't comment on it, only nodding again.

Mike turned on the recorder. "Please state your full name and your role in the Windstanton Players."

"Emily Shaw," she said crisply. "I'm the stage manager for the Windstanton Players."

"And outside of the theatre?"

"I'm a project manager for a construction firm," she replied, shifting her position a touch.

So Em was used to managing people, dealing with logistics, and problem-solving under pressure. A good person to have running a production. *But something about her tone seems… off.*

Mike leaned forward a little. "Let's focus on your role as stage manager. Could you walk us through your responsibilities?"

Em exhaled slowly. "I handle the practical side of the production. I make sure rehearsals run smoothly, props are where they need to be, the set is built and functional, and that everything backstage operates like clockwork. If there's an issue, I deal with it."

"And acquiring equipment? How does that work?"

The stage manager's shoulders tensed, and her fingers curled around the edge of her chair. "It depends on what we need. Some props we already own, some we borrow, and others we… source."

"Source from where?"

She folded her arms across her chest. "Local shops, donations, that sort of thing."

What's she so defensive about?

"And the cigarette case and prop cigarettes. Where did they come from?" Mike asked.

Em hugged her arms ever tighter over her chest. "I've no idea. We've had them for years. We don't use them much these days unless it's a period piece we're doing."

Mike moved on. "So the props were at the hall on Wednesday for rehearsals, correct?"

Em nodded.

"So were they the same ones taken to the theatre, or were they different props?"

"The same ones." Em unfolded her arms and straightened as if relieved by the change in subject. "We packed everything up Wednesday night after rehearsals finished. I locked the hall up afterwards when Colin and I left."

"What time was that?"

"About eleven."

"And you had the keys on you the whole time after that?"

A flicker of hesitation. "Yes," Em said, then her eyebrows lifted. "Why? Am I in trouble for something?"

"Not that I'm aware of," Mike replied smoothly. "I'm attempting to establish a timeline."

There was a shift in Em's shoulders as she exhaled sharply. "No one else had access to the hall after that."

Why was she worried?

Mike pressed on. "So what time did you go back the next day?"

"I met Colin at the hall on Thursday at four-fifteen to move it all to the theatre. We loaded everything into my estate car and drove to the theatre. We got there about ten to five, then we unpacked it all. After that I went to sort out the scenery while Colin prepped the props for rehearsals."

Bea felt a small thrill of satisfaction. Unless Em herself was involved, their window for when the props could've been tampered with had shortened considerably.

"Where was that, and how long were you there?"

Em crossed her arms again. "I was in the basement. When I finished, I went up to make sure everyone had arrived for the six o'clock call."

"And what time was that?"

"Shortly before six. Perry and Noel arrived just as I got up there. Kurt and Tom were already there."

"And you began rehearsal on time?"

She shifted and unfolded her arms. "I tried to, but Stella appeared just as we were about to start. She seemed to have got confused about her call-time. By the time we'd sorted that out, we were probably five minutes late."

"And how did Noel seem during rehearsal?"

Em's eyes narrowed, and her chin turned down. "A little jumpy, I guess. But that's normal. First time rehearsing in the actual theatre always feels different."

Bea's eyes narrowed. There was no doubt Em was much more at ease now. But earlier, when Mike had mentioned the props… she'd panicked. *Why?*

"Did you see anyone near the props table before or during rehearsals who shouldn't have been there?"

"No," Em said quickly. "I was too busy directing."

"And what was your relationship with Noel Ashworth like?"

Em's reaction was immediate. Her lips pursed, and she shifted in her seat. "He was a good actor. He'd been here for years."

That isn't an answer…

Mike didn't press her on it, but Bea noted the tension in Em's jaw. *She didn't like Noel.*

"Any reason you can think of why someone might want to harm him?" Mike asked.

Em snorted. "He could… er, get people's backs up."

People like you?

Em continued, "You know, rub them up the wrong way." She turned her palms up. "But that's not a reason to kill someone, is it?"

It could be…

"And Stella Vance? What did you think of their relationship?"

Em waved her hand dismissively. "As far as I knew, it was over before this production began. They still managed to keep it professional from what I could see."

Mike smiled. "Thanks, Ms Shaw. That's all for now. Could you send in Kurt Grant, please?"

He leaned over and switched off the recording device. As the door clicked shut, he turned to Bea. "What do you think?"

Bea pulled a strand of her long red hair out of her face and tucked it behind her ear. "She knows something about those props she's not telling us. The question is, what?"

Mike exhaled. "Agreed. But whether that's linked to the murder or not is another question."

Knock! Knock!

"Come in," Mike responded.

Kurt Grant shuffled through the door, his unruly brown hair looking as if he'd just rolled out of bed. Bea watched as he nervously adjusted his glasses, which seemed determined to slide down his nose. He hesitated before sitting down. His dark eyes flicked between her and Mike with thinly veiled unease.

"This is Lady Beatrice," Mike said, gesturing to Bea. "She's assisting with our inquiries."

Kurt's hazel eyes widened behind his lenses, his expression hovering somewhere between polite and wary. "A consultant? Like they have in cop shows on TV?"

Mike's lips twitched. "Something like that."

Bea suppressed a smile. She'd seen the type of shows he was referring to, and she rather liked the idea. *Although, I'm not sure there's much call for specialist knowledge of the royal family within police investigations.*

Mike gestured for him to sit. "Thanks for coming in, Mr

Grant." He leaned over and switched the recorder on. "Just to make you aware, this interview is being recorded."

Kurt gave Bea another quick look before sitting down on the wooden chair.

"I need your full name and your role in the Windstanton Players for the record, please," Mike instructed.

Kurt's fingers fidgeted with his rumpled shirt. "Kurt Grant. I play Canon Chasuble and Lane. I'm also Jack's understudy."

"And what do you do outside of the theatre group?"

Kurt frowned. "Do you mean my job?"

Mike nodded.

"I'm a freelance science tutor. I also occasionally lecture at the local college."

Kurt's fingers tapped an irregular rhythm on his knee. Bea felt the nervous energy practically radiating off him. *Is it just because of the police presence, or something more?*

"How long have you been with the Players?"

"Three years."

"And how well did you know Noel?"

Kurt's eyes darted away. "I looked up to him. He was such a natural actor, you know?"

"Were you friends?"

Kurt's mouth opened, then closed. "Not exactly. I'd say we were more like work colleagues."

That hesitation again...

"So you didn't see him outside of the Players?"

"No," Kurt mumbled, looking down at his hands.

Bea's eyebrow arched. *Is he lying, or is he simply uncomfortable in this situation?* He lacked the charisma she expected from an actor. *Is it possible he comes to life when he's pretending to be someone else?* She paused, recalling what Perry had said about him earlier. Hadn't he described Kurt's delivery as very flat? That made more sense...

"Was there anyone that you know of who didn't get on with Noel?"

Kurt darted a look at Bea, but as soon as she met his eyes, his chin dipped, and his gaze rested on the table. *He knows something!*

"Mr Grant?" Mike prompted.

Kurt looked up reluctantly. "He could be quite rude to people," he said slowly.

"Anyone in particular?"

"Em. Colin. Stella. Take your pick," he replied, a trace of bitterness in his tone.

Another one who didn't like Noel...

"Any particular incidents you can recall?" Mike pushed, but Kurt shook his head and again looked away.

I knew it! What's he not telling us?

Mike clearly thought the same as he didn't reply immediately, instead letting a long pause linger. But Kurt continued to stare at the wall. Mike let out a sigh. "Okay. If you *do* recall anything, please let me know."

Kurt didn't react.

Mike continued, "So you arrived at the theatre at twenty past five even though your call time, I believe, wasn't until six. Why did you get there so early?"

Kurt leaned back, his eyes still fixed on the wall. "I wanted to have a bit of time to familiarise myself with the stage again. I knew my marks back on the makeshift stage area at the hall, but it's different when you're actually in the theatre. You have to make sure the audience can see you, for a start. As I was first on, I wanted to be ready." He crossed his arms.

"And who did you see when you arrived?"

"Only Colin, I think," Kurt replied. "He was fiddling around with the lights. Tom arrived after me and then Em appeared at about the same time as Noel and Perry."

"And how did Noel seem to you these past few weeks?" Mike continued.

Kurt unfolded his arms, his gaze now moving from the wall to a spot over Mike's left shoulder. "Same as usual, I guess. He needed prompting, but that's normal… I mean, was normal for Noel, but he was always word perfect by the dress rehearsals."

"And Thursday night?" Mike asked. "How did he seem then?"

"A bit nervous, I guess," Kurt replied. "But we all were. First time rehearsing in the theatre is a big deal."

Mike shifted the questioning. "Tell me about the cigarette case. You handled it as Lane?"

Kurt nodded. "Yeah, I handed it to Perry… you know, as Algernon, when prompted."

"Did it look tampered with?"

Kurt squinted, pushing his glasses up his nose. "No. It looked normal to me."

Mike hadn't mentioned anything about the cigarette being the murder weapon. *Does Kurt know? Or is he pretending not to?*

"Were you normally onstage when Jack handed Algernon a cigarette, Mr Grant?"

Bea leaned forward. Kurt might be able to confirm if Noel took the prop cigarette from the same place in the case before he offered it to Perry.

Kurt shook his head. "No. I hand the case to Algernon and then I leave."

Rats!

"But you watch from the stage, do you not, as you were acting as a prompt for Noel?"

Good point!

Kurt paused, his eyes distant. "Er, yes… I suppose so." He ran his fingers through his unruly mop of hair.

"So did Noel always take the cigarette from the same position before he offered one to Perry?"

Kurt's eyes flickered for a moment, then he looked down at the floor and shrugged. "I've no idea. I wasn't close enough to see."

Bea's stomach clenched as she pressed her lips together. She really wanted to be able to reassure herself that Perry couldn't possibly have been the intended target.

Mike leaned back, his chair creaking. "Alright, Mr Grant. Thanks for your time. Could you send in Tom Hatlee, please?"

As Kurt slouched out, his shoulders hunched, Bea caught Mike's eye. There was a moment of shared understanding between them. Mike switched off the recording machine and rolled his shoulders. "That wasn't really very useful, was it?"

Bea shook her head, her lips quirking into a wry smile. "Indeed. But sometimes it's what people don't say."

Mike inclined his head.

Bea continued, "I think he knows a lot more about Noel and his rudeness to some of the cast than he's letting on." His nervous energy, the careful way he'd answered questions about Noel—it all added up to something. *But what?*

17

A FEW MINUTES LATER, SATURDAY 2 OCTOBER

The storeroom at Windsham Village Hall felt smaller and more claustrophobic as the interviews wore on. Bea shifted slightly in her chair, stretching her legs out as she waited for Tom to arrive.

The door opened, and Tom Hatlee strode in with theatrical flourish, as if stepping onto a stage rather than into a police interview. He was taller than Bea had expected. His blond hair was carefully styled, and he wore a fitted maroon blazer over a patterned shirt that screamed 'look at me'. The way he looked around, his lips curling slightly as his gaze landed on Bea, immediately set her on edge. She'd heard enough from Perry to know Tom was a right—

"Ah, Mr Hatlee. Thank you for joining us," Mike said, his tone neutral. He gestured at Bea. "This is Lady Beatrice. She'll be sitting in on the interviews."

Tom's eyebrows shot up as he glanced between them, his lips pursing as if he was sucking a lemon. "Can I ask why?"

"Lady Beatrice is an observer," Mike said smoothly. "She assists the police in some cases."

Tom's mouth twisted as if he wanted to protest, but he thought better of it. Bea caught the flicker of irritation in his eyes before he sat down with a dramatic sigh. Bea disliked him even more.

Mike turned on the recorder. "This interview is being recorded. Please state your full name and your role in the Windstanton Players, please."

"Thomas Lyle Hatlee. I've been with the Players for almost four years now. One of the troupe's veterans, you might say." He preened, smoothing the lapels of his jacket.

"And what's your occupation outside of the theatre, Mr Hatlee?" Mike asked.

"I'm a graphic designer," Tom declared importantly. "I specialise in posters, branding, event invitations. If it needs flair, I make it happen."

Bea resisted the urge to roll her eyes. Perry's description of Tom as "hammy" was spot on.

"In fact, I designed the poster for this very production of *The Importance of Being Earnest*," he said with a self-important air.

What? That garish pink-and-orange thing she'd seen outside the theatre the other week? She'd thought a child had won some sort of competition to have their design used!

"And you're Algernon's understudy?"

"I'm Merriman the butler, *and* I understudy for Algernon." Tom's face pinched in irritation. "Though I should have had the part of Algernon outright. Four years with the troupe, and Liv brings in some complete novice instead."

He waved a dismissive hand. Bea's hackles rose. *Perry may be new to this, but he's a much better actor than you!*

"And now she's gone and done it again! Giving the role of Jack to some complete unknown after Noel's death. By all rights, that part should have been mine. The utter gall!" Tom's voice rose with each word, his face reddening.

Bea wondered if he might actually stomp his foot like a toddler. She studied him through narrowed eyes. Could his bitterness run deep enough to actually sabotage the play? Did he try to get rid of Perry or Noel to snag a starring role? It seemed absurd. This was only an amateur production, after all.

Mike cleared his throat, drawing Tom's attention. "As far as I understand it, it's the director's prerogative to cast as she sees fit, isn't it?"

Tom sniffed. "That doesn't make it right. It's nepotism, that's what it is!"

Mike cut in smoothly before Tom could work himself into a full-blown rant. "Speaking of Noel... What was your relationship with him like?"

Tom leaned back. "I didn't really know him that well. But the man had a tongue sharper than a guillotine. I made it a point to steer clear."

"And how did Noel get on with everyone else from what you observed?"

Unlike the others, Tom made no attempt to soften his words. "He was a bully through and through. Always putting people down, and he was sly about it too. Hiding barbs behind a smile or pretending to help." Tom's lips twitched. "He used Stella mercilessly. He showed no respect to Em when she was directing, questioning everything she said. And he was constantly needling poor Colin about props being out of place or him being too slow. The man was a menace."

Did anyone like Noel Ashworth?

"And how was he in the days before his death?" Mike asked, leaning forward. "Did you notice anything unusual about his behaviour?"

"He was as jumpy as a cat on hot bricks, and he looked like something the dog had dragged in."

Bea suppressed a grin. Did the man only talk in idioms?

"He was practically vibrating out of his skin," Tom continued, shaking his head. "My guess? He was zooming on something. Uppers, probably. He had all the signs."

Tom wasn't pulling any punches. Bea might not like the man much, but so far he was turning out to be the only one who didn't seem to be hiding anything.

"So according to your statement, you arrived at the theatre at five thirty-five. Your call time was six. Was there any reason you were so early?"

Tom's eyes widened, then he said scornfully, "Unlike some others, I take my role seriously, and I think it's disrespectful to arrive only just in time to start."

He really is pompous!

"So what did you do when you got there?"

Tom put his hand to his chin and looked upwards. "I said hello to Colin, who was doing something with the stage lighting, then I sat in the auditorium and read the script."

"And did you see Kurt?"

"Yes." His forehead wrinkled. "He was onstage wandering around, mumbling, I recall."

"And then the others arrived?" Mike prompted.

"Yes. Em appeared, with Perry and Noel right behind her, and I went up onto the stage, ready to prompt. We were about to start when Stella turned up. She'd misread her call time apparently. Noel basically told her to scoot. She did, and we started."

"One last thing," Mike said. "You're obviously watching the whole act every time. At the point where Noel takes a cigarette from the case and then offers one to Perry, did you notice if Noel always took the same cigarette from the case?"

Tom shrugged. "No idea."

Bea clenched her jaw. *Useless.*

Mike stood. "Right then. Thanks for your help, Mr Hatlee. Can you ask Colin Myatt to join us, please?"

With a showy bow, Tom swept from the room. Once he'd gone, Mike clicked off the recorder and turned to Bea. "So that confirmed what Kurt said—Noel had a habit of tearing into Em, Colin, and Stella in particular."

Bea exhaled. "He's a pillock who—"

Mike smirked as he cut in, "Agreed."

The door opened, and Colin poked his head in, his eyes darting between them with unmistakable wariness. "You wanted to see me?"

"Yes. Please come in and take a seat," Mike replied.

Colin hesitated for the briefest of moments before stepping inside, his lanky frame moving with a kind of restless energy. He dipped his chin politely to Bea as he folded himself into the chair across from them. His auburn hair stuck up at odd angles, like he'd been running his hands through it.

Mike turned on the recorder and gave the standard spiel about the interview being recorded, then introduced Bea. Colin gave a tight nod, his gaze flicking over her before returning to Mike. If he was surprised by her presence, he didn't show it.

"Can I have your full name and your role in the Windstanton Players for the record, please?" Mike said.

"Colin Myatt," he said in a slightly shaky voice. "I'm the lighting technician and assistant stage manager."

He's nervous. Is it because he's being interviewed by the police? Or is it something more…

"And your day job?"

"I'm a lab technician. I work at a water treatment facility outside Fawstead."

A lab technician? Bea sat forward slightly, intrigued. That meant he had at least some knowledge of chemicals. That could be important given how Noel had died.

Mike moved on, "I understand the props were left overnight at the rehearsal hall and moved to the theatre on Thursday. Is that correct?"

Colin nodded. "Yeah. Em and I packed up on Wednesday night after everyone else had left. I locked up the hall, then met Em there at four-fifteen on Thursday. We loaded up the car and drove everything to the theatre."

"And the fake cigarettes and the case were there?"

Colin nodded again, shifting in his seat. "I put all of them in sterilising liquid on Wednesday night."

Sterilising liquid? Perry will be relieved...

"And how many are there?"

"Ten in total."

"And you cleaned all of them?"

"Yeah, after each use, I soak them all in a sterilising solution. Then I take them out and rinse them so they're ready for the next time they're needed."

"And when did you take them out this time?"

Colin hesitated, his fingers tapping an uneven rhythm against his thigh. "I left them in it until we got to the theatre on Thursday, then washed and dried them before I put them in the case and onto the prop table at about ten past five." He swallowed, his Adam's apple bobbing.

Bea sat up straighter and exchanged a look with Mike. This was a crucial detail. If the cigarettes had been in the solution until Colin had put them on the props table, then they couldn't have been tampered with *before* ten past five. That gave them a much smaller window of opportunity. *Unless, of course, Colin himself is involved.*

"And what did you do after that?"

He twisted his neck from side to side as if it was stiff. "I went to sort out the lighting on the stage."

"Did you see anyone?"

Colin frowned. "Er… Kurt appeared about fifteen minutes later and started wandering around, going through his script. He didn't speak."

"Go on," Mike said softly.

"Tom arrived about ten minutes later. He came and said hello, then went down and sat in the auditorium. Then Em came up onstage, and everyone else arrived almost at the same time."

"And during that time you were on the stage dealing with the lights, were you able to see the props table at all?"

Bea held her breath. *Did Colin see someone?* That would explain why he was so nervous…

He cleared his throat. "No. I was over the other side mainly. Why?"

Mike hesitated for a moment, then he shifted in his seat. "I'm interested if anyone could have tampered with the cigarette props—"

"Is that how he died then?" Colin blurted out. "Something to do with the fake cigarette he used? It said in an online report just now that he was poisoned."

So the news has got out already…

"We believe the fake cigarette could've been the means to deliver the poison that killed him, yes," Mike confirmed.

Colin let out a sharp breath, his foot tapping faster against the wooden floor.

Does he know something about it?

"You're familiar with the props. Is that possible, in your opinion, Mr Myatt?"

Colin's eyebrows drew together. "I… er, I suppose so. You put something in the chamber that would be inhaled…" He rubbed his face. "Yes, I suppose so…" he repeated.

He seemed to be really thinking about it from what Bea could see. *As if it was only occurring to him this minute.* Did that make him innocent? Or did Colin have a hidden talent for acting? She pushed the thought away, focusing on Mike's next question.

"Tell me about your relationship with Noel."

Colin exhaled slowly and raked his hand through his already-mussed hair. "We weren't… er… close."

Mike pressed on, "So you were not friends then?"

"Look, Noel was a good actor, yeah? But he knew it. He also made a sport of making others feel inferior." Colin's fingers drummed lightly on his thigh. "I tried to stay out of his way."

Another one who avoided Noel!

"Would anyone want to harm him, do you think?" Mike asked, his tone neutral.

Colin's foot-tapping intensified. "Harm him? No. I mean, he got on people's nerves, sure. But not—" He cut himself off, shaking his head. "Not like that."

Bea's eyes narrowed. There was something off in the way he'd said it—like he was trying to convince himself more than them.

"And how did Noel seem in the days before his death?" Mike asked.

Colin's gaze dropped to his lap. "Same as always," he muttered, his voice tight.

"Some others have mentioned he seemed strung out. Possibly on drugs even."

The question hung in the air as Colin's face paled. *What does he know? Is he somehow involved?*

Colin stiffened. For a few seconds, his eyes settled on the

door like he was weighing up an escape route. "No. I don't think so," he said, his voice a little too controlled.

Liar! He knew something.

Bea's eyes flicked to Mike, waiting for him to ask about the cigarettes. To her surprise, he thanked Colin and moved to dismiss him.

"Er, wait," Bea blurted out, unable to stop herself. She caught Mike's eye and gave him an apologetic smile. "I have a question."

Mike dipped his head. "Go ahead, Lady Beatrice."

She gave him a grateful smile, then turned to Colin, who was staring at her, his mouth open a fraction. "The fake cigarettes," she said. "Did Noel and Perry always use the same two from the case?"

Colin blinked rapidly, then scratched his head. "I... I think so," he said slowly. "I think Noel took the first one on the left as he held the case, then offered one to Perry, and he took the one next to it."

Bea's shoulders relaxed. So Noel *had* been targeted. *Perry isn't in danger...*

"Are you certain?" Mike pressed.

Colin swallowed heavily. "Not one hundred percent. No. I never really paid much attention, to be honest."

Rats! So close, yet so far...

Mike thanked Colin again, and the man lumbered out.

Mike leaned over and switched off the recorder. "Good catch, my lady. I'd completely forgotten to ask him that," he said. "Shame we couldn't get a definitive answer."

Bea chewed her lip. "I can't shake the feeling Colin knows more about Noel's drug use than he's prepared to say."

Mike's eyebrows rose. "How so?"

"His reaction, for one. And with his background... could

he know who was supplying them to Noel? Or could he even be the supplier himself?"

Mike's blue eyes twinkled. "Now there's an interesting theory. It's definitely worth looking into." He stood, stretching. "How about we grab a coffee?"

She smiled. "Coffee would be great."

As they stood, Bea glanced at the door, wondering how Perry was getting on with his undercover endeavours.

18

TWENTY MINUTES LATER, SATURDAY 2 OCTOBER

P erry sat in the dimly lit auditorium, watching as Gabe Rossi, the new Jack Worthing, delivered his lines with an ease that made it look effortless. Earlier in the act, Perry had found himself completely swept up in the scene with Gabe. The newbie's delivery had been flawless, his timing impeccable, and—best of all—he hadn't needed prompting once. For Perry, it was like a dream come true—sparring with a co-star who made the dialogue feel natural and alive. *And having someone that good-looking opposite me onstage certainly doesn't hurt either!*

Across from Gabe on stage, Ralph, as Lady Bracknell, was in full command of the scene, his booming voice filling the empty rows of seats. Perry smirked. As sad as it was that Noel had died, it was clear that the production was going to be the better for it.

A rustle of fabric caught his attention as Stella slid into the seat beside him. Her perfume, a heady mix of jasmine and vanilla, wafted over him.

"How did it go with the police?" Stella whispered, her dark eyes wide with concern.

Perry turned his head a fraction. He made a face, pretending to be unsettled, and lowered his voice. "Not great. I think they suspect me."

Stella's perfectly manicured hand flew to her mouth. "What? Why?"

"I was onstage with Noel when he collapsed." Perry let the words sink in, watching her reaction carefully.

"But that doesn't mean anything!" she whispered fiercely. "How do they think he was killed?"

"They didn't say," Perry replied. "But they asked a lot about the fake cigarettes."

A flicker of something—apprehension?—crossed Stella's face, but she quickly composed herself. Perry knew the most important thing now was to keep her talking. "How are you holding up, Stella? I know you and Noel were... er, close."

She exhaled shakily. "I'm still numb. I can't believe he's really gone. I keep expecting him to waltz in, fashionably late as always." She gave a sad smile, her eyes shining with tears, and Perry nodded sympathetically. She swallowed and seemed to compose herself. "And now they're saying it wasn't natural? That someone killed him?"

Perry leaned closer, his blue eyes fixed on Stella's face. "What did *you* think happened?"

"I assumed it was a heart attack."

Perry hesitated for a beat before saying, "He was too young for that, surely?"

She pressed her lips together but didn't respond. Perry took that as his cue to push a little harder. "I mean... there were rumours, weren't there?" *Subtle, remember, Perry...* He tried to sound casual. "People said he was taking something."

Stella inhaled sharply, her nails digging into the fabric of the seat. For a second, Perry thought she might shut down completely, but then, after glancing around to make sure no one else was listening, she exhaled. "I think so too." The words came out quiet and confident. "When we were together, I was sure he was on something. He was always so… wired. It wasn't simply the energy. It was too much— too fast, too sharp. I saw the same thing with some of my uni friends who were taking speed. The same restless energy. The same mood swings."

Perry blinked slowly as if thinking it through. "Did you ever ask him about it?"

Her mouth twisted. "I did once. He laughed and said he was 'high on life' and that I was boring." She swallowed hard. "He shut me down completely. After that, I didn't bother to ask him again."

"Any idea where he got the stuff?" he asked, trying to keep his tone casual. If he could find that out, the others would really be impressed.

Stella shook her head. "No clue. Noel was intensely private about certain things."

Perry nodded. He needed to steer the conversation to her early arrival at Thursday's rehearsal, but how?

As if reading his mind, Stella asked, "What do you think the police will ask me?"

Perry saw his chance and took it. "Well, first they asked me my name and what I did, that sort of thing." Come to think of it, he didn't know what Stella did for a job. "What *do* you do for a living?"

Stella took a compact out of her bag and tossed her dark waves over her shoulder as she looked into the mirror. "I'm a marketing executive for a luxury cosmetics company in Fenswich. Charming clients, promoting brands—that sort of thing."

I suppose that makes sense, he thought, looking at her stylish dress-and-boots combo.

"Sounds fancy," he replied. "They also asked about my relationship with Noel."

She fumbled with her compact mirror, snapping it shut.

"Simply tell them the truth, Stella," Perry soothed, placing a reassuring hand on her arm. "Oh, and they were interested in everyone's whereabouts before... you know, before Noel collapsed."

He watched her closely, waiting for her to volunteer the information. Suddenly, she was fascinated by her manicured fingers.

"You arrived early that evening, didn't you?" Perry prompted gently.

Stella's gaze darted away. "I misread the call sheet," she muttered.

Not very convincing. Perry's mind raced. Had she come early to tamper with the cigarette? Or had she merely wanted to see Noel?

"What did you do after you left the stage?" Perry asked, recalling her storming off backstage after Noel had told her to leave.

"I went to one of the dressing rooms to wait," she blurted.

Perry raised an eyebrow. "Did you see anyone?"

She hesitated for a second too long. "Er... No."

She glanced at him then, as if trying to gauge his reaction. "You don't think the police will find that suspicious, do you?"

Before Perry could respond, the door at the back of the auditorium opened, and Millie Trent slipped in. She spotted them and hurried over.

"Stella," she said, slightly out of breath, "the police want to see you now."

Stella's face drained of colour. She stood, smoothing her dress with shaking hands, and shot Perry one last glance before scuttling off towards the exit.

Millie plopped down next to Perry, her blue eyes sparkling behind her glasses. "So," she said brightly, "that was interesting."

Perry turned to her. "How did it go?"

Millie shrugged. "Not what I expected. I was surprised to see Lady Beatrice there. You work with her, don't you?"

Perry kept his tone light. "Yeah."

"Why does she help the police?" Millie asked, her eyes sparkling with interest.

Perry gave a vague shrug. "Probably something to do with her fiancé being a senior police officer." He changed the subject quickly. "What did they ask you?"

She leaned back. "Same as you, I imagine. How well I knew Noel—which, let's be honest, wasn't very well at all. He was a bit snarky for my tastes."

"Did you tell them that?"

"Yes," Millie admitted. "And you know what? I hated how he treated Stella." She paused, glancing around before asking, "You don't think... Stella killed him, do you?"

Perry's eyebrows shot up. He'd thought it, of course... But then, Stella didn't seem like the murdering type. Not that any of the killers he and Bea had met in the past had seemed like the murdering type... "Well, I—"

"I wouldn't blame her, you know," Millie interrupted, her words tumbling out. "I overheard them arguing as I arrived at the theatre."

So Stella was lying when she said she'd been waiting the whole time in a dressing room. "What time was that?"

"About half-six. I don't think they saw me. I came in through the stage door."

Perry frowned. That would have been when they'd taken their first break. Noel had left to go outside.

"Did you hear what they were saying?"

Millie tipped her head to one side. "Not much. They were doing that angry whispering thing. He said something about how could she have been so stupid. She was sort of crying. I remember she reached out to touch his arm, and he jerked it away and said something like, 'I need to think about this.' She didn't look happy at all."

"Do you think she was angry enough to kill him?"

Millie hesitated. "She seemed pretty upset."

Perry took a second to digest that. "I don't know..." Could this be Millie trying to distract him from what she had been doing so early at the theatre on Thursday? But he wouldn't be distracted... "The police were really focused on where people were between five and six-forty weren't they?"

Millie tilted her head. "Why?"

"I don't know." Perry forced a laugh. "But I hope you've got an alibi."

Millie gave a tight smile. "I didn't get here until six-thirty and after was watching you rehearse from the auditorium. Didn't you see me?"

Perry shook his head. "You can't see much from the stage with the lights on. Did you see anyone else other than those onstage?"

"Er... I waved at Colin. He was standing in the wings, but he didn't wave back. I suspect he couldn't see me either."

Convenient or unfortunate?

He studied her closely. "Why did you get here that early? You weren't due onstage until later."

"Yes, I know. My call time wasn't until seven-thirty."

Perry tapped his fingers against the armrest. *So?*

Millie hesitated.

Perry met her gaze. *Tell me! Tell me!*

"I wanted to talk to Em," she said finally. "I didn't know

she'd be directing. Once I was here, it seemed a bit pointless to go home just to have to come back again later."

Before Perry could probe further, Liv's voice rang out. "Five minutes to Act Two, everyone!"

Millie stood. "That's me."

She scurried off as Ralph lumbered down the steps from the stage and joined him. "Have you been interrogating young Millie?" he whispered as he lowered himself into the seat next to Perry. He raised two bushy eyebrows. "Did she do it?"

19

IMMEDIATELY AFTER, SATURDAY 2 OCTOBER

P erry shifted in his seat in the dimly lit auditorium as the murmur of quiet conversation filled the space around him. He stared at Ralph with wide eyes. "What? No, I don't think—"

Ralph smirked. "Relax, my dear, I'm only joking." His blue eyes twinkled with mischief. "Unless that *was* what you were thinking? Are you sleuthing, young Perry?" He wiggled his eyebrows. "I can practically see the gears turning in that beautifully-styled blond head of yours."

He's too perceptive, this man... Perry forced a laugh, keeping his expression light. "I'm just interested, that's all."

"Mm-hmm," Ralph murmured, clearly unconvinced. He opened his mouth as if to press further, but at that moment, Liv shouted, "Places, please, ladies."

Millie swept onstage as Miss Prism, followed by Gina, playing Cecily. As they began their scene, Ralph nudged Perry again.

"Gina's heart isn't in this," Ralph muttered, nodding at the stage. "Not like it used to be."

Perry glanced at him. "Really?"

"She's been phoning it in for weeks. I think all she cares about these days is planning her wedding."

Ralph wasn't wrong. Perry had noticed it himself—Gina's disengagement, the way she went through the motions. She appeared flat compared to Millie's energetic performance.

All of a sudden, a uniformed police officer appeared at the auditorium doors and caught Liv's attention. She lifted her eyes to the ceiling, held up a hand to pause the scene, then walked over. He whispered something, and she nodded, "Take five, everyone. Gina, you're needed, please."

Gina hurried offstage and followed the police officer out of the hall.

Perry turned back to Ralph. "Have you spoken to the police yet?" he asked.

Ralph shook his head. "No, dear boy. I imagine they're seeing the people who were actually here at the time of Noel's demise first." He glanced over at the door Gina had left through. He waggled his eyebrows. "I'm next up for the hot seat, I imagine." His busy eyebrows rose as he lowered his voice. "Did they tell you how Noel died?"

Perry hesitated, wondering how much to reveal. He didn't want Ralph blabbing to the entire cast, but the older man could know something useful. He needed to get his head into undercover-spy mode. *What would I say if I didn't know anything?*

"Well," Perry said, keeping his voice low, "they asked about the fake cigarettes we used."

Ralph's head snapped around so fast, Perry started. "Aha!" the older man exclaimed, fanning himself dramatically with his hand. "That must be it! Something was in the cigarette, wasn't it? Oh, how deliciously devious!"

Perry grunted noncommittally, letting Ralph run with his theory. Ralph's eyes sparkled with excitement.

"You know who I think did it?" Ralph leaned in, his voice a conspiratorial whisper. "Colin!"

Perry blinked, genuinely surprised. "Colin? Why?"

Ralph tapped the side of his nose. "Think about it, my boy. He works in a laboratory, doesn't he?"

Does he? "Really? I didn't know that…"

"So it goes without saying that he must have access to all sorts of nasty chemicals," Ralph said with a knowing look.

Perry had to admit it was a good point.

"And," Ralph continued, warming to his theme, "he's always fiddling with the props. It wouldn't be hard for him to tamper with one of the cigarettes, would it?"

"Okay. But *why* would Colin want to kill Noel?"

Ralph hesitated, less certain now. "Noel was always horrible to him. He made snide remarks all the time."

"He did that to a lot of people, Rafe."

"True." Ralph tapped a finger against his chin. "It could be something we don't know about." He grinned. "Maybe they were having a torrid affair."

Perry couldn't help but chuckle at the absurdity of the idea. "Somehow, I doubt Colin is the torrid type."

Ralph exhaled dramatically. "There's a chance I'm wrong. But wouldn't it be exciting if I'd cracked the case already?"

Perry smiled, patting Ralph's arm. "You never know," he said. There could be something in what Ralph had said about Colin having access to chemicals through his job. He made a mental note to discuss it with Bea and the others later. "Any other theories, Rafe?" The older actor was proving quite helpful with his observations.

Ralph's eyes twinkled mischievously as he leaned in closer. "Well, my dear, there's always the obvious suspect." He paused for dramatic effect. "Stella."

I suppose she is *the most obvious suspect motive wise…*

"A woman scorned and all that," he continued. "And did you know she was here early on Thursday? More than an hour before she was needed!"

"Yes, I was here when she turned up. She said she must've got her call time wrong." He already suspected Stella had been there early to see Noel.

"Rubbish!" Ralph's eyes widened. "Obsession, darling, I'm telling you. Pure and simple. I bet Noel finally told her to leave him alone, and she just... snapped!"

Perry frowned. That didn't quite fit. It didn't feel like a crime of passion. The murder had to have been planned—getting hold of nicotine in that concentration wasn't something you did in the heat of the moment. And anyway, how easy was it to get hold of? Would Stella have had the means to do it?

Before he could respond further, Gina appeared beside them, her long braid swinging as she turned to Ralph. "The police would like to see you now, Rafe."

Ralph stood, straightening his waistcoat. "Ah, my moment in the spotlight! Wish me luck." He struck a dramatic pose, lifting his face to the light. "I'm ready for my interrogation, Mr DeMille."

Perry laughed as Ralph strolled off in the direction of the exit. "I'd like to be a fly on the wall in that interview," he said to Gina as she slid into Ralph's vacated seat.

She smiled shyly, her soft brown eyes meeting Perry's as she toyed nervously with a charm bracelet dangling from her wrist.

"How did you get on with the police?" he asked gently.

"Oh, fine," Gina replied, her voice a tad too high. "I didn't have much to tell them, really. I was getting ready to leave home for rehearsals when Liv texted about the accident and told me not to come in. Imagine my shock when she rang later to say Noel had died."

Perry watched her closely. There was something off about her demeanour, a hint of nervous energy that seemed out of character for the usually laid-back Gina.

"Did you know Noel well?" he asked.

Her nose wrinkled a little. "Not really. When I first joined the Players two years ago, he flirted with me, which made me uncomfortable, so I kept my distance after that. Fortunately, when I got engaged last year, he lost interest." She paused, fiddling with her bracelet again. "Though he told me once I'd 'lost my edge' since getting engaged."

Perry thought back to Ralph's earlier observation about Gina's recent lacklustre performances. Perhaps Noel had had a point.

"He might not have been my favourite person around here, but it's so sad," Gina continued, her voice softening. "And poor Stella. Noel treated her terribly."

Perry wondered if she, like Millie, thought Stella had been justified in getting rid of Noel.

Gina's eyes darted around the auditorium before she leaned in closer to Perry. "Can I ask you something?" she whispered.

Perry's pulse kicked up a notch. "Of course," he replied, trying to keep his voice casual.

"Did you... tell the police everything you know? I mean, even if it wasn't what they asked?"

Perry stifled the urge to lean in even closer. "What do you mean?"

Gina bit her lip. "They asked if I knew anyone who might want to harm Noel. I said no because I don't, but…" She trailed off, her lips pressed together in a slight grimace.

But what? "What do you know, Gina?"

Gina hesitated, clearly torn. "I heard a conversation between Noel and one of the cast… But I don't think it's really my business to say anything to the police."

Tell me! "Tell me," Perry urged, trying to keep his voice calm. "And I can help you decide if it's worth mentioning."

Gina paused for a moment. As she opened her mouth to speak though, the auditorium door swung open with a loud *creak*. Liv bustled in, her clipboard clutched to her chest. "Oh good, Gina, you're back!" she chirped. "We can carry on now. Perry, don't forget you're in this scene too. Come on now. Chop! Chop!"

Gina jumped up. "Don't worry," she said lightly, patting Perry on the shoulder. "I'm sure it's not even relevant."

Perry clenched his jaw as she disappeared towards the stage. *But it could be!* And now he'd have to corner her on her own again later to find out…

20

10:15 PM, SATURDAY 2 OCTOBER

The salty breeze rolled in from the sea, carrying the crisp bite of early October. Perry Juke zipped up his stylish leather jacket and tucked his hands into his pockets as he strolled along the Promenade. The air was cool, but not unpleasantly so, and the quiet murmur of the tide washing against the shore was a comforting backdrop for his late-night walk.

He glanced at his watch. Hopefully, Simon wouldn't be too shattered after a busy evening at SaltAir. Perry's eyes softened, recalling the worried text he'd had from his step-daughter, Isla, earlier today. She'd said her dad had sounded distracted and exhausted on the phone when she'd rung him that morning. Perry pulled his shoulders back. *Time for an intervention with my overstretched husband.* Perry needed a little heart-to-heart with Simon before he worked himself into an early grave.

He passed the now dark shopfronts lining the main road, their colourful awnings flapping in the breeze. Most of the day-trippers had long gone, leaving only the locals and a few late-night stragglers lingering outside pubs and restaurants, their laughter drifting in the air. Streetlights cast long golden reflections on the pavement, and somewhere down an alley-way, a seagull screeched, indignant about something or other —probably food related.

Perry's mind wandered back to rehearsals. He couldn't believe he'd missed Gina before she'd left—she'd been about to tell him something before they'd resumed the second act. He wanted to know what juicy bit of gossip she might have overheard. His pulse sped up at the thought. *It could be important.* And now he had to wait until tomorrow to find out...

He sighed, adjusting his stride as he neared SaltAir. The restaurant's exterior was dark save for a few lights still on inside. He tapped on the glass, and Simon appeared almost instantly, scanning the street before opening the door. "Ah, double-oh-six-and-a-half," Simon said, his eyes darting left and right dramatically before he stepped aside to let Perry in. "Were you followed?"

Perry smirked. "Doubtful, unless you count a rather suspi-cious-looking seagull that's lurking in a shop doorway over there."

Simon grinned as he locked the door behind them. They stepped further into the restaurant. The smell of herbs, garlic, and something buttery still clung to the air. Two of the kitchen staff—a man and a woman in chef's whites— emerged from the back.

"Kitchen's all sorted, boss. We're heading out," the woman said.

"Thanks, both of you. See you next week," Simon said, and they waved as they left through the side exit.

Perry's stomach dropped as he took a moment to really look at Simon—the shadows pooled beneath his eyes, the weight behind his movements. He was shattered. "How was service?"

"Buzzing and busy." He gave a weary smile as he plucked at his beard. He gestured to the now spotless dining room. "Ryan and Fay have already headed up to their flat. I thought I'd give them a break and finish locking up myself."

No wonder he was so tired if he'd supervised the clear-up on his own. *But what can I do?* "I could murder a coffee after all that undercover work," Perry said breezily. "What do you say to me playing barista for a change?"

Simon let out a weary sigh, then smiled. "That would be much appreciated, Mr Bond."

As Perry disappeared towards the bar in the far corner, his phone beeped.

Bea: *Breakfast at The Dower House tomorrow? Compare notes on today's sleuthing?*

He typed back quickly.

Perry: *Yes, please. I've got stuff to share. See you in the morning.*

Not long after, he returned with two steaming mugs and plonked one in front of Simon before collapsing into a chair opposite him.

Simon cradled his coffee and inhaled heavily. "Mmm... that smells good."

Perry sipped his drink. *Here goes…* "Right. So this is me saying I'm worried about you."

Simon groaned. "Perry—"

"No, shush. Isla texted me earlier. She's worried about you too. And she's your daughter, so she trumps me."

Simon drew his eyebrows together, rubbing his face. "I'll be fine once I get through this deadline."

"You said that last time." Perry shook his head. "And then there will be the next deadline, and the next. It never ends. And forgive me for saying so, but you don't seem to be enjoying it anymore. Any of it."

"I feel like I'm trying to keep too many plates spinning," Simon admitted reluctantly.

Perry reached across the table to take Simon's hand, giving it a gentle squeeze. "If you had to choose," he asked softly. "Right now. Writing or the restaurant—which would it be?"

Simon met his gaze. His lips softened into a smile. "Writing," he said without hesitation. "It's my passion." He shrugged. "Don't get me wrong, I love cooking and the restaurant, but... it was more fun when it was merely a hobby. Now it feels like a job. Writing though? That never feels like work, no matter how challenging it gets. It's part of who I am."

"Then we'll figure out a way for you to focus on your writing," Perry said firmly. "Whatever it takes. You can't kill yourself trying to do both. Your happiness is non-negotiable, love. We'll make it work."

Simon's eyes shone as he tilted his head to one side. "Have I mentioned lately how lucky I am to have you?"

"Once or twice," Perry smirked. "But you can always tell me again."

Simon exhaled and rubbed his face. "I don't want to leave Ryan in the lurch."

Perry softened his voice. "Ryan's your friend. Have you actually told him how you feel?"

Simon gave a half-shrug.

I thought not...

His husband stared down at the dregs of his coffee. "What I really want is to take some time next year, properly focus on writing. Do the US book tour. Go for a while—explore the country." He hesitated, then glanced up at Perry. "Come with me."

Perry blinked, caught off guard. *Go to the US with him?* His pulse raced.

Simon smiled, a little self-conscious. "Wouldn't it be fun? We could hire an RV. Drive around."

Perry's gut twisted. "What, like a camper van?"

Simon snorted. "No. These are American RVs. They're like travelling hotel suites. All the amenities. Think about it— road trips, great food, music, no responsibilities for a bit. Just us. Seeing new places, having adventures."

Perry's mouth was dry. He took a sip of lukewarm coffee. *Could we?* He was already thinking about it—really thinking about it. He'd barely left Fenshire since he'd started working at Francis Court at the age of nineteen. The idea of getting away for a while, of being with Simon somewhere new, somewhere exciting… it was tempting.

In fact, it was more than tempting.

Only... Perry narrowed his eyes. "Will there be sharks?" *Don't Americans get bitten by sharks all the time?*

Simon made a choking sound, then gave a small shake of his head. "No sharks."

Perry sat back, still a little dazed by the offer. But there was something else nagging at him now. "I don't want to leave Bea to do everything by herself."

"Hey," Simon said gently, reaching across and squeezing Perry's hand. "There will be plenty of time to plan your sabbatical. Besides, with her upcoming nuptials to Rich, I suspect some changes are on the horizon for her too."

Perry nodded slowly, considering Simon's words. "You're right. I'll talk to her soon. But" —he fixed Simon with a pointed look— "only if you promise to have that chat with Ryan about the restaurant. Deal?"

Simon held out his hand, grinning. "Deal." Perry shook it firmly.

"Sorted," Simon said, finishing his coffee. "Now, tell me, how was your sneaky-beaky spying this evening?"

Wouldn't you like to know… Perry's eyes twinkled. "Oh, I've got some theories brewing. But I'm dying to hear what Mike and Bea have dug up too." He glanced at his phone. "Speaking of which, we're all having breakfast at The Dower House in the morning to compare notes."

Simon pushed back his chair. "In that case, let's go home."

As Simon turned off the lights and locked up, Perry felt happier than he had for a while. Hopefully, this was the first step on the road for Simon to get back to what he loved doing. And it could come with an American adventure for them both to boot.

But first, he needed to concentrate on his acting debut and catching Noel's killer.

21

THE NEXT MORNING. SUNDAY 3 OCTOBER

T*he Daily Post* online article:

End of the Fairytale: Prince and Princess of Wales Finalise Divorce

By Victoria Harcourt, Royal Correspondent, The Daily Post

After months of speculation, Gollingham Palace has today confirmed that the divorce between His Royal Highness, The Prince of Wales, and Anika, Princess of Wales, has been finalised. In a statement released by the Palace, it was announced that Prince Robert has been granted full custody of the couple's twin sons, who will remain in the UK under his care, while the Princess will have access to them during school holidays.

In keeping with royal precedent, Anika will retain the title Princess of Wales but will no longer be styled as Her Royal

Highness, marking her formal departure from the royal family. Sources close to the Princess say she intends to return to her native South Africa, where she hopes to live a quieter, more private life after struggling to adjust to the demands of royal duty.

Once hailed as a modern royal romance, the couple's whirlwind courtship thirteen years ago captured the nation's imagination. The dashing, duty-bound Robert—ten years Anika's senior—fell hard and fast for the glamorous conservationist during a royal tour of Africa, and their engagement was announced just six months later. But while their grand wedding was a spectacle watched by millions, behind the palace walls, cracks were already beginning to show.

Friends of the Princess say she never truly settled into royal life, feeling stifled by the constant scrutiny and rigid expectations. "Anika tried, she really did," one close source revealed. "But she was never cut out for the endless public engagements, the protocol, the expectations. She wanted to be a wife and mother first and a royal second—but in that family, duty always comes first."

It is understood that Anika had been unhappy for some time but was waiting until the twins turned 11 and went off to boarding school before deciding to walk away from royal life for good. The divorce, though painful, has reportedly been "amicable", with both parties committed to co-parenting their sons and maintaining a respectful relationship.

The King and Queen are said to be deeply saddened by Anika's decision to leave but are understanding of her wish for privacy and a return to her roots. A palace insider said, "They respect her choice, and while they wish things had turned out differently, they want her to be happy. The Queen, in particular, is very fond of Anika, but she knows that royal life isn't for everyone."

The Prince of Wales, meanwhile, has remained character-istically stoic, focusing on his duties and raising his sons. Palace sources say he is not seeking to remarry soon, with his priority firmly on his children and his role within the royal family.

Anika, Princess of Wales, is expected to settle in Cape Town, where she will be close to her parents and her siblings. There are no plans for her to give interviews or speak publicly about her marriage, and she is said to be looking forward to a peaceful life away from the royal spotlight.

But with the departure of such a high-profile royal, questions remain about what this means for the monarchy. With the working royal family already slimmed down, and the Prince of Wales now shouldering the weight of future duty alone, he will be grateful when his cousin, Lord Frederick Astley, and his fiancee, Summer York, begin their full-time royal duties after their wedding in November.

While their addition is expected to ease the burden on Prince Robert, royal commentators have questioned whether the current lineup of senior royals will be enough to maintain the institution's presence at home and abroad. Could there be further changes on the horizon?

———

"I'm glad to hear Mike is taking a day off. He needs it," Simon said as he leaned under the table and held out a piece of bacon to Daisy, who was lurking by his leg. A soft snuffle, and the food disappeared.

"Simon!" Bea gave him a look. "Remember, no treats. She still needs to lose a little of her bulk."

Simon gave Daisy a sympathetic look. "But it was only a tiny bit, wasn't it, little girl?" The small white terrier looked up at him, her head tilted to one side. "How can I resist that cute little face?" Simon said, looking over at Bea.

"Try!" she replied with a smile.

Perry stifled a laugh, but Bea caught the guilty look he exchanged with Simon. She looked at his plate where he'd cut up some small morsels of sausage. *Not him too!*

"That goes for you too, Perry," Rich chimed in, pointing at his plate.

Perry feigned innocence, his eyes twinkling. "Who, me? I would never break Daisy's diet."

"Um…" Rich clearly wasn't convinced.

"Okay," Simon said, buttering a piece of toast. "Let's consolidate what we know." He turned to Rich. "Did anything come up on the background checks?"

Rich put down his cup of coffee and tapped on his tablet. "Nothing too juicy, I'm afraid. Emily Shaw seems to make a tidy income selling items on eBay. I'm not sure what exactly. I'm still looking into it, but it's probably not relevant. Colin and Kurt both have chemistry backgrounds. That could be promising."

Perry perked up. "Promising for poisoning people?"

"I was thinking more along the lines of providing the victim with drugs. But, yes, that too." Rich picked his cup back up and took a sip.

Bea recalled her interviews from the day before. "Colin works at a water treatment plant, which could grant him access to various chemicals. Kurt is a freelance science teacher. I'll be honest, I didn't make the connection yesterday, but you're right, he likely has some access too."

"And what was your impression of the interviewees?" Perry asked. "Did anyone jump out at you as being especially suspicious?"

Bea huffed. "To be honest, with the exception of Tom

Hatlee, who was almost brutal in his honesty, they all seemed like they were hiding something, although, of course, it could've simply been nerves around being interviewed by the police." She continued, "It felt like Liv was hiding something she knew about Noel, but I don't know what. Em got cagey when theatre props were mentioned. Kurt straight out denied that Noel was on drugs, which seemed odd when so many others mentioned it as a possibility. Colin was very edgy throughout the interview, as if he was hiding something. And Stella and Millie were both vague about why they each got there early that night."

"They didn't give any reason?" Rich asked Bea.

"Stella said she misread the call sheet, and Millie told us she wanted to talk to one of the other cast," Bea replied. "Neither of them seemed convincing to me."

Perry nodded. "Stella told me she went to wait in the dressing room, but Millie said that when she arrived at about half-six, Stella and Noel were outside arguing, and Stella seemed pretty angry."

Ah... Bea's eyes widened. "Really? So Stella might have been there to confront Noel."

"My thoughts exactly," Perry replied, then he smirked. "Gina Bernet also told me she overheard Noel and a cast member having a conversation about something that she thinks might be relevant."

Bea frowned. Gina had said very little when she and Mike had interviewed her and certainly nothing about Noel's relationships with other members of the cast. "Which is?" she prompted him.

Perry tossed his head. "Unfortunately, she didn't have a chance to tell me before we were called on the stage to rehearse, but I'll catch her tonight and get the full story."

"What about the timeline, Bea?" Simon asked. "Your text

said it could be narrowed down to a period between ten past five and six-forty. Is that right?"

Bea explained to them about the fake cigarettes being in a sterilising solution from the night before until Colin got them ready and laid them out on the prop table.

"So that rules out anyone who wasn't at the theatre between those times," Simon said.

"Indeed. Mike and I narrowed down the suspects based on who had access to the props table during that window to: Em the stage manager; Colin the lighting tech; Stella, Noel's ex; Kurt, who plays Lane; Perry's understudy Tom; and Millie, who plays Miss Prism."

"I can vouch that the props were left on a table back-stage," Perry added. "So there was plenty of opportunity for skulduggery without being spotted from the stage."

"And none of them have an alibi for that time?" Rich asked.

Bea shook her head. "They were either on the stage, back-stage, or on their own for some or all of that time. So unless we can narrow that window, then the only person with an alibi is…" She smiled. "Guess…"

"Perry!" Rich laughed.

"Yes, Perry, you were the only one who was seen by at least one other person since the time you arrived a few minutes before six until Noel collapsed at six-forty-five."

Perry gave an exaggerated swipe of his hand across his brow. "Phew, that's me off the hook then!"

"So to summarise," Simon said, taking a sip of coffee, "we have six suspects. Two of them have a chemical back-ground. At least one of the six we know was lying about where they were during the window when the prop was tampered with. And another of the six is withholding poten-tial important information from the police. And finally, the rest all seem to be holding back info, with the exception of Tom?"

Bea's eyebrows rose in silent agreement.

"It doesn't sound like much when you say it like that," Perry said, sounding disappointed.

"It's early days yet. I think the best thing we can do at this stage is pass on what Perry found out to Mike tomorrow and see what he wants to do next," Rich said.

Bea knew he was right, but like Perry, it felt a bit slow to her. Normally by now in an investigation, they'd be speculating about who the most likely suspect was and—

"For what it's worth, my money is on Colin," Perry blurted out. "He's got a background in chemistry, so could presumably make up a fatal dose of nicotine. He's familiar with how the fake cigarettes work, and he had access to them. After all, it would have been super easy for him to add the nicotine before he put them out on the props table. We only have his word about the timings."

That's means and opportunity. Recalling Colin's fidgeting hands and darting eyes during his interview, he could be guilty. *But...* "What about motive?" she asked. "Colin said he didn't really know Noel that well. Why would he want to kill him?"

"Ralph claims Noel was always being mean to Colin. I saw it myself a few times. Maybe it was enough..." He trailed off, sounding a little less convinced now.

Isn't there an obvious suspect? "What about Stella? She could have gone backstage while you were rehearsing and fiddled with the props. We know she lied about where she was at the time. And she seems to be the only one we know for sure who was upset and possibly angry at Noel. She seems to have a strong motive."

Perry dipped his chin. "I agree. But would she really have

the resources to obtain the nicotine dose and know how the fake cigarette worked so that Noel would inhale it?"

That's a fair point. Stella was a marketing guru, wasn't she? Would she have the capability to kill Noel that way?

Simon, ever the voice of reason, held up a hand. "Hold on, I think we're jumping to conclusions. At this stage, they're all suspects until we can prove them otherwise."

Rich shrugged. "True. Although if either Colin or Kurt turn out to be Noel's drug supplier, that would certainly bump them up the list for me."

They all murmured in agreement. "Okay. I'll talk to Mike tomorrow," Bea said. "And Perry, see what more you can find out from your castmates. They may open up to you."

"Yes, Miss Moneypenny," Perry said in a Sean Connery voice.

Bea rolled her eyes at him, looked at her watch, then at Rich. "We'd best be off. We can't keep the king waiting!"

She'd had a call last night requesting she and Rich attend her uncle, the king, at Gollingham Palace in Surrey this afternoon. She had no idea why, but of course, they had to go. She'd told Perry and Simon about it when they had arrived for breakfast.

Perry leaned in, a cheeky glint in his eye. "Perhaps there's been a royal scandal—a murder, even—that the king wants to keep under wraps. He's probably summoning you two to discreetly investigate."

Bea failed to suppress a smile, while Rich shook his head, laughing. "Let's hope it's nothing so dramatic," he said.

Simon chuckled. "Are you taking Daisy with you? She can keep the royal corgis entertained while you talk business."

Daisy perked up at the mention of her name, her tail wagging enthusiastically.

Bea grinned. "Funny you should say that, but do you think—"

Simon held up a hand. "Yes, I'll have Daisy. She can keep me company while I'm holed up in my office all day writing."

"Thanks, you're an angel," Bea said, rising and patting Simon on the arm. "But no stuffing her full of treats, alright?"

22

THAT AFTERNOON, SUNDAY 3 OCTOBER

Perry was browsing the greeting card section in Windstanton's independent bookshop when he spotted Gina Bernet at the counter, paying for a stack of magazines. She looked a little flustered, fumbling for the right coins as she chatted to the cashier.

Perry hesitated. *What a piece of luck!* Yesterday, just as she was about to tell him something interesting about Noel, they'd been interrupted, and he hadn't had a chance to follow up. If she was hesitating to go to the police, it was possible she'd feel more comfortable telling him now.

This was the perfect chance to talk to her.

He strolled over as Gina was stuffing her purse into her handbag. "Hey, Gina."

She blinked, startled, then gave him a small smile. "Oh! Hi, Perry. Sorry, I didn't see you."

"Fancy a coffee?" His mouth tugged into a half-smile as he nodded in the direction of the café across the street. "I know *I* could use one."

She hesitated for a fraction of a second, then smiled back. "Yeah, okay. I've got time."

The café was bustling, the hum of conversation and the hiss of the espresso machine blending into a comfortable background noise. They found a small table near the window, and after ordering two cappuccinos, Gina said, "Did you get the message that we're back in the theatre for rehearsals this evening? It feels a bit weird, doesn't it... you know, knowing that's where..." She trailed off as she gave an exaggerated shiver.

Perry gave a thoughtful hum. He'd also had the text from Liv saying the police had finished with the theatre and they could go back in this evening. "It will be a bit strange, but I suppose we'll have to get used to being on that stage again."

Perry let the moment settle before steering the conversation to what he really wanted to ask. "So..." He leaned back, watching her stir sugar into her coffee. "Yesterday, you were about to tell me something about Noel and one of the cast. You weren't sure whether to go to the police?"

Gina froze mid-stir. A flicker of hesitation crossed her face, but then she relaxed her shoulders, putting her spoon down. "Yeah... it's been on my mind."

"Why don't you tell me, and I'll let you know what I think."

She bit her lip, glancing at the window as if checking no one could overhear them. "It was months ago," she said finally. "June time, in fact. We were doing final run-throughs for *Noises Off*. Anyway, I'd got there early, so I was in one of the private boxes, scrolling on my phone, when I heard voices down below. It was Noel and Colin."

Colin? A tightness crept into Perry's chest. "Go on."

Gina exhaled slowly. "Noel was asking Colin where he could get some drugs."

Perry's stomach knotted. He'd expected something along

these lines, but hearing it confirmed sent his thoughts racing. "Noel simply… asked outright?"

"Yeah. And he sounded pretty confident. Like he knew Colin could help him. I remember his exact words—" She lowered her voice. "'With your background, you can probably hook me up with something.'"

Perry felt a cold prickle on the back of his neck.

"And?" Perry pressed. "Did Colin say yes?"

Gina hesitated, then gave a quick shake of her head. "I don't know exactly. I couldn't hear everything. But Colin didn't seem surprised. He didn't freak out or tell Noel to get lost. From what I caught, Noel kept pressing, saying he needed a little something to help him focus on opening night."

Perry rubbed his chin. If Colin hadn't outright refused, that meant he could have been Noel's supplier. And if Colin had been supplying him, then maybe…

Gina fidgeted with her spoon. "At the time, I didn't think it mattered. Yeah, Noel was asking for drugs, but you know…" She shrugged. "And Colin… well, he didn't say much. But now—" She sighed. "Now Noel's dead, and I heard that the police found drugs on him. What if Colin gave him something dodgy? What if it went wrong?"

Perry stared at his coffee, his mind churning. *But that's not what killed him. It was the nicotine in the fake cigarette.* But if Colin had been trying to cover his tracks, then… Perry tapped his fingers against the table. "I think you should tell the police."

Gina bit her lip. "You think it's relevant then?"

"I think it could be," Perry said carefully. "If Colin was Noel's supplier, then the police need to know."

Gina looked troubled. "I don't know… I don't want to throw accusations around if I got it wrong."

Perry softened his voice. "I get it. But don't worry. All the police will do is investigate. If they find it's nothing to do with the case, then they'll not take it any further."

"Really?" Gina nodded slowly. "Okay. I'll do it."

As they finished up their coffees, Perry's mind was already working overtime. Colin was now their major suspect, surely.

————

Perry practically flew through the front door of Rose Cottage, tossing his keys onto the hall table with a *clang*. He'd spent the entire drive home turning Gina's words over in his head. Noel had asked Colin for drugs. Colin hadn't outright refused. The police had found drugs on Noel's body. It wasn't all a coincidence, was it?

What shall I do? It was only a partly heard conversation. He needed more—something solid—before he shared it with the others. Otherwise, they'd tell him he was jumping to conclusions.

Which, in fairness, I probably am.

And anyway, Bea and Rich were in London. Mike was on a well-deserved day off, and Simon was holed up in his office at the bottom of the garden, trying to get another chapter completed. Perry knew better than to disturb him when he was writing.

He was on his own.

He glanced at his watch. It was still early. Rehearsals didn't start for almost an hour. But with the move back to the theatre, there was a good chance that Colin and Em were already there getting it all set up. It would be the perfect time to talk to Colin before the rest of the cast arrived. *But hold on.* Hadn't he heard Em say to Liv that she might be a bit late tonight? Something about a family dinner? So Colin could be there alone…

His expression turned firm. *I need to be sensible.* He couldn't simply confront Colin on his own, could he? That would be reckless. After all, Colin *could* be the killer…

Perry grabbed his phone and dialled.

"Perry, my dear," came the sing-song greeting, "you do realise I'm about to sit down with a rather lovely bowl of pasta and a small glass of rosé?"

"But we have rehearsals in less than an hour."

"Not me, dear boy. I'm not called until later."

Perry stifled a groan. So that was his plan out of the window.

Ralph's voice turned serious. "What's wrong, Perry?"

"I wanted to talk to someone in the cast," Perry reply, pacing the length of the hallway. "But I wanted someone with me."

There was a pause. Then a sigh. "Are you channelling Miss Marple, old boy?"

Perry exhaled. He may as well tell Ralph everything. It was probably the only way he would get his help. "I think Colin might have been Noel's drug supplier. And if so, it's possible he might have killed him to cover his tracks."

That got Ralph's attention. "Go on."

Perry rushed through the conversation he'd had with Gina, barely stopping for breath. "I need to talk to him before he gets spooked and clams up."

"And you think doing this now, in the dead of night, rather than waiting until tomorrow, when you could bring in, oh, I don't know, maybe *actual* detectives, is the best course of action?"

Perry rolled his eyes. "It's not the dead of night; it's

barely five-fifteen. And I want to talk to him. That's all. Just a chat."

"And you want me there to stop him from killing you?"

"Yeah. Something like that."

There was a long silence.

Then Ralph muttered, "I'm warning you now, I'll be practically useless in a fight…"

Perry grinned. "So you'll come?"

"Obviously. Someone has to keep you from getting murdered. But you owe me dinner in that lovely restaurant of your husband's."

"Of course."

"And a bottle of wine."

"Fine."

"And it has to include dessert. I hear they do a chocolate bombe that's to die for."

Perry huffed. "I'll meet you at the theatre in fifteen minutes."

"I'm on my way."

Perry hung up, grinning. He grabbed his coat, ignoring the niggling voice in his head that sounded suspiciously like Simon's, telling him he should call the police first.

I'm only talking to him… That should be okay, shouldn't it?

23

MEANWHILE, SUNDAY 3 OCTOBER

B ea sat stiffly in the back of the car as they passed
through the grand wrought-iron gates of Gollingham
Palace. Even though she'd been here countless times before,
she still felt a nervous flutter in her stomach. Her mind raced.
What could her uncle possibly want? They'd already
discussed wedding plans with the king and queen last month.
Her mother had been infuriatingly vague when Bea had asked
what this summons was about. "Please keep an open mind,
darling," she'd said airily.

As the car progressed up the sweeping driveway, which
was lined with towering oaks that led up to the imposing
palace entrance, Bea glanced at Rich. He looked completely
at ease beside her, one arm resting casually on the back of the
seat, his gaze flicking idly out of the window as the palace
grounds unfolded before them.

She shook her head slowly. "How are you so calm?" she
murmured.

He turned to her with an amused glint in his eyes. "I used
to work here, remember?" he said. *Of course!* He'd blended

into her life so easily over the last six months that she'd forgotten he'd been around royal palaces during his years of working for PaIRS, the Protection and Investigation (Royal) Service.

"Although, coming in this way is a bit of a novelty. The security wing is hidden around the back," he added.

She nodded. She'd been involved in an investigation with him earlier in the year and had spent time in that part of the palace. She shuddered. It had also been where he'd been shot.

"Are you alright?" He smiled at her as he reached over and gave her hand a squeeze.

She couldn't help but return his smile. They were together. *It will be alright.* "I'm wondering what my uncle wants."

"Search me." Rich shrugged, keeping hold of her hand. "But your brother was acting very chipper at dinner last night. He and Summer could barely contain themselves over something."

Bea had noticed it too but had assumed it was excitement over their upcoming wedding.

"And when they left, Fred wished us luck for today. Why would we need luck?" Rich looked puzzled.

Bea frowned. "Yes. And what was that he said to you as they left? It sounded like, 'This could be the solution to your problems.' What was that about?"

"I assume he was talking about the fishing spot we're setting up at Three Lakes. He thinks I need a hobby."

He could be right... When Rich returned to work, a relaxing activity like that could help him deal with the frustrations of his job. Bea didn't really get fishing—all that sitting around with the hope that you *might* catch something seemed like a waste of time to her, but it was a sport of patience, strategy, and technique, according to her father, who loved to fish.

Rich had certainly seemed in better spirits these last few days, since he'd decided to take the following week off. He'd been animated in the car, chatting about his plans with Fred to set up this fishing lake at the Three Lakes rehabilitation centre. It was going to add another tool to the recovery program for the military personnel and veterans. *It's good to see him so excited about something.*

The car came to a smooth stop at the palace entrance. A tall, dignified butler in a pristine morning suit was already waiting for them. A footman glided forward and opened the car door. Bea stepped out, taking a steadying breath and forcing a serene expression onto her face.

They followed the butler inside, their footsteps echoing against the polished marble floor. As they walked through the palace corridors, Bea's gaze swept over the familiar grandeur —vaulted ceilings, enormous oil paintings, and ornate tapestries. They passed the gilded double doors leading to the state rooms.

If they weren't being taken there, then this wasn't a formal audience. This was a family matter.

The butler led them through a set of grand oak doors, and they stepped into the private wing of the palace. The atmosphere changed immediately—less ornate, more comfortable, with soft lighting and a sense of home rather than duty.

They stopped in front of a large mahogany door, and the butler knocked sharply.

A footman opened it, stepping aside as they were announced.

"The Countess of Rossex and Superintendent Richard Fitzwilliam, Your Majesty."

They stepped inside. The sitting room was warm and inviting, a far cry from the formal state rooms—plush armchairs and shelves lined with books instead of ceremonial regalia.

Her uncle, the king, stood as they entered, a welcoming smile on his face. Beside him, grinning like the cat who'd got the cream, was her brother, Fred. Bea's pulse quickened. *What's he doing here?*

Bea curtsied, and the king, still smiling, came forward to embrace her lightly. "Beatrice, my dear. Thank you for coming."

She straightened, smoothing her dress. "Of course, Uncle."

The king turned to Rich, extending his hand. "Richard. Good to see you again."

Rich gave a short bow, then shook it firmly. "You too, Your Majesty."

"Sit, sit." The king gestured to the sofas opposite him.

Fred looked fit to burst. Bea shot him a quizzical glance as she perched beside Rich on the offered sofa.

The king settled opposite them and steepled his fingers. "Thank you for coming on such short notice. I have a proposition for you both."

———

The black Bentley glided through the gates of Gollingham Palace, Fraser expertly navigating through the swarm of photographers camped outside. The press surged forward, their cameras flashing, shouting questions that were swallowed by the purr of the engine.

Bea flinched reflexively, shielding her eyes. She'd never get used to this—the hungry lenses, the intrusive shouts.

"We may need to get used to this," Rich said wryly, his thumb tracing soothing circles on her wrist, "if we take your uncle up on his offer."

She blinked absently, barely noticing as they pulled away from the frenzy and into the quieter streets beyond. Her mind was still replaying every word of the conversation they'd just had with the king.

"The fact is, the monarchy is at a crossroads," he'd begun. "Robert desperately needs support now that Anika is going back to South Africa, and he's basically raising the children alone. The old guard simply can't shoulder the load. It's time to pass the torch."

He had turned to Fred and grinned. "Why do you think I've recruited this reprobate and his lovely wife-to-be into the working family? Needs must!"

"Steady on now, uncle," Fred had responded, and they'd all laughed.

"So how would you two feel about taking up royal duties too?" the king had continued.

Bea had blinked, stunned. *Working royals? Me and Rich?* She hadn't expected that…

Her uncle had laid it out carefully. They would start gradually, taking on limited duties while they were engaged, then transitioning to full-time working royals after their wedding.

Fred had been practically bouncing in his seat with enthusiasm. "Think of all we could do together—you, Rich, Summer, and me," he had said to Bea, his excitement palpable. "Charities, worthwhile causes—"

"And overseas tours, of course," her uncle had jumped in. "Robert won't want to leave the boys during term time, at least not for a few more years yet."

She'd felt a flicker of something then. Memories of the early days. Before James' death. She'd loved it then, being a working royal—the sense of purpose, the ability to use her position for something meaningful. She'd been useful.

Until everything had gone so wrong.

Her uncle had acknowledged that too. "I know it hasn't been easy for you, Beatrice. The press were... relentless after James died."

Relentless was an understatement. After her husband's death, she'd become their favourite subject—every movement of hers scrutinised, every aspect of her grief picked apart, the never-ending speculation about the female passenger who'd died in the earl's car with him when it had crashed.

And now, here she was, being asked to step back into the fire.

She felt Rich's hand squeeze hers. She glanced at him next to her. His profile was calm, but she knew his mind must be racing too. The press had already dragged his name through the mud this summer, digging up every skeleton they could find—his estranged father, his ex-wife. Could she really ask him to walk into this life with her?

Their eyes met. "How are you feeling about all this?" Rich asked, his voice gentle.

Bea sighed, running her free hand through her thick red hair. "Honestly? I'm torn. Part of me remembers how fulfilling it was before... You know, before everything changed."

Rich nodded, understanding in his eyes. After all, he'd been there as part of the team investigating James's death. He knew what she'd been through.

"But the press," Bea continued, her voice dropping. "After James... and then this summer, with us. Your ex-wife. Your father. I can't help but worry." She glanced at him. "And you'll have to leave the police force too."

"I know." He blew out a breath. "It's been my whole life. It's what I do. Walking away from it…"

She studied him, seeing the conflict in his expression.

His lips pressed into a line. "It's a big thing. But…"

She had a feeling there was a 'but'. She'd seen the way Rich had lit up when the king had described the philanthropic side of being a working royal, the difference they could make highlighting good causes. Like Fred, Rich hadn't been able to hide his excitement. "But?" she prompted.

He hesitated. "I won't lie. The idea of working with Fred on projects, doing something meaningful beyond simply chasing criminals—there's appeal in that. And overseas work? That actually excites me."

He definitely looked more animated than he did when talking about his current job. "Really?"

"I enjoyed that part of my career when I was in royal protection. And if we do this, we'd be together. That's what matters to me the most."

Her throat tightened.

"What about you?" he asked.

Me, a working royal again?

She hesitated, then admitted, "I don't know. The work itself—I loved it. I felt like I was actually doing something worthwhile. But the press? The scrutiny? I don't know…"

Rich squeezed her hand again. "Then we take our time. We think it through properly."

Can I do it? It would be different this time. She would have Rich by her side through it all. Could *they* really do this? Turn their lives upside down and step into the spotlight?

Bea exhaled, nodding. She would need to talk to Sam. The inevitable attention would fall on him too if they agreed. And there was one other person whose counsel she should seek. *I need to talk to my mother.* Her mother had lived this life for decades. She was in a good position to help them navigate this decision.

And as much as Bea hated to admit it, her mother was usually right.

24

MEANWHILE, BACK WITH PERRY,
SUNDAY 3 OCTOBER

Perry and Ralph slipped through the unlocked stage door, into the dimly-lit backstage area of Windstanton Theatre Royal. The heavy door swung shut behind them with a soft *click*.

"Unlocked," Ralph whispered dramatically. "Ominous."

Perry rolled his eyes. "Of course it's unlocked. Colin will be here setting up."

"You say that," Ralph muttered, peering into the gloomy corridor, "but I swear all theatres are haunted. It's a rule. All those old actors who never quite got the standing ovation they wanted…" Glancing around, he continued, "This place gives me the creeps when it's empty."

Perry shot him a look. "You're an actor, Rafe. You should be used to dark theatres."

"Yes, well, usually there's an audience and a bar."

A faint *thump* echoed from somewhere above. Both of them froze.

Then there was a shuffle.

Ralph grabbed Perry's arm. "What's that?"

Perry rolled his eyes, questioning his decision to bring the older actor. "It's most likely Colin. You know, because he *is* the lighting guy?"

"Yeah," Ralph whispered back. "But what if it's not?" He raised his other hand to his throat and muttered, "It feels a bit murdery in here."

They had instinctively lowered their voices. *This is ridiculous!* They were whispering like children sneaking into the neighbours' back garden to steal apples. "What are we doing?" Perry muttered. "Are we whispering because they can't see us if we're quiet?"

"Shut up," Ralph whispered back, gesturing for Perry to follow.

They moved carefully past racks of costumes and stacked scenery flats. As they neared the stage, the theatre's house-lights were on, casting long shadows across the floor. The vast auditorium stretched out before them as they crept forward, stepping cautiously onto the stage.

Another noise. A rustle near the footlights.

Ralph gasped. "I tell you—it's a ghost," he said, stopping.

"Don't be silly; it's just Colin," Perry said as he turned. "See."

A figure stood at the edge of the light on the other side of the stage.

"Perry, Rafe," Colin called out. "How are you—"

There was a creak above them. Perry looked up. The lighting rig! A tremor ran through his chest. The enormous metal frame above them swayed dangerously. *Something's wrong.* The rig wasn't supposed to move—not like that.

"Colin, get out of the way!" Perry cried, grabbing Ralph's velvet jacket and dragging him backwards.

Ralph yelped as they stumbled right as the rig came crashing down with an ear-splitting bang. It smashed onto the stage where Colin had been standing. The impact sent dust and splintered wood flying into the air.

For a moment, nothing moved.

Then Ralph coughed violently, waving dust from his face. Perry forced himself to breathe through the adrenaline surge.

"Colin!" Perry cried, rushing towards the body. He dropped to his knees.

The assistant stage manager lay spreadeagled on the stage floor, his body twisted, one arm outstretched as if he'd tried to grab at something in the darkness.

Ralph let out a strangled noise as he joined Perry. "Oh my god—is he dead?"

Perry's hands hovered uncertainly over Colin's shoulder. He leaned in, watching for the rise and fall of his chest.

It was moving up and down.

"He's alive," Perry breathed in relief. "Help me get him onto his side."

Perry rose from his knees, and Ralph leaned down beside him, fumbling with Colin's limp body. They shifted him further along the stage, into the pool of light, and positioned him into the recovery position as Perry had seen the paramedics do on TV.

Colin groaned softly, his eyelids fluttering.

"Colin? It's Perry. Can you hear me?" Perry bent down and tapped his cheek gently.

Colin's face twitched. "Up there," he murmured, his arm raising a few inches off the floor. "Footsteps…" He faltered, then went quiet.

"Colin. Who did you see?" Perry asked urgently. *Was whoever it was still in the building?*

Colin didn't respond.

"We need to call an ambulance," Ralph said, already reaching for his phone.

Perry didn't answer. His mind was racing. His pulse pounded as he looked down at Colin, then across to where the twisted wreckage of the rig now covered the exact spot where Colin had been standing moments ago.

Perry swallowed hard.

Ralph's breathing was ragged as he dialled. "That… that nearly killed all of us."

Perry nodded slowly, the blood rushing in his ears. His gaze snapped back to Colin. A thin trickle of blood now seeped from a fresh gash on his forehead. A light lay next to him, its thin metal cover spotted with blood. *Colin!* Perry's heart jumped into his throat as he noticed that Colin's breathing, once shallow but steady, was now erratic.

He frantically looked around for Ralph. He was over by the steps, his voice frantic as he told the operator what had happened. "Please send an ambulance immediately." His words echoed Perry's desperate thoughts.

Someone had tried to kill Colin. *And they almost killed me and Ralph too!*

25

THE NEXT DAY. MONDAY 4 OCTOBER

T*he Windstanton Echo* online article:

The Importance of Being Earnest *Production Cursed?*
Another Accident Rocks Windstanton Players

The Windstanton Players' latest endeavour, Oscar Wilde's The Importance of Being Earnest, *has been marred by yet another calamity, fuelling whispers of a production cursed from the outset. Hot on the heels of the shocking death of lead actor Noel Ashworth—now at the centre of a murder investigation—comes a harrowing incident involving the company's lighting technician, Colin Myatt.*

During a recent rehearsal, Myatt suffered a head injury when a lighting rig catastrophically collapsed. He is currently hospitalised at King's Town Hospital, where he remains in a stable condition.

Speculation is rife among cast and crew members, with some fearing that the production is jinxed. One anonymous source confided, "First Noel's tragic death, and now this? It's as if the play is cursed. We're all on edge, wondering who's next."

Despite the turmoil, director Olivia Belmont remains steadfast in her commitment to see the show through. In an exclusive statement, Belmont asserted, "Our hearts are heavy with concern for Colin. We are doing everything in our power to support him during this critical time. In honour of both Noel's and Colin's dedication, the Windstanton Players are resolute in our decision to proceed with the production."

Fenshire Police continue to delve into the circumstances surrounding Ashworth's untimely demise. Detective Inspector Mike Ainsley provided a brief update, stating, "Our investigation into Mr Ashworth's death is ongoing. We are meticulously examining all evidence and encourage anyone with pertinent information to come forward."

As the Windstanton Players forge ahead amidst adversity, the local community watches with bated breath, hopeful that the company's resilience will culminate in a triumphant opening night, scheduled for Wednesday 27th October.

26

11 AM, MONDAY 4 OCTOBER

As Bea climbed out of the back of the car, Daisy leapt out behind her and bounded over to Simon, who stood waiting for them outside Rose Cottage. Rich closed the door and thanked Fraser before he joined them.

"Thanks for coming," Simon said as he kissed Bea's cheek, his usually laid-back demeanour replaced by a tense frown.

"How's he doing?" she asked.

"He's pretty spooked and didn't sleep much. Come on in." Simon ushered them through the front door.

The kitchen was warm and inviting, but Perry's haunted expression shattered the cosy illusion. He sat hunched at the dining table, his normally impeccable hair mussed, and dark circles shadowed his eyes.

Bea's heart clenched. She hurried over and enveloped him in a tight hug. "Oh, Perry, you poor thing."

Daisy yipped and pranced around Perry's feet until he reached down to scoop her up. She showered his face with sloppy kisses.

"Dealing with attempted murder is much worse when

you're not there with me," he said to Bea as he managed a weak smile.

She grabbed his hand as she sat next to him. "Well, stop doing things without me then," she replied as she squeezed his fingers and grinned at him.

"Coffee?" Simon called from the kitchen counter.

"Absolutely," Rich said, settling into a chair opposite Perry. "So what happened, Perry?" Rich fixed Perry with an intent gaze. "We only got your garbled voicemail when we turned our phones back on after leaving Gollingham Palace."

Bea shivered, remembering the panic that had gripped her when she'd heard Perry's frantic message saying that there had been an accident at the theatre, and Colin had been taken to hospital. Thank goodness, when she'd rung Simon, he'd assured them that everything was under control.

Simon joined them at the table and poured out four steaming mugs before passing them around. The rich aroma filled the air. Bea dropped Perry's hand, then grabbed the offered cup and took a grateful sip of the hot, somewhat bitter coffee.

Perry took a shaky breath and recounted the harrowing events from the night before. As he spoke, Bea watched him closely, her heart aching at the haunted look in his eyes. She exchanged a troubled glance with Rich across the table. From what Perry was saying, it sounded like someone had tried to kill Colin.

Perry's voice wavered as he finished recounting his story. "If I hadn't shouted out to him… that rig would've crushed him. He'd be dead." He let out a sigh and looked away as if trying to dislodge the thought.

Rich leaned forward, his brow furrowed. "So you think it was a deliberate attempt on Colin's life?"

"Yes. No. I mean…" Perry hesitated, his eyes darting

around the room. Bea's instincts prickled. There was something more, something he wasn't saying.

"What is it, Perry?" she prodded gently. "What's that look about?"

He turned and met her gaze, his blue eyes dancing. "This is going to sound crazy, but... what if the target wasn't Colin? What if it was meant for me or Ralph? If I hadn't stopped and looked up, then grabbed him, it could've been us underneath it."

Bea's breath stalled mid-chest. The air grew still and tense.

But why?

Perry scrubbed a hand over his face and continued, "If someone was watching us from above, ready to drop it on Colin, why didn't they stop when they saw us?"

Simon cleared his throat. "It was dark up there and quite a distance. If someone was watching, they might not have seen you both until it was too late. Or perhaps it was set up in advance."

Perry shook his head vehemently. "Ralph and I definitely heard someone scurrying around when we first arrived."

"That could've been Colin," Simon pointed out.

"Colin said he heard someone up there," Perry persisted.

"Colin had been hit by a bit of rig. He could've been confused."

Bea turned to Simon, trying to read his expression. "So you think Colin's injury could've been an accident?"

Simon shrugged. "It's possible."

An accident? After everything Perry had described, it sounded far too deliberate to be mere chance. *Why is Simon downplaying this?* Bea bit her bottom lip, then opened her mouth to argue, but Simon was already rising from the table.

"I've got some cookies in the oven. Bea, would you mind giving me a hand?"

She hesitated, torn between pursuing the conversation and the pleading look in Simon's eyes. "Of course," she said at last, placing down her half-empty mug and following him into the kitchen.

As soon as they were out of earshot, Simon lowered his voice. "I'm trying not to feed into Perry's fears," he said, his expression grave. "He's convinced that he was the real target and that even Noel's death was somehow aimed at him."

Bea gasped. "What?" It seemed like an enormous leap, but then again, if anyone could leap that far, Perry could. She studied Simon's face, expecting to see a relaxed grin; but instead, he looked deadly serious. Her heart tumbled over. "Do you really think he's the target, Simon?" she asked in a quiet voice. *Please say no...*

"I honestly don't know," Simon muttered, pulling on oven mitts and retrieving a tray of golden-brown cookies from the oven. The warm, buttery scent did little to soothe Bea's nerves. "Perry thinks he must've seen something, or he knows something that someone wants to keep quiet. He thinks someone is trying to silence him."

Bea's mind reeled. "Is that likely?" She recalled Mike was going to look into any possible connections Perry might unknowingly have in the area. *Surely, he would've said if he'd found anything?*

Simon let out a deep sigh. "Noel's a more believable candidate from what we've learnt so far, but then there's this Colin thing…" He placed the tray on the side and flicked the oven door closed with his foot. "I want to think it's the shock and the lack of sleep that's making Perry talk like this. But…" He trailed off again.

Bea puffed out a breath. "Look, maybe we should do

some digging just to be sure. Mike was going to look into the background of the suspects and see if any of them have a connection to Perry. I'll chase him up."

Simon nodded as he carefully transferred the cookies to a large serving plate. "In the meantime, to stop Perry worrying, we need to keep him focused on Noel's case."

"Agreed," she said as she picked up the plate of warm cookies. She walked over to the table with them. As she passed Daisy, who was in her favourite chair by the large bifold doors that looked out over the garden, the little dog stirred and sniffed the air. *I don't think so, little girl...* Bea gave her a stern look, and Daisy curled back up into a ball with a huff.

As Bea reached the table, Rich was mid-sentence, his tone measured and reassuring. "...and until the police finish their investigation, we can't be certain it wasn't simply a terrible accident," Rich said, his gaze fixed on Perry.

A wave of gratitude washed over Bea. Rich had clearly picked up on Simon's concerns about Perry's state of mind.

Perry frowned as his lips thinned and his jaw tightened. "So you're saying it's a coincidence?" He leaned forward, his knuckles white as he gripped his mug. "Colin just *happened* to be standing right in that spot, and then the rig just *happened* to fall exactly where he'd been?"

Bea winced inwardly. *When he puts it like that, it does sound rather far-fetched.*

"And correct me if I'm wrong," Perry continued, a hint of triumph in his voice, "but don't the police always say there's no such thing as a coincidence, Rich?"

Bea's eyes darted to Rich, who looked like someone heavy had trod on his foot. *Oh, Perry's got you there.* In all the cases they'd worked together, Rich had always scoffed at the mere suggestion of a coincidence.

Rich opened his mouth, then closed it again, looking thoroughly scuppered. Bea jumped in. "Look," she said, her voice calm but firm as she met Perry's troubled gaze. "Until we hear from Mike, I think we should continue to focus on Noel's death."

She turned to Simon, silently pleading for backup. He nodded. "Bea's right. Let's go over the statements and evidence, see if we can piece together a timeline. We should start from when the cigarettes were taken out of the sterilising fluid until Kurt took them onstage."

For a long moment, Perry stared at them, his expression unreadable. Then with a heavy sigh, he gave a reluctant grunt. "Okay, fine. I suppose there isn't anything else we can do right now."

"Indeed," Bea agreed, pushing the plate towards him. "Except possibly have a cookie?"

He reached over and took one. "Yeah, that might help."

27

THIRTY MINUTES LATER, MONDAY 4 OCTOBER

B ea leaned back in her chair next to Perry as he grabbed another cookie from the platter. She smiled. He was eating. That was always a good sign. His colour had improved too. As they'd gone through the timeline for Noel's death and their suspects, he'd seemed more engaged. And Simon's and Rich's gentle encouragement had worked wonders, restoring Perry's usual confidence.

Over by the French doors, Daisy let out a gentle snore, and Bea's shoulders relaxed. This was the process she was comfortable with—looking at each suspect and considering means, motive, and opportunity. Any gaps would point them in their next direction.

Simon cleared his throat. "Right, let's review our findings, shall we?" He glanced down at his laptop. "So the window of opportunity for someone to tamper with the fake cigarette was between ten-past-five and six-forty. Agreed?"

They all nodded.

"We've ruled out Liv Belmont, Ralph Harvey, and Gina Bernet," he continued. "Not one of them was in the building during that time, and they've all provided alibis to Mike."

"Assuming the police confirm those alibis, of course," Rich added.

Hopefully, Mike would update them on that soon.

Simon moved on to the remaining suspects. "Emily Shaw arrived with Colin Myatt a tad before five. After helping Colin unpack, she went off to do her own thing in the basement until nearly six. No one can confirm her whereabouts during that time."

Perry leaned forward as he brushed his mouth with a napkin. "I can vouch for her from the moment I arrived until Noel collapsed. She was onstage with me and never left my sight."

"Great. So we can narrow down her opportunity to between five-ten and just before six."

That's still quite a long time...

"So now motive. Em doesn't have a motive that we know of."

"Indeed," Bea acknowledged, "but she was awfully nervous when Mike asked about the props. I think we need to follow up on that."

"Agreed," Simon said, typing a note onto his laptop. "Next up, we have Kurt Grant. He claims he arrived early at five twenty-five and was onstage from then until Noel's collapse. Colin Myatt confirms seeing Kurt onstage when he was dealing with the lights, and Tom confirmed Kurt was there when he arrived ten minutes later."

So Kurt couldn't have done it?

"So if Kurt's our culprit, he must have lied about his arrival time and tampered with the cigarette earlier." Rich leaned back, folding his arms across his chest.

Of course!

"Exactly," Simon agreed. "We don't know of any motive

for Kurt though. I think we need to dig deeper into his history with Noel, see if there's any underlying tension."

"And let's not forget, he's got a background in chemistry. He certainly had the means to pull it off," Rich added.

Bea exhaled sharply, running a hand through her hair. He had the opportunity and means too. *But why kill Noel? No one so far seems to have a good enough reason…*

"Agreed," Simon said, scanning his notes on the screen. "Right. Tom Hatlee next. He arrived at five thirty-five. Colin saw him around then and watched him head into the auditorium. Now it's possible Tom snuck out before everyone took to the stage at six without Kurt or Colin noticing—"

Or… "He's another one who could have been lying about when he arrived." Bea looked at Rich diagonally opposite her, and he gave her a slow smile. She was learning…

Perry's eyes widened as if a memory was sparking to life. "Wait a minute! Tom left the stage during that unexpected break at six-thirty. He could've tampered with the cigarette then…"

Rich frowned, turning to Perry. "Was it normal to take a break so soon after starting?"

Perry shook his head, a rueful smile playing at his lips. "No, it was highly unusual. Noel was struggling with his lines. I think Em hoped a reset might work for him."

So… Bea chimed in, "Unless Tom knew there would be a break, it doesn't make sense for him to have relied on that opportunity, does it?"

Perry exhaled slowly. "No. I hadn't thought of that. Ignore me," he said, picking up the coffeepot and pouring himself a refill. "And anyway," he said as he raised the cup to his lips. "Tom's another suspect without an apparent motive."

"That we know of," Rich said. "So again, we need to look more closely at Tom's relationship with Noel as well."

"And that leaves Millie Trent," Simon said. "She arrived during the unscheduled break and said she spotted Stella and Noel arguing. That was just after six-thirty, according to her."

"But no one saw her arrive," Bea pointed out. "She could also be lying about the time she got there to cover her tracks."

Rich drew his brows in, considering the possibility. "True, but if she wanted to get to the cigarette, she would've been cutting it awfully close to arrive that late. Without that unexpected break, the cigarettes would've already been onstage for what, ten, fifteen minutes?"

Good point. She would've had to arrive quite a way before she said she did to be sure she would have had time to tamper with the props.

"So if Stella confirms the argument with Noel, it corroborates Millie's presence at the time she said she was there, and we can rule her out?" Bea asked.

"And like me, Millie is new to the troupe," Perry added, his eyes meeting Bea's. "It's unlikely she had a long enough history with Noel to want to harm him."

Another good point.

"So we agree?" Simon asked. "If Stella confirms she and Noel were arguing during the break, then Millie's an unlikely suspect?"

Murmurs of assent rippled through the four of them.

"And that brings us to Stella Vance. She's the only one with an obvious motive, and her story about why she arrived so early doesn't quite add up."

Rich scratched his chin. "And if Millie's telling the truth, Stella also lied about where she was during that crucial window of time."

"She was definitely vague about it in her interview," Bea said, twirling a strand of her hair. She recalled Stella's stumbled response when Mike had asked her what she did after being asked to leave the stage. She'd told him she'd gone into one of the dressing rooms, but had claimed not to remember exactly which one. At the time, Bea had been suspicious that she wasn't telling the truth. Now it seemed she could have been hanging around backstage. "I think Mike needs to interview Stella again."

Rich and Simon nodded.

Perry's shoulders slumped. "So that's it. Stella is the most likely candidate. Kurt, Tom, and Em are possibles if we can find a motive for any of them, and Millie seems like she not only has no motive but not much opportunity either."

Is that it? She couldn't help feeling like their list of suspects had shrunk a lot since they'd first discussed everything. *That's good, isn't it?* So why did she feel like they were overlooking someone?

"What about Colin Myatt?" Rich asked.

Of course! She resisted the urge to slap her forehead. She'd forgotten all about the poor man currently in the hospital.

"I mean, before yesterday's incident, he was a pretty viable suspect, don't forget," Rich continued.

Bea's heart skipped a beat. But after what happened last night, surely, they could rule him out now…

Rich continued, "In fact, Perry, he was your number one suspect, wasn't he?"

Perry looked aghast. "I mean, he was… but now… You can't still consider him a suspect after what happened last night, can you?"

Rich's shoulders lifted a touch, his expression thoughtful. "If it was an accident, then no, we can't rule him out. Noel asked him to supply him with drugs. With his background in chemistry, he had the means to kill Noel. And when it comes to opportunity, he had the advantage over the others as he was the one who'd set up the props."

Bea's mind raced. Rich was right. But was it likely that Colin was both the victim of an accident *and* a potential perpetrator?

Perry puffed out his cheeks. "I suppose so, but—" The chirping of his phone interrupted his sentence. "It's from Liv," he announced, his eyes scanning the message. "Rehearsals are going ahead this afternoon. We're back at Windsham Village Hall."

As if on cue, Bea's own phone buzzed with an incoming text. She glanced down, her breath catching as she read Mike's name on the screen. *What news does he have?*

DI Mike Ainsley: *I'm on my way over. Are you at home?*

"Mike's on his way," she said, looking up at Simon and Perry. "Is it alright if I tell him to come to Rose Cottage?"

They both dipped their chins in agreement, and Bea quickly typed out a response. As she hit send, a flurry of questions raced through her mind. Did Mike have news about Colin? She rested her hand on her thigh to stop her leg jiggling. Was what happened last night truly an accident... or something far more sinister?

28

FORTY MINUTES LATER, MONDAY 4 OCTOBER

D aisy, her fluffy white tail wagging furiously, bounded over to greet Detective Inspector Mike Ainsley. Bea smiled as he crouched down, his face softening as he ruffled Daisy's fur. "Hello there, Daisy. I'm pleased to see you too."

As Mike continued to fuss over Daisy, Bea was pleased to see that his face, which had been creased with worry the last time she'd seen him, seemed smoother today. The skin under his eyes was less dull and sunken than it had been. *Whatever he did on his day off has clearly done him a world of good.*

Daisy, satisfied with her warm welcome, trotted back to her favourite armchair by the window, jumped up, and settled herself down again. Mike accepted a steaming mug of coffee from Simon with a nod of thanks and joined them at the dining table.

Perry, his leg bouncing with nervous energy, couldn't contain himself any longer. "How's Colin?" he blurted out, leaning forward in his seat.

Mike took a sip of coffee. "He's fully conscious and out of danger."

Thank goodness! Next to her, the tension in Perry's shoulders visibly eased. Bea licked her dry lips and reached for her glass of water.

"He has a nasty cut and bruise from where the metal light-casing hit him, but the CT scan came back clear—no bleeds. He has a few other bumps and bruises from the lighting rig debris, but he'll mend quickly."

"Have you been able to talk to him? Did he see anyone?" Bea asked, her mind already racing with possibilities. *If he saw who it was, or even recognised something about them, then—*

"I had a brief chat with him," Mike answered. "He says he heard footsteps in the rafters above as he lay on the floor, but he couldn't open his eyes. Before that, he thought he was alone in the theatre, so it was all unexpected."

Bea's stomach clenched. *Really?* "Could he tell if they came from a man or a woman?"

Mike shook his head. "He says not."

Rats! They couldn't rule anyone off their suspect list then.

"And the rigging?" Rich asked.

Mike took a sip of coffee, then said, "Crime scene officers confirmed the rope had been untied. Presumably deliberately. Bolts that hold the pully-system stopper had been removed and were lying on the ground. A screwdriver was found abandoned on the floor by the side of where the rig had been. It looks like whoever did it didn't have time to clear up afterwards."

I wonder if once they realised Colin was still alive, and Perry and Ralph were there, they made a run for it?

"Any fingerprints?" Rich asked.

That would be really helpful.

"No. Sorry. Whoever did it was wearing gloves. There are no prints anywhere."

Can't we catch a break? A murder and an attempted murder, and nothing in the way of evidence yet!

"Did Colin know why someone might want to hurt him?" Simon asked, leaning forward, a look of intense concentration on his face.

Mike's lips thinned. "He claims he has no idea, but…" He trailed off, shaking his head.

"But you don't believe him," Bea finished, meeting Mike's gaze.

Mike gave a wry smile. "I'm not buying it. He's scared of something. Or someone."

The hairs on Bea's arm prickled. *Does Colin know who did this to him?*

"I will try again with him when he's feeling a bit better," Mike said.

"So we can assume Noel's death and Colin's attack are connected then?" Rich's tone made it more of a statement than a question.

Mike drained the last of his coffee and set the mug down with a decisive *thunk*. "That's how we're treating it for now."

At least that was good news. They'd already narrowed the suspects down to five—Kurt, Tom, Em, Millie, and Stella, so they needed to find out what they'd all been doing last night. They should share what they had with Mike. "We've not been idle, Mike. Perry's been playing the sleuth among the cast members, and we've been able to go through and eliminate some of our original suspects."

Mike's eyebrows shot up, a hint of a smile playing at the corners of his mouth. "That's great because I'm still with no extra staff at the moment. Tell me all about it."

———

"So Stella was lying about her movements at the theatre, eh?" Mike said when they had finished filling him in on what they knew. "I'll need to interview her again to find out where she was last night. We'll see if she tells us the truth a second time around." He rubbed his chin. "It's interesting what you said about Gina overhearing Noel asking Colin to supply him with speed. That's not something Mr Myatt has mentioned. It could be why he's so reluctant to talk."

Simon nodded. "Of course, until Colin got attacked, we were wondering if he was Noel's supplier and that was a motive, but now…" He trailed off.

"He could still have been. But it might not be relevant to Noel's murder," Mike pointed out.

It's possible…

"I have to say you've done a great job," Mike said to them. "You lot could give my regular team a run for their money."

Bea felt a surge of pride. *We're actually helping!*

"You were right to knock Liv, Ralph, and Gina off your list. We've confirmed their movements on the evening Noel was killed. We also had a bit of luck with a CCTV camera at the shop down the road from the theatre."

They all leaned in with anticipation.

"It confirms Millie's and Kurt's statements about when they arrived that night. Unfortunately, it only catches people going past on the main road, so Tom and Stella must've come in from the side street. We've not got anything that shows them arriving."

That clears Millie now too. We're down to four… Suddenly, her heartbeat quickened. *CCTV!* "What about last night, around the time of the attack? Did the CCTV pick up anything then?"

Mike grimaced. "Only Colin arriving at five, then Perry

and Ralph half an hour later, and, of course, the ambulance later on. No sign of our mystery assailant."

Bea swallowed. *That would've been too easy...* She slumped back in her chair. They were so close, and yet, the truth still felt just out of reach.

Mike rubbed the side of his face as he turned to Bea. "I could still use your help, if you don't mind. I need to re-interview Stella, Kurt, Em, and Tom. We can dismiss Millie as far as I'm concerned. I want to see what they have to say about where they were yesterday when Colin was attacked. I also need a statement from Ralph about last night." He looked at Perry. "I'll need an official statement from you as well, of course."

"No problem."

"When do we start?" Bea asked.

"Three this afternoon, Windsham Village Hall. Before rehearsals begin." Mike turned to Perry. "And I hope you will continue to keep those eyes and ears open around the theatre for me? Any little scrap of gossip or drama—I want to know about it."

Perry grinned, looking for all the world like a kid who'd been given free rein in a sweet shop. "I'm on it, inspector. Covert intelligence gathering is my speciality now."

Simon snorted, then coughed to cover it up. Bea caught Rich's eyes, and he smirked back at her.

Mike turned to Rich. "Actually, Fitzwilliam, I was hoping I could have a quick word with you before I leave."

What's that all about?

Rich blinked, surprised, but recovered quickly. "Sure. I need to get going anyway." He turned to Simon and Perry with a smile. "Thanks for the coffee. I'm meeting Fred. We're off to look at some equipment for the rehab centre."

"I can give you a lift back to Francis Court if that helps, and we can talk on the way," Mike offered.

Rich nodded. "Thanks, Mike, that will be great." He rose and moved to Bea. He leaned down and gave her a swift kiss. "I'll ring you later, darling."

She smiled back at him. "Have fun."

As Rich and Mike headed for the door, Simon checked his watch and cursed under his breath. "I've got to run too. I'm meeting with Ryan and Fay at their flat."

He shot Perry a wry smile.

"Good luck, love," Perry said, blowing Simon a kiss.

"You too," Simon said as he turned and rushed out of the door.

Bea frowned. *What does Simon need good luck for? And for that matter, why does Perry need good luck?*

29

TEN MINUTES LATER, MONDAY 4 OCTOBER

B ea scooped up Daisy and settled into the armchair by the French doors, the little dog curling up contentedly on her lap. Early October sunlight streamed in, illuminating the riot of red and gold leaves blanketing Rose Cottage's lawn.

As she gazed out, Bea's thoughts turned to the unexpected audience with the king yesterday. *Now is the ideal moment to tell Perry about it…*

The prospect of resuming royal duties stirred a mix of excitement and apprehension within her, but the enormity of the decision she and Rich faced weighed heavily on her. If she accepted, what would it mean for the design business she shared with Perry? Especially with the shock of what had happened to Colin at the theatre, she worried the news might unsettle him further. *Should I leave it for later?*

As Perry clattered around behind her, making them coffee, Bea chewed her lip, gazing out at the kaleidoscope of foliage. She hated keeping something so monumental from him. With a sigh, she scratched Daisy behind the ears, trying to settle her roiling thoughts. *Of course you have to tell him... He's your best friend. He'll understand... won't he?*

Perry sauntered over, balancing two steaming mugs. His usual buoyant demeanour seemed subdued, a slight furrow creasing his brow. Handing her a cup, he settled into the chair beside her, his fingers tapping nervously against the ceramic.

Bea accepted the mug, inhaling the comforting aroma. *Do it now! It'll be fine...* "Perry, there's something I need to discuss with you—"

"Bea, we need to talk," Perry blurted out.

Their eyes met, and they burst out laughing, the tension dissipating like smoke. Bea leaned back, shaking her head. This was Perry, her rock, her confidante. Whatever lay ahead, their friendship would endure.

"You first," Perry said with a grin.

Bea took a fortifying gulp of coffee, then placed it on the table between them. "So you know how Rich and I met with the king yesterday…"

Perry slapped his forehead. "Blimey, I completely forgot! Some friend I am. What with Colin's attack and everything…"

"It's fine, Perry, really." Bea placed her hand on his arm. "It's been a crazy time for you."

"Thanks," he said as he patted her hand. "But, tell me, what happened?"

Taking a deep breath, Bea recounted her uncle's proposal: her and Rich transitioning into royal duties, then gradually increasing their responsibilities leading up to their marriage.

Perry's eyes widened with genuine excitement. "Bea, that's brilliant!" He beamed. "You two will be phenomenal at it."

"He wants us to support my cousin Robert while he raises his children," she continued. "So we'll also be doing overseas engagements alongside Fred and Summer. Fred's desperate for us to say yes."

"And you? How do you feel about diving back in after such a long time?"

Bea gazed into her mug, pensive. "Honestly? I used to love that side of things when James and I were married. It was only after he died and the press…" She trailed off and took a deep breath. "Talking with Fred and my uncle about it reminded me that it had given me a sense of purpose, you know? I could make a difference."

Perry nodded. "I remember seeing you two on the telly, out and about. The people adored you, Bea. You were a natural."

Aw, that's sweet… She breathed in slowly.

But then there's Rich. "I'm not sure about Rich though," Bea said. "It's a massive leap for him, leaving his career behind."

"Bea, the man's been positively glowing when he talks about his involvement with Three Lakes. If that's any indication, I don't think you'll need to worry."

Is Perry right? Rich was certainly loving getting involved with Fred's passion project. But would he feel differently if it became his job?

But then there's the press… "But I'll be honest, the thought of being constantly scrutinised by the press… I don't know, Perry."

"I get it." He nodded slowly. "But you've been getting better at coping with that over the last six months or so, haven't you?"

I suppose so… It was definitely easier than it had been before, now that she had Rich at her side, but even so, there were still days when she felt physically sick at the thought of what the press might say about her and those she loved.

And then there's you... She looked at Perry, sat back in his chair, smiling as he took a sip of his coffee. *He hasn't realised yet the impact this will have on our business.* She swallowed. *Here goes...* "Perry, I don't know what this means for the company yet. But you could easily handle things on your own, don't you think?"

Perry's smile faltered. Bea's stomach churned. *Oh no. Perhaps I shouldn't have said anything? We haven't even decided yet...* "Perry, I'm sor—"

"It's my turn now," he interrupted, holding up a hand. Bea clamped her mouth shut, her pulse quickening.

He gave her a nervous smile. "I want to take a break from the business, Bea. I didn't know how to tell you."

Bea's jaw dropped. *What?* "Why?"

"It's Simon." Perry's eyes sparkled as he said his husband's name. "He's spread himself too thin. SaltAir is taking up too much of his time, and he's struggling to write. That's where he's gone now—to hash it out with Ryan and Fay."

Oh my goodness. "But Simon loves cooking."

"I know. But as a hobby. Not a full-time job. He wants to focus on his crime writing."

Well, then... "Of course, then yes, that's what he should do. But why does that impact you and your job?"

"I want to support him." Perry beamed. "Crime writing is his passion, and Simon is mine. He wants me to join him on his book tour of the USA next year. We'd make a road trip of it. Apparently, you can get these things called RVs that are like hotels on wheels."

Bea grinned. Knowing how Perry felt about 'roughing it', that would cost Simon a pretty penny!

"I might even dabble in a bit more acting," Perry continued. "Minus the homicidal maniacs, of course."

They laughed, then Bea reached for Perry's hand. "How about after we wrap up Three Lakes, we take a sabbatical? No new clients, no commitments. Just a break to explore other options?"

Perry squeezed her fingers. "I'll miss seeing your face every day, partner."

"Rubbish. You can't get rid of me that easily. After everything we've been through together, we're family. Now and always."

Daisy, clearly not wanting to be left out, sat up and pawed at Bea's and Perry's hands.

"Too right. You almost got me killed at least half a dozen times," he replied, grinning, his eyes sparkling as he ruffled Daisy's head.

Our paths might diverge, but our bond? Unbreakable.

Bea pulled back, wiping a stray tear. She gently placed Daisy on the floor and stood, taking her phone from her jeans pocket. "Right. Why don't we go and have lunch at The Dower House, then we'll go to Windsham?"

Perry rubbed his hands together, his eyes twinkling with mischief. "Yes. It's undercover time!"

Bea stopped with her phone halfway to her ear. "After what happened to Colin, you will tread carefully, won't you?"

"Don't worry," Perry said as he stood and scooped up their empty cups. "Discretion is my middle name, remember?"

30

2:55 PM, MONDAY 4 OCTOBER

I nside Windsham Village Hall, they found Em pacing, her face etched with worry. As they approached, the stage manager looked ready to burst into tears.

"Em, how are you holding up?" Bea asked gently. *Please don't cry...*

"I've got so much to do without Colin, and—" Em choked out before abruptly turning and marching away.

Bea exchanged a worried glance with Perry. "Poor thing. Colin's accident must've hit her hard," she said to him as they made their way to the storeroom cum incident room they'd used previously, Daisy trotting at their heels.

As they entered, DI Mike Ainsley stood up to greet them and thanked them for coming.

Bea gestured to Daisy, who was sniffing everything in sight. "Sorry about Daisy," she said as they joined him at the table. "Perry will take her for a walk once we start."

Mike waved a hand. "No worries. But listen, I've got news." He lowered his voice as he gestured for them to be seated. "When we got Colin's clothes from the hospital, we found a packet of uppers inside the pocket of his jeans. They are the same kind we found on Noel Ashworth."

Bea's stomach dropped.

Beside her, Perry stiffened. "Wait, are you saying Colin was Noel's supplier, after all?" he asked.

Bea's heart fluttered.

Mike shook his head. "Colin swears he's never taken or supplied drugs. He admitted that Noel had asked him to get him drugs, but Colin says he turned him down flat."

Mike sounded unconvinced.

"Do you think he's lying?" Bea asked him.

The DI rubbed a hand over his face. "I don't know. But he's definitely hiding something if you ask me."

Does Colin think he knows who tried to kill him? Then another thought occurred to Bea. She met Mike's gaze. "You don't think... Could someone be setting Colin up?"

Mike's jaw tightened. "Funny you should mention that. I've been considering the same possibility."

Bea's mind whirled as she worked it through in her head. She turned to face Mike and Perry, determination etched on her features. "Right, let's think this through logically," she said. "If Colin was being framed, how would the killer have done it?"

Perry leaned forward, pressing his lips together, then said, "Could the rigging falling have been made to look like an accident?"

Mike grimaced. "It's possible if the killer had had more time and hadn't been interrupted."

"Interrupted by me and Ralph," Perry said, his face paling. "Oh my goodness, if we hadn't shown up when we did…"

Bea laid a comforting hand on his arm, then turned to Mike. "What did the crime scene officers find exactly?"

"A screwdriver and a large file," Mike replied. "They reckon the file might've been used to make the bolts look worn down, like they'd sheared off on their own."

Bea's eyes widened. "So the plan was to stage it as an accident, then the drugs would make Colin seem guilty by association. But why Colin?"

A slow smile played on Perry's lips. "His access to the fake cigarettes? His chemistry background? He's the perfect scapegoat if you think about it. After all, we suspected him for those things too, remember?"

I suppose so... Bea wrung her hands. "But is it enough? Unless... Mike, what if Colin knows something?" Her stomach dropped. "Something that makes him a threat perhaps?"

Mike's blue eyes crinkled. "I'll push him harder when he's stronger. See if he can shed light on who'd want to frame him. In the meantime, Perry, I need your statement, please."

Bea took her seat in the corner, with Daisy perched on her lap. Her mind churned. If someone had succeeded in killing Colin, and had had time to make it look like an accident, then they must be pretty upset right now knowing their plan had failed. Would it show when they interviewed them? *I hope so...*

After formalising Perry's statement, Mike thanked him, and he departed with Daisy.

Bea rose. "Mike," she said as she walked over to him. "Is it possible that Perry or Ralph was the actual target and not Colin?"

"Ralph Harvey?" Mike's eye's widened, then he shook his head. "I can't see any reason why anyone would want to hurt Mr Harvey. He wasn't there when Noel was killed, and we can't find any connections in his background that would suggest he's in anyway involved. No, I don't think so."

"And Perry?"

Mike hesitated.

Bea's pulse rate rose. *Oh no, what does Mike know?* She was almost afraid to ask. "Mike?"

"I can't rule it out at this stage, my lady. I wish I could. But we have nothing definite that confirms that Noel always took the same cigarette, so I can't ignore the possibility that Perry was the target." He added quickly, "However, nothing we've found so far suggests any link between Perry and any of the cast, so I still think it's unlikely."

But not impossible….

"At this stage, we're continuing the investigation based on Noel being the intended victim as we believe everything we have discovered so far points in that direction," he finished.

Bea swallowed, focussing on what Mike had said about them having not found anything in anyone's background connecting them to Perry. So no motive for anyone to harm him… *That's good, isn't it?* So why did she still feel uneasy?

As if sensing her mood, Mike moved a little closer. "If it helps, I passed all the updated information we have on every-one's background, including Perry's, to Fitzwilliam earlier, and he's going to review it and check we haven't missed anything, alright?"

Bea gave him a slow smile. "Thanks, Mike. Yes, that helps." *If there is anything, Rich will find it.*

The door opened, and a constable escorted Ralph into the room. Bea returned to her chair. She studied the normally flamboyant actor as he entered and was struck by how different he seemed from their first meeting. Gone was the mischievous twinkle in his eye and the joie de vivre he'd exuded so effortlessly. Now Ralph looked worried and worn down.

"How's Colin?" he asked immediately, sinking into a chair.

"He's a bit battered and bruised, but he'll make a full recovery," Mike assured him.

Ralph slumped in relief.

Mike flicked on the recorder. "Mr Harvey, please walk us through the events of Saturday night to the best of your recollection."

As Ralph began his account, his dramatic flair temporarily resurfaced, but he seemed on edge, distracted. And when he mentioned having heard someone moving around when he and Perry had first arrived, his voice faltered. He swallowed hard. "Someone tried to kill Colin, didn't they?" he asked in a small voice.

Mike hesitated, then inclined his head. "It would appear so, yes."

Ralph closed his eyes briefly. "Poor lad," he whispered.

Bea and Mike exchanged a glance. Bea's intuition was screaming at her—Ralph was definitely holding something back.

Mike gave her a subtle nod, then leaned forward. "Mr Harvey. Do you have any idea who might want to hurt Colin? Or why?"

Ralph shifted uncomfortably in his seat, not meeting their eyes. He seemed to wrestle with himself. Finally, he sighed heavily and looked up. "I don't want to believe she'd ever do something like this, but…" He took a deep breath. "I overheard Em and Colin having a blazing row on Friday night after rehearsals."

A prickle swept across Bea's skin. *Em and Colin arguing?* She exchanged an alarmed glance with Mike, then leaned in, intent on Ralph's every word. *What had they been fighting about?* And could it have driven Em to attempt murder? A chill ran down her spine as she waited with bated breath for Ralph to continue.

"I'd popped offstage to… er, powder my nose, you see. On my way back, I heard raised voices coming from the storeroom." He fidgeted with a loose thread on his sleeve. "It was Colin and Em. I was surprised to hear her—I thought she'd left earlier as it was Colin's turn to lock up."

So why did Em stay behind?

"I couldn't make out everything, but Colin… he sounded quite resolute. He told Em he couldn't ignore it anymore, that he'd have to tell the police."

Bea's eyes widened. *Tell the police? About what?*

"Em, she… she was begging him not to. She said her life would be over if he did." Ralph's face was pale. "She reminded him that they'd been friends for years and that she'd always had his back."

A chill ran down Bea's spine. What could Colin possibly know about Em that would warrant police involvement? Could it be connected to Noel's death? Had Colin seen something incriminating?

"Did you hear any more?" Mike prompted him.

"Just then, a door slammed down the hall." Ralph swallowed hard. "I scarpered quickish, not wanting to be caught eavesdropping… But as I left, I heard Colin tell Em it wasn't over and that they'd talk about it again tomorrow."

Bea sat back, her mind spinning with the implications.

Ralph looked at them beseechingly. "Look. I'm sure Em wouldn't hurt Colin, but… well, I thought you ought to know."

Mike nodded solemnly. "You did the right thing. Thank you for telling us."

As Ralph left, his shoulders sagging with relief, Bea turned to Mike, her eyes wide with shock. "So are we thinking that Colin knew something about Em? Something to do with Noel's murder?"

Mike dipped his chin. "It's possible. It could explain why he's not talking. I wonder if he suspects Em tried to silence him permanently."

Bea shook her head in disbelief. "I simply can't picture Em as a killer. But if she killed Noel, and Colin found out…" She trailed off, the unspoken implication hanging heavy in the air.

Mike exhaled heavily. "Let's not get ahead of ourselves. This could have nothing to do with Noel's death." He stood up, his jaw set with determination. "We need to talk to Em. Confront her with what we know and see how she reacts."

As Mike left to instruct the constable outside the door, Bea sat alone, her thoughts churning. *Could this really be it? If Em was the killer, had her botched attempt to silence Colin left her exposed?*

31

MEANWHILE, MONDAY 4 OCTOBER

Perry strolled along the windswept beach of Windstanton, Daisy trotting beside him, her white fur ruffled by the sea breeze. The rhythmic crashing of the waves provided a soothing backdrop, yet his mind churned with unsettling thoughts. The image of Colin, pale and vulnerable as they'd loaded him into the ambulance, haunted him. If he and Ralph hadn't arrived at the theatre when they had, would Colin be dead? The thought tightened his chest, and he gave a quick headshake, trying to dispel the grim possibilities. *Best not to dwell on it.*

Instead, he wondered how Simon's meeting with Ryan and Fay was going. Simon had been so much more at peace since he'd decided to focus on his writing and treat cooking as a cherished hobby rather than a parallel career. Perry hoped they could find a solution that allowed Simon to pursue his passion without guilt or obligation.

Should he swing by SaltAir just to 'accidentally' check on them? He changed course, leaving the promenade and heading in the direction of the town centre. As he rounded a corner, he spotted Stella Vance exiting the pharmacy. Her hurried steps and the way she was clutching a small paper bag caught his attention. Without considering the potential danger of approaching someone who might be involved in a murder, Perry quickened his pace, Daisy half-running to keep up.

Now is my chance to confront her about why she really showed up early to rehearsals on the night of Noel's death. "Stella!" he called out, forcing a cheerful tone.

Stella Vance, her dark hair blowing dramatically in the breeze, halted, her eyes widening as Perry jogged up beside her, a little out of breath. Daisy circled them curiously.

"Oh, hi, Perry," Stella said, nervously flipping her hair as she gripped her pharmacy bag tight. She glanced around as if looking for an escape route. At that moment, the traffic light changed, and Stella seized the opportunity to hurry across the street. Perry followed doggedly, Daisy at his heels.

"Stella, please," he called out, wincing as his shoes pinched with each step. "I want to ask you the real reason you turned up for rehearsals early the night Noel died."

She slowed her pace, allowing him to catch up. "Fine," she sighed, her shoulders slumping in defeat. "But not here. Let's sit."

She led them to a nearby bench overlooking the beach. As they settled, Daisy hopped up between them, nuzzling Stella's hand. To Perry's surprise, Stella's tense expression softened as she stroked the little dog's silky ears.

"Daisy seems to like you," Perry observed, hoping to break the ice. "She's an excellent judge of character, you know."

Stella laughed half-heartedly. "I suppose that's something." She took a deep breath, staring out at the rolling waves. "The truth is, I went to the theatre early that night to confront Noel. He'd been ignoring my calls, and I desperately needed to talk to him."

Perry leaned forward, intrigued. "About what?"

"I can't say." Stella's jaw tightened. "It's personal. But believe me, I had no choice. He left me no other option."

Perry studied her carefully. Could this really be the face of a killer? Daisy certainly didn't seem to think so as she was now contentedly dozing with her head in Stella's lap.

"Stella," he said gently, "I understand wanting to keep some things private. But if you don't tell the police the whole truth, it's going to look really bad for you."

She met his gaze, her dark eyes glistening with unshed tears. "You don't understand, Perry. It's complicated. If I tell them everything…"

Just then, the rich aroma of frying bacon wafted over from a nearby café, mingling with the salty air. Stella suddenly turned pale. "Excuse me," she mumbled, shooting to her feet. "I think I'm going to be ill."

With that, she fled down the promenade, one hand pressed to her mouth. Perry hurried after her, with Daisy trotting at his heels. He caught up to her near another bench overlooking the sea. She sat down heavily, looking miserable.

"Stella, are you alright?" Perry asked, concern lacing his voice as he sat beside her.

She shook her head, tears spilling down her cheeks. "Oh, Perry, I've made such a mess of things."

He patted her shoulder awkwardly. "Hey, it can't be that bad. You deserve so much better than a jerk like Noel anyway."

Stella let out a bitter laugh. "It's not that… simple." The words caught in her throat. She gazed out at the waves. "I thought maybe... he would change. That we could make it work somehow."

Fat chance of that, Perry thought.

"I don't know how I'll manage now without him." Stella's voice cracked. She sounded so lost, so broken, that for a moment Perry couldn't believe she was involved in the murder at all.

He squeezed her hand. "Stella, I know it's hard, but you have to be honest with the police. Someone saw you arguing with Noel that night. If you keep lying, they're going to think…"

She whipped her head around, her eyes wide. "They think I killed him?"

Perry hesitated. "They might if you don't come clean."

"But I could never hurt Noel! Not now, not when…" She clamped her mouth shut, going white again. "I'm sorry. I need to go home. I'll see you later."

Perry watched her retreating figure, pieces of the puzzle clicking into place. The nausea, the emotional swings, the urgency to speak with Noel… *Oh my goodness!* Could Stella be pregnant with Noel's child? The revelation hit him like a tidal wave. It all made sense.

But hold on… If she was expecting his baby, it seemed unlikely she'd harm Noel, knowing she'd have to raise the child alone. *Can we dismiss Stella as the killer now?*

Determined to share this new insight with Bea and Mike, Perry turned back towards Windsham, with Daisy trotting faithfully beside him. As they walked along the side road leading to the theatre's back entrance, Daisy suddenly veered into a narrow alleyway. She tugged on her lead, nearly yanking Perry off balance. She scrabbled at a greasy fast-food bag, trying to stick her nose inside. Perry hauled her back, huffing.

"Really, Daisy? A takeaway?" he said, scolding her gently. But as he pulled her away, something that had been underneath the bag caught his eye—an empty small glass vial about the size of his little finger sat inside a plastic bag.

Perry shivered, unease prickling down his spine. It could be nothing. Probably some teenager's science experiment or an essential oil or something.

But then again, they were beside the theatre where Noel had been killed and Colin was attacked. This alleyway would be the perfect place to dump something—something like the container the murderer had used to carry the nicotine he'd put into the prop cigarette.

And in a murder investigation, Perry had learnt that you could never be too careful…

32

BACK AT THE VILLAGE HALL,
MONDAY 4 OCTOBER

Emily Shaw shuffled into the room, looking like she'd seen a ghost. Her usually neat black hair stuck out in tufts from under her baseball cap, and her hands trembled as she took a seat. Her face was pale, her eyes rimmed with redness. She offered them a weak smile.

"I must inform you that this interview is being recorded, Ms Shaw," Mike said, reaching over and switching on the machine.

Em's gaze flickered between Bea and Mike, then settled momentarily on the recording device before her. "Is there any update on Colin?" she asked, her voice wavering. "I called the hospital, but they wouldn't tell me anything since I'm not family."

She seems genuinely concerned, Bea thought as tears welled up in Em's eyes. If Em had harmed Colin, she was certainly putting on a convincing act.

Mike's response was measured. "Mr Myatt is fortunate to be alive."

At this, Em's composure crumbled, and she began to sob quietly. Mike shot Bea a panicked look that screamed,

"Help!" Suppressing a sigh, Bea grabbed a box of tissues and handed it to Em.

"Thanks," Em sniffled, blowing her nose loudly.

"You and Colin must be close," Bea said, watching Em's reaction carefully.

Dabbing her eyes, Em nodded. "We've worked together for three years. We're a team, you know? I can't believe the rig fell; Colin was meticulous about maintenance."

Bea leaned back, considering. Em's defensiveness of Colin didn't exactly scream murderess... *But you never can tell.*

Bea exchanged a glance with Mike, who leaned forward a bit. "We believe someone deliberately sabotaged the rig to harm Mr Myatt."

Em's eyes widened, shock flickering across her face. "But... why would anyone want to hurt Colin?" She looked from Bea to Mike, seemingly bewildered.

"We were hoping you could help us with that," Mike replied.

"Of course, I'll do anything I can to help. But I honestly can't imagine who'd want to do that to him."

Mike's voice was calm. "We understand you had a disagreement with him the night before the incident?"

Em's face paled, and she seemed lost for words for a moment. Then, taking a deep breath, she straightened in her chair. "Yes, we argued, but I would never, ever hurt him."

"Even though he was threatening to report you to the police?" Mike pressed gently.

"I didn't harm Colin. I swear it," Em insisted vehemently, her voice thick with emotion.

Bea was inclined to believe her, but glancing at Mike, she could tell he was still sceptical. "What were you arguing about?" he asked, his gaze unwavering.

"It was merely a misunderstanding," Em mumbled, picking at a loose thread on her combat trousers.

Mike shook his head. "That's not good enough, Ms Shaw. And, of course, I can always ask Mr Myatt later…" He trailed off, his look pointed.

Em's shoulders slumped.

Was the argument connected to Noel's death somehow?

After a long moment, Em spoke, her voice quiet, "I've been selling old props on eBay. Props we don't need anymore or that have been replaced. And I... I kept the money."

Bea felt a pang of disappointment, remembering Rich's mention of Em's eBay income. So this was the secret Em had been hiding.? Nothing to do with Noel…

"Colin found out recently," Em continued, sounding exhausted. "He came across a listing for something he recognised from our prop inventory. He confronted me, said he'd go to the police. I begged him not to." She pulled out her phone with a shaking hand, opening her text history. "He messaged me later. He said he wouldn't turn me in if I shut down the account and made a donation to the theatre."

Mike scanned the messages before returning her phone. "Oh, and one more thing. Where were you yesterday between four and six in the afternoon?"

Em blinked, surprised by the sudden change in topic. "Er… I was having dinner with my parents, my sister, and her family. I wasn't due in until seven. Colin had the early shift, so he was opening up."

Bea's mind raced. If Em's alibi checked out, and if Colin's accident was linked to Noel's death... they could rule Em out. The suspect list was dwindling. Only three left now.

Mike switched off the machine as he thanked Em for her time. As the stage manager closed the door behind her, he turned to Bea. "Seems like that's another one we can cross off the list," he said with a sigh. His phone beeped, and he looked down at the message just as the door burst open, and Perry entered, Daisy galloping excitedly at his heels.

His face was flushed with urgency. He took in a deep breath and announced dramatically, "I've got big news!"

33

A FEW SECONDS LATER, MONDAY 4 OCTOBER

P erry was practically vibrating with energy as he stood before them. Daisy trotted over to greet Bea.

"I spoke with Stella," Perry said in a rush. "And I think— I think she might be pregnant with Noel's baby!"

Bea, who had bent over to fuss Daisy, shot upright. "What makes you say that?"

"Simply a hunch based on a conversation I've just had with her. Plus, she's feeling sick. And she's very emotional. Oh, and she admitted she was there early the night Noel was killed to talk to him about something 'personal'." He emphasised the word personal with his fingers, then gave her a triumphant look.

Bea's stomach fluttered. That would explain a lot if Perry was right.

"I'll need to talk to her, of course, confirm that is the case and—"

"She's going to tell you the truth about why she was there that evening as soon as she gets here today," Perry jumped in. "She promised me."

"Okay, that's great. Thanks," Mike said. He took a sip of

water, then continued, "I got a message that you've found something in the alley next to the theatre?"

"It was actually Daisy who found it," Perry admitted, grinning at Bea. He handed his phone to Mike. "Here's a photo."

Bea bent down and patted her little terrier on the head. "Have you been sleuthing again, little girl?" Daisy's tail swept the floor at speed while she looked into Bea's eyes. "Good girl," Bea said.

"The PC who was at the theatre is dealing with it," Perry added.

"Well done, Perry," Mike said, handing his phone back. "As you say, it might not be anything, but we'll get it looked at. You never know; it might be important."

Perry began pacing, his hands gesticulating. "Back to Stella. So here's the thing—I don't think she killed Noel. It was in her best interest to keep him alive to help raise their child. I don't think she's our killer."

Bea tipped her head. "If you're right, then that leaves us with only two viable suspects—Kurt and Tom."

Perry frowned. "What about Em?"

Bea and Mike quickly brought him up-to-date.

"So that explains the extra income Rich mentioned," he said when they'd finished. He glanced at his watch. "Right. I've got to dash as rehearsals start soon. I can keep Daisy with me if that helps. Between you and me," he added with a wink, "she'll probably give a more convincing performance than Tom."

At that moment, the door swung open and Tom walked in. *Oh no, did he hear that?*

An awkward silence descended as Tom directed an icy glare at Perry.

That would be a yes then…

Perry's cheeks flushed as he scooped up Daisy and scuttled out of the room.

The hostility radiating off Tom was palpable, his eyes shooting daggers at Perry's retreating back. Bea had sensed the tension between them before, but this raw animosity took her by surprise. *What on earth had happened to cause such bad blood?*

"Mr Hatlee. Thanks for coming. Please have a seat," Mike said calmly, gesturing to the empty chair. He switched on the recorder as Tom sat. "Can you tell us where you were between four and six yesterday afternoon, please?"

Tom examined his nails with an air of boredom. "I was at home."

"Alone?"

Tom cocked an eyebrow. "Yes," he sneered.

Bea fought the urge to roll her eyes. If Tom turned out to be the murderer, she wouldn't be that disappointed.

"I heard the most dreadful rumour," Tom continued, his posh Fenshire accent dripping with affected concern. "Is it true someone's attacked our dear Colin?"

"Mr Myatt is in hospital, but fortunately, he will make a full recovery."

"Good. Good." Tom bobbed his head, then tilted it to one side. "So when will we be allowed back in the theatre? This delay is frightfully inconvenient. We're missing desperately needed time on the real stage."

Mike's jaw tightened. Bea had rarely seen him so visibly annoyed. "The theatre will reopen when the police have finished their investigation, Mr Hatlee," he replied curtly.

Tom's eyebrows shot up. "I was only asking."

Mike ignored his comment and pressed on, "On the night Mr Ashworth died, where were you during the unscheduled break that happened at around six-thirty?"

"Oh, I popped to the loo," Tom said breezily, waving a hand. "Nature called. You know how it is."

"Did anyone see you?" Mike pressed.

Tom pursed his lips, thinking. "Not that I recall. But I was only gone for five minutes tops."

Five minutes. Long enough to tamper with Noel's cigarette… But no—as loathed as she was to admit it, she had a gut feeling Tom was telling the truth. Pompous and aggravating, yes. But a murderer? She suppressed a smile. *Not unless Perry was the victim!*

"Alright, thank you, Mr Hatlee," Mike said, switching off the machine in front of him on the table. "Could you please ask Kurt Grant to come in?"

Tom stood up, smoothing his garish shirt. "Of course. I do hope you sort this mess out soon. The show must go on, as they say!" With a final hair flip, he strutted out of the room.

Bea let out a loud breath. "I don't like that man one bit!"

Mike chuckled ruefully. "I have to agree. You know, part of me wishes it was him just so I can wipe that smug look off his face when I arrest him."

Bea grinned. "As long as I can be there to watch."

Mike rubbed his temples. "In all seriousness though, we've got nothing concrete on him. He has no alibi for Colin's attack, and he could've sabotaged the prop." He shook his head. "But it's not enough without hard evidence."

There was a sharp rap on the door, and Kurt entered, looking mildly rumpled as always, his glasses slipping down his nose. He pushed them back up nervously as he took a seat across from Mike who reminded him he would be recording the conversation again.

"How's Colin?" Kurt blurted out as Mike started the recording. "Is he alright?"

Mike's expression remained neutral. "He'll make a full recovery."

Kurt's shoulders relaxed a little. "Did he... did he say what happened?"

"I haven't taken a full statement yet," Mike replied, his tone guarded. "But it would appear not."

Bea watched Kurt carefully, but he merely nodded.

Mike continued, "Where were you between four and six yesterday afternoon, Mr Grant?"

"At home," Kurt said quickly. "I was due in later, but Liv texted to cancel rehearsals before I left."

"Was anyone with you?"

Kurt swallowed loudly, then shook his head. "No."

So he had no alibi either... *We still have our two suspects.*

"Did Noel ever ask you to get him drugs?"

Mike's question caught Bea off guard. *Does he know something he's not told me?*

Kurt's head snapped up, his eyes wide behind his glasses. For a split second, Bea thought she saw a flash of something. But just as quickly, his face shuttered closed again, calm and collected. "No," he replied. "As I told you before, Noel and I weren't friends."

Mike pressed on, "But you knew he was on something, didn't you?"

Kurt paused, his gaze dropping to the table. "I... suspected. The way he acted... I thought he might be on speed, but it was merely a hunch."

"Any idea where he might have got the drugs from?"

Ah... She could see what Mike was doing now.

There was a slight hesitation. "Er... No."

Bea and Mike exchanged a glance. Kurt was holding something back; that much was clear. Mike's eyes narrowed. "I find that hard to believe, Mr Grant."

Kurt seemed to deflate. He took off his glasses, rubbing his eyes wearily. "Alright, look. I didn't want to say anything, but…" His shoulders drooped a little. "I think it might have been Colin."

Bea's eyebrows shot up. But Colin had denied it. She chewed her lip. But perhaps it was true, and the drugs were a distraction, a red herring. Perhaps Noel's death had nothing to do with them at all. But then what was the motive?

"What makes you think it was Mr Myatt?" Mike asked, interrupting her racing thoughts.

Kurt shifted uncomfortably in his seat. "I saw them together a few times, whispering in corners backstage. They didn't seem to know each other well, so it struck me as odd. But hey, you asked for my opinion. I could be way off base." He looked away as if he was suddenly disinterested in the conversation.

Mike leaned over to switch off the machine. "Alright. Thank you for your time, Mr Grant. You can go now."

As Kurt left, Bea turned to Mike, narrowing her eyes. "Is it possible that the drugs and Noel's death aren't actually connected?"

He spread out his hands. "I don't know, but at this point, we have to consider all the angles."

A knock at the door interrupted them. Stella poked her head in, looking uncharacteristically timid. "Have you got five minutes, inspector?"

Mike waved her in. "Of course, Ms Vance. Come in."

Stella walked in and sat down. She looked pale and drawn, with dark circles under her usually vibrant eyes. It seemed to Bea that Perry could be right. A wave of sympathy washed over her. She remembered how exhausting and emotional those first few months of pregnancy could be.

Stella took a deep breath, twisting her hands in her lap.

"I'm sorry," she began, her voice a bit wobbly. "I wasn't completely honest with you the last time we spoke."

34

THAT EVENING, MONDAY 4
OCTOBER

The clinking of crystal and soft laughter filled the elegant dining room at Francis Court, her parents' home, as Bea sipped her wine and listened intently to the animated conversation flowing around the dinner table.

"The king and queen opening Three Lakes next year will be incredible publicity," her brother, Fred, said, his eyes shining with enthusiasm.

Rich nodded vigorously. "Having them cut the ribbon will draw so much positive attention to the work we're doing there with the rehabilitation of our military and veterans."

The work we're *doing?* There was no doubt Rich had thrown himself into this project of Fred's.

"I'm glad James and Olivia are giving you their support," her mother, Her Royal Highness Princess Helen, said as she took a sip of water. "But then, perhaps it's not such a big surprise. My brother has fond memories of his time in the Royal Air Force when he was younger."

Bea speared a roast potato and popped it into her mouth. It was lovely to sit down and eat with her family like this. Since she'd moved to The Dower House, even though it was on the estate and only a fifteen-minute walk away, she didn't come and visit as much as she should do. Even so, the invitation to dinner tonight had come out of the blue. She looked across the table at her mother. Princess Helen's eyes sparkled with that familiar gleam—the one that always meant she was up to something. Bea knew her mother too well and suspected she had an ulterior motive for having invited them to this little family soirée beyond discussing the rehab facility.

As if on cue, her mother gave Bea a sideways glance. "How's Sam doing, darling? I feel like I haven't seen that grandson of ours in ages."

"Oh, you know, teenage boys." Bea set down her glass, suppressing a sigh. "Always on the go. I'm lucky if I get five minutes on the phone with him these days. That's if he can fit me in between school and sports."

"Fred was the same at that age," the princess said, spearing a bite-size piece of chicken. "Never around to chat, always dashing off to rugby or polo. I'm afraid it only gets worse when they toddle off to university." She sighed dramatically before brightening. "But don't despair, they circle back to family once they've had their fun and need somewhere to live."

Fred rolled his eyes good-naturedly. "I don't know what you're talking about, Ma. I've always been a devoted and dutiful son."

Summer York giggled, nudging her fiancé. "Oh, yes, a perfect angel."

As the table erupted into a lively discussion of Fred's behaviour as a teenager, Bea took another fortifying sip of wine. Her mother was a master of steering conversation exactly where she wanted it to go.

Princess Helen's voice cut through the laughter. "Speaking of Sam, when is he next home, darling?"

Here we go…

"Not until half-term, I'm afraid. But Rich and I are going to watch him play rugby on Saturday. We've been given permission to take him out for an early dinner afterwards."

Rich chimed in with a grin. "And by 'him', of course, we mean Sam *and* Archie. Those two are practically joined at the hip."

Bea smiled. Rich was right; they would no doubt take Sam's best friend with them, and she could guarantee he would have lots of questions about Noel's murder. Archie's second love after celebrity gossip was true crime.

The table chuckled knowingly, but Bea noticed her mother's eyes narrowing slightly. Princess Helen smiled. "And have you spoken to Sam yet about your uncle's proposal?"

The clinking of cutlery ceased abruptly.

And there it is….

Rich's hand found Bea's under the table, and he gave it a reassuring squeeze. *Thanks.* She cleared her throat. "No. Not yet. It doesn't seem like something we can discuss over the phone or FaceTime. We're hoping to talk to him on Saturday if we get a chance."

Princess Helen's mouth twitched a touch. "And have you two given it any more thought yourselves?"

A double whammy!

Bea glanced at Rich, who squeezed her hand again. "We're still thinking about it, Ma," she said. "It's only been twenty-four hours. We need some time…"

"Is it the press that worries you?" her mother asked pointedly.

Bea felt a twinge of irritation at her mother's persistence. "It's certainly a consideration," she admitted, trying to keep her tone neutral.

Summer, perhaps sensing the tension, jumped in. "You

know, I still get terrified of public appearances. Isn't that ridiculous, considering I've been a TV presenter for so long?"

Bea shot her soon-to-be sister-in-law a grateful look as Summer continued, "But it's also been so rewarding. And think how great it would be to have you and Rich working alongside us, Bea."

Fred nodded enthusiastically. "Absolutely! You'll both be brilliant at it."

"A fresh, youthful face for the monarchy," Princess Helen declared, beaming. "And Robert would be over the moon to have your support."

I know all of this! These were all points her uncle himself had made. Had he asked her mother to test the waters to gauge her and Rich's receptiveness?

As the conversation swirled on around her, Bea retreated into her own thoughts. It was a monumental decision, one that would irrevocably change the course of their lives. She'd been initially relieved when Perry had told her he wanted to take a break from their business, but afterwards, she'd realised that their business was one of her last barriers to saying yes. *No excuses now.* But was she ready for that? And what about Rich? When she'd told him about her conversation with Perry and how that, if she wanted to, she could step away from the business without letting Perry down, Rich had said, "That's good." That was all. She'd no idea what was going through that head of his. Was he reluctant to give up the career he'd worked so hard to achieve? *That must be it...*

Bea swallowed, her throat suddenly dry. "The biggest consideration is Rich's job," she said, her voice wavering a tad. "It would be an enormous decision for him to give that up. What if... well, what if it doesn't work out for us?"

Fred snorted. "But Rich doesn't even *like* his job."

Bea's head snapped towards Rich as she dropped his

hand. *He's discussed this with Fred? Without telling me?* Rich squirmed under her gaze, looking sheepish.

"Fred, Helen," Charles Astley interjected, his voice gentle but firm. "Let's not put undue pressure on Bea and Richard. This decision is theirs, and theirs alone."

Gratitude swelled in Bea's chest. Trust her father to be the voice of reason.

"Yes, darling, of course." Princess Helen smiled at her husband. "But if I may, just one last thought?" She turned to Rich. "Have you considered requesting a sabbatical from work? Say, six months? That way, you and Bea could give this a proper go without burning any bridges."

Bea hated to admit it, but her mother's suggestion was a good one. A trial run of sorts. Bea glanced at Rich, trying to decipher the emotions flickering in his eyes. *Excitement? Hope? Both?*

"That's… not a bad idea," he said slowly, his mouth curving ever so slightly as his hand found hers again. "Thank you, Helen. We'll think about it."

As his fingers laced through hers and squeezed reassuringly, Bea knew that whatever path they chose, they would walk it together. Hand in hand. She smiled back at him. *Although, I* will *be talking to you about confiding in my brother and not me about your job!*

35

LUNCHTIME THE NEXT DAY.
TUESDAY 5 OCTOBER

B ea shifted in her seat at the kitchen table at The Dower House, a half-eaten plate of sandwiches sitting in the centre. She and Perry had just finished telling Simon and Rich about Stella's pregnancy and Em's side business of selling props.

Daisy sat ever hopeful at Perry's feet as he munched his way through his food.

"So that explains Em's extra income," Rich said. His dark eyes narrowed as he reached for another sandwich. "But it also gives her an excellent motive to get Colin out of the way."

"Except he agreed later that evening not to report her," Bea pointed out, tucking her hair behind her ear. "And although Mike's team is still confirming it, she has an alibi for the time he was attacked."

"So we think we can rule her out?" Simon asked as he absentmindedly threw Daisy a morsel of cheese.

"Simon!" Bea raised an eyebrow.

"Sorry," he said, looking only mildly contrite.

She carried on, "Unless her alibi fails, then yes, I think we can, and Mike was of the same opinion."

Perry stuffed the last piece of his sandwich into his mouth, then swallowed noisily. "Then there's the plot twist that Stella's pregnant. I think that rules her out too." He reached over and grabbed another one.

Bea's mind drifted back to yesterday's conversation in the village hall storeroom. The fluorescent lights had cast harsh shadows across Stella's sickly face as she'd made her confession to Bea and Mike. "Hold on, I've remembered something she said that might be useful."

"Go on," Rich said through a mouthful of food.

"She admitted she went to rehearsals early specifically to see Noel. After Em asked her to leave, she didn't actually go to the dressing rooms like she originally claimed. Instead, she stuck around backstage and watched the rehearsals from behind the scenery. Mike asked her about the props desk, and she said she was right beside it the whole time."

Simon tapped his fingers on the wooden table. "If she's telling the truth, then it narrows our window for when the fake cigarette could have been tampered with to between ten to five until just after six."

Simon leaned forward. "Did you and Mike believe her?"

The question hung in the air. Bea considered it carefully, remembering Stella's trembling hands and the mascara that had begun to smudge beneath her eyes during their conversation. *She looked sincere… but then…*

"Yes. I think so," Bea said. "I know she's a good actress, but the pregnancy…" She paused, weighing her words. "That changes things."

"How so?" Rich asked.

"It gives her a motive to keep Noel alive rather than kill him," Bea said.

"But it could also be a motive to harm him if he rejected her and the baby," Simon pointed out.

I suppose so… "She told us that Noel had agreed that they needed to discuss it further, and they were planning to do that later that evening. I think it depends on if we believe her or not."

"And you do?" Simon asked.

"I believe her when she says she wanted Noel to raise the baby with her."

Under the table, Daisy whined softly and nudged Perry's hand. Perry broke off a corner of his sandwich for her.

"Don't," Bea warned too late.

"Sorry," Perry said, not looking sorry at all.

"Okay, can everyone stop feeding Daisy, please?" Rich cried, sounding exasperated. "You're undoing all the good work I've done at getting the weight off her."

You? Bea coughed and stared at him.

"Sorry, I mean we…" Rich added quickly and winked at her.

The group fell silent for a moment. The only sound was Daisy's contented chewing coming from under the table.

Rich pushed his plate away and grabbed his coffee. "I've been doing some further background checks. And—" he paused for effect "—Tom and Noel were at school together."

Bea shot him a look. "I'm fairly certain he claimed not to know Noel very well when Mike and I interviewed him." She pressed her lips together. *What had he said about Noel?*

"But?" Rich prompted.

Ah, that was it. "He called Noel a menace. I specifically remember him using the word as it struck me as an odd choice. You don't hear it often, do you?"

Simon's eyes narrowed thoughtfully. "So maybe they

knew each other better than Tom's letting on? Perhaps Tom was on the receiving end of Noel's bullying at school?"

"That was years ago though," Rich pointed out. "Is that really a strong enough motive to hurt someone now, all these years later?"

"Yes!" Bea and Perry cried simultaneously, then looked at each other.

"Lucinda," Perry said simply.

Bea nodded, memories of a past case rushing back. "Rich, a few years ago, Perry and I were involved in a case where the motive turned out to be revenge for school bullying nearly twenty years after it had happened."

"Some wounds never heal," Perry added, uncharacteristically serious. "Especially the ones inflicted when you're young and vulnerable."

Rich considered this. "Point taken. I'll let Mike know."

Perry shifted in his seat, his slim frame practically vibrating with frustration. "The irony is that Tom himself has turned into a bully," he said, jabbing a finger at the table. "During rehearsals yesterday, he was giving me daggers the whole time."

Bea watched her friend's face flush with indignation, the blond spikes of his hair seeming to stand even more on end with his agitation.

"Every time I paused for even half a second, he'd jump in with line prompts when I didn't need them! It's like he's trying to make me look incompetent."

Well, it is sort of your own fault if he was mad at you yesterday... Bea cleared her throat delicately. "You did say Daisy would be a better actor than him."

At the sound of her name, the terrier, who was sprawled at her feet, looked up at Bea. Bea patted her on the head, and she settled down again.

Perry's eyes widened dramatically. "We can't know for sure he heard me."

"Oh, he heard you, Perry. You should've seen his face as you scuttled out."

"And now he's determined to get me out of the production one way or another," Perry insisted, his blue eyes flashing.

Bea exchanged a quick glance with Simon, who was watching his husband with exasperated affection. "Perry, love," Simon said gently, trying to contain a smile. "Don't you think you might be reading too much into this? Tom was probably simply hacked off that you didn't rate his acting any better than a dog's."

Perry opened his mouth to protest, but Rich interrupted. "How was the atmosphere during rehearsals yesterday, Perry?" he asked, wisely steering the conversation away from Perry's wounded pride.

Perry sighed, deflating a little. "Subdued. Everyone was whispering about the production being cursed." His shoulders slumped just a little. "Gabe and I were doing what we could to perk everyone up, but no one's looking forward to going back to the theatre later."

I can't say I blame them. A murdered cast member and a hospitalised lighting technician would act as a deterrent for most people.

Simon's phone buzzed. He glanced at it and raised an eyebrow. "It's a message from Roisin," he told them. "The vial Perry and Daisy found had traces of nicotine in it. They think it was discarded by the killer."

Good girl, Daisy! Yet again, Daisy had sniffed out a clue that could be useful.

"They're still testing it for fingerprints," Simon continued. "She also says the bag of pills found in Colin's pocket was completely clear of prints."

"Which suggests they were planted," Rich murmured.

Perry frowned. "Why does that matter?"

"If they truly belonged to Colin," Simon explained, "they would have his fingerprints on them. But if they're clean…"

"Whoever handled them used gloves. I get it now," Perry said.

A chill ran through Bea. Someone had carefully planned this.

Rich got up from the table and stretched his back. "I'm going to ring Mike and let him know about Tom and Noel being at school together." He moved towards the stairs, then disappeared up them.

Bea shifted her focus to Simon, who had set his phone aside and bent down to stroke Daisy's head. The dog was sprawled contentedly across his feet under the table.

"How did your chat with Ryan and Fay go?" she asked. "About the restaurant?"

Simon's beard twitched with a half-smile. "They were disappointed," he replied, straightening up and running a hand through his light-brown hair. "They said they love working with me, which was nice to hear. But they understood where I'm coming from."

I'm so glad… They'd all watched Simon struggle to balance his writing career with the demands of running the restaurant for months.

"Are they going to buy you out?" she asked.

"They're thinking about it. They don't know if they can afford it. It's an enormous investment for them."

"And how do you feel about it all?"

He considered for a moment, his brown eyes thoughtful.

"Equal parts relieved and sad, honestly. I'll miss being part of the restaurant. We built something special there."

"Indeed. Although I sense a but…"

A genuine smile spread across his face. "But I'm looking forward to concentrating solely on my writing career."

"And me," Perry added, his blue eyes twinkling as he reached over to squeeze Simon's hand. "Don't forget you'll be concentrating on me too."

"How could I forget you, love?" Simon replied, grinning.

Bea felt a surge of affection for her friends. Despite everything happening with the case, these moments of warmth were a lifeline.

Simon rose. "So talking about writing. I really need to do some. My book is due to go to my editor in two weeks, and she's being increasingly vocal about how she can't push the deadline out beyond that. "

Perry glanced at his watch and stood up too, unfolding his slim frame. "And I'd better be off to rehearsals."

Today? "I'd have thought after everything…"

"Liv's asked those of us who are free to be there this afternoon," Perry said. "With all the disruption over the last few days, we're falling behind schedule."

Bea couldn't help notice a flicker of unease crossed his face. *Is he dreading another encounter with Tom.* "Ignore Tom, Perry. He's merely jealous because you're so much better than Daisy."

———

Bea placed a steaming cup of coffee on the desk in The Library of the Dower House and smiled at Rich, who was hunched over his laptop. "I thought you might want one?"

He smiled up at her, and she enjoyed the familiar flutter in her tummy that a smile from Rich always produced. "Mike told me you're doing some further checks on the background information they gathered."

He nodded. "So far, apart from the Tom and Noel school connection, I've not found much more, I'm afraid."

"So nothing on Perry then?"

Rich shook his head. "I've not uncovered anything to support the theory that Perry was the target. Even the background checks I've done on him—there are no links whatsoever to any of the cast."

Phew! If Rich had found nothing, then the chances were that there was nothing to find.

He paused, his expression turning thoughtful. "Wait a sec. I had an email a few minutes ago that I haven't looked at yet. I doubt it has anything new to add, but just in case." He tapped on the screen and scrolled through his emails. "Here it is." Rich's eyes scanned the screen, then he paused. "Darling, what's the name of the man who owns the tea shop in Francis-next-the-Sea?"

"Peter Tappin," Bea replied, a flutter in her belly. "Of Tappin's Teas. Why?"

Rich lifted an eyebrow. "It turns out that Tom Hatlee used to lodge in a house owned by Peter Tappin."

Bea's eyes widened. "Peter really doesn't like Perry. Perry has this theory that Peter is still firmly in the closet but had an unrequited crush on Simon. So when Perry appeared on the scene, Peter gave him the cold shoulder and now blatantly ignores him whenever he eats there." She gave a wry smile. "It's become a bit of a running joke." But as the words left her mouth, a thought struck her. "Wait a minute. What if it's not a joke? What if Peter poisoned Tom against Perry and then Perry got the role Tom wanted? That would explain why Tom dislikes him so much."

Rich nodded slowly, his expression thoughtful. "I agree—dislike him, yes. Want to kill him? It doesn't seem like a strong enough motive to me."

Is he right? People kill for all sorts of reason, but even so...

She felt Rich's hand take hers. "Try not to worry, Bea. I still think the poison was meant for Noel. But" —he raised her fingers to his mouth and lightly kissed them— "I'll let Mike know, and he will no doubt want to talk to Tom about it."

As Rich dropped her hand, she looked at her watch. "Well, I'm meeting Mike at the theatre soon, so I look forward to sitting in on that conversation."

She was a bit early, but it wouldn't do any harm to go now and see how Perry was getting on.

36

MEANWHILE, TUESDAY 5 OCTOBER

Perry sat in the comfy red chairs in the auditorium of Windstanton Theatre Royal. Stella was onstage with Gabe and seemed to be delivering her lines with a newfound energy. The harsh stage lights softened her features, making her look more like the Stella he'd come to know—confident, radiant even.

Next to him, Ralph sighed heavily. "I don't care what anyone says about this production being cursed; it's good to be back in the building."

Perry's eyes lit with understanding. He, too, had been pleased to receive Liv's text earlier to say the police had released the theatre back to them. The light onstage moved a touch, and Perry peered ahead of him to the base of the stage. *Colin?* "Is Colin back already?" he whispered to Ralph.

Ralph dipped his chin. "Yes. They released him from hospital last night."

Well, that's dedication for you. If he was Colin, he wouldn't want to go anywhere near a lighting rig for a very long time!

"Stella's looking better today," Ralph said. "Almost... glowing."

Was it the pregnancy or had a weight been lifted off her shoulders since she'd confessed all to Mike and Bea? Perry recalled how Stella had cornered him when he'd arrived for rehearsal earlier.

She'd pulled him into the empty green room, her dark waves bouncing as she'd squeezed his arm and smiled. "Perry, I need to thank you," she'd said. "Talking to the police was exactly what I needed. I feel... lighter."

"You certainly look blooming," he'd replied.

She'd studied his face. "You guessed yesterday, didn't you?"

Perry had hesitated, then had given her a half-smile. "How are you feeling?"

"Well, the tablets have controlled the sickness, and I managed to get a full night's sleep."

"And becoming a mother?"

"I'm coming to terms with it." She'd glanced at the door nervously. "Would you mind keeping it to yourself, Perry? Just for a little while longer."

"Of course," he'd promised.

Now, as she delivered her lines with perfect timing, Perry could see the subtle change in her demeanour. The way she carried herself was different. There was a *swoosh* behind him, and the spotlight moved onto her again. She looked confident and strong. *She'll be fine.* He turned to Ralph. "Like us, she's probably excited to be back in the theatre."

Ralph exhaled dramatically, fanning himself with a discarded script page. "So... I have something juicy to tell you about our leading man."

Gabe? Perry raised an eyebrow. "Please tell me you've found out something that he's not annoyingly good at?"

"Well, actually. Funny you should say that…" Ralph leaned in closer. "My niece is at Nottingham, you know," he whispered, his eyes never leaving the stage. "Same uni Gabe was at."

Perry tilted his head to one side. "Really? Do tell…"

"She said he was kicked off his course a few weeks ago," Ralph continued, the words practically dancing off his tongue. "Well, 'asked to reconsider his choices' was how the university phrased it."

Perry blinked. "Seriously?" He glanced up at the stage, where Gabe was mid-monologue, a perfect blend of charm and arrogance that made the role of Jack Worthing feel like it had been tailored to him by Wilde himself. *So he's not perfect, after all…*

"Oh, yes." Ralph's eyebrows arched theatrically. "Missed a major assignment. Third one he'd been late with, apparently. They warned him—turn this one in on time or you're out. And guess what?"

"He didn't?"

"He didn't," Ralph confirmed, his eyes gleaming. "Too busy trying to get himself into a professional theatre company. Auditions and stuff. His law tutors weren't impressed. And his parents?" Ralph said, drawing back from Perry and putting his hand over his heart. "Furious, my dear! Apparently, they wanted to wash their hands of him. So who had to drive all the way to Nottingham to collect our boy?"

"Marco, his uncle?" Perry guessed.

Ralph nodded smugly. "And our lovely director. Nephew duties."

Of course! Liv was late to rehearsals on the day Noel died because she'd been to Nottingham… to collect Gabe.

"They brought him here so he could think about what he wants to do. Law or no law."

Perry folded his arms, thoughtful. "Do you think that's why Liv cast him in the lead? To give him a chance to see if this really *is* what he wants to do?"

"Well," Ralph said with a dramatic sigh. "She's not daft. She knows talent when she sees it. But yes, I think this is his shot. His real shot." Ralph dipped his head. "Lucky for him an opportunity came along…"

Perry gave Ralph a look. "Not so lucky for Noel though…"

"Of course," Ralph said, putting his hand to his chest. "Talking of poor Noel, have you figured out who killed him yet, Miss Marple?"

"What do you mean?" Perry gave him a sly smile.

"Oh, come on, you've got that detective gleam in your eye, my dear."

"Detective gleam?" Perry feigned vagueness. "I'm simply here to act, Rafe."

"Oh, please." Ralph rolled his eyes dramatically. "You can't kid a kidder, sweetie. Your brain's been working over-time since the moment Noel's body was found. Now tell me everything."

Perry's heart sank to his feet. *And for a minute, I thought I was doing a good job undercover…* But then, this was Ralph. "Fine," he said. "We've narrowed it down to two viable suspects."

"We?"

"I mean, you know, the police."

Ralph leaned in, his eyes twinkling. "And who are they?"

"Tom and Kurt."

"Ooooh." Ralph fanned himself faster. "And did one of them also try to flatten Colin?"

Perry shrugged. "It seems likely. Then frame him so that it looked like Colin was the killer."

"Well," Ralph whispered. "My money is on Kurt. After all, he was in Windstanton that afternoon."

"What afternoon?"

"The one Colin was almost dumped on."

Perry's eyes widened. "When was this?"

"Oh, not long after we spoke. I was walking to the theatre. So around twenty-past-five, I suppose."

"And where was he?"

"In his car. He drove right past me, going in the same direction."

Perry frowned. Hadn't Bea said that both Kurt and Tom had said they'd been at home between four and six that day? So Kurt had been lying... Perry's stomach clenched. He'd rather hoped that Tom would turn out to be the killer, not Kurt.

As if summoned by dark magic, Tom appeared at the far edge of the wings, his blond hair catching the stray stage light. He was staring into the auditorium, his eyes—behind those ridiculously bright-orange frames—fixed on Perry with unmistakable coldness.

A shiver ran up Perry's spine. *What is his problem?*

Ralph followed his gaze. "Now, of course, if you were suddenly found dead backstage, my dear, I'd believe it was Tom in a heartbeat." He patted Perry's arm. "The way he looks at you... It's like you've stolen his favourite toy and his ice cream in one fell swoop."

Perry ran a hand through his blond hair, feeling strangely vindicated. "So I'm not imagining it? The way he looks at me?"

"Not at all, dear boy." Ralph's voice dropped to a theatrical whisper. "You need to watch your back! I've seen daggers drawn backstage before, but Tom's glares could slay Richard the Third!"

Perry glanced back at Tom right as another light swept across from the bottom of the stage and lit up his understudy's face. *If looks could kill...*

Perry rubbed his clammy hands together. "I was beginning to wonder if I was merely being paranoid."

"The way that man glares at you, it's a wonder you haven't combusted on the spot!" Ralph chuckled, but then his weathered face grew serious, his rosy cheeks contrasting with his furrowed brow. "What I can't work out, though, is why either Tom or Kurt would want to kill Noel and frame Colin. What's the motive?"

"One thought is that Kurt was providing Noel with drugs, and it all went wrong."

Ralph raised an eyebrow but didn't say anything.

"The other's not so obvious, but we do know that Tom and Noel were at school together."

"Really?" Ralph stroked his small white moustache, his eyes widening with intrigue. "Now that's interesting. Old grudges can fester for decades—believe me, I've held on to a few myself in my time." He fanned himself dramatically. "Was there bad blood between them?"

Before Perry could answer, the scene onstage shifted. Gabe, looking impossibly dashing with his tousled dark hair catching the stage lights, dropped gracefully to one knee before Stella.

"Gwendolen, will you marry me?" Gabe asked as Jack, his voice carrying perfectly to the back of the theatre, his eyes fixed adoringly on Stella.

"Of course I will, darling," Stella replied, her voice clear and confident.

Then silence fell. Her face froze in a mask of panic.

Gabe remained on one knee, confusion flickering across his chiselled features, though he maintained his character's composure. His hands, still outstretched towards Stella, gave the slightest of trembles.

From the front of the stage, Liv's voice called out, "Line, please!"

More silence. Perry glanced around, noticing the prompt book was abandoned on a small desk.

Seconds ticked by.

Then from the shadows near the back curtain, Kurt's slightly breathless voice floated out: "How long you have been about it. I'm afraid you have—"

Stella's face relaxed. "I'm afraid you have very little experience in how to propose."

The scene continued, flowing smoothly once again.

When the scene concluded, Liv's voice rang out, "Great work, everyone! Let's take five minutes."

Colin appeared on the stage. He said something to Liv. She nodded, and he disappeared. She looked out into the auditorium, her hand shielding her eyes. "Rafe, you're up next, please."

Ralph dramatically clutched his chest as he rose. "Ah, the stage calls! How can I resist?" He winked at Perry before sashaying off to the set. "Try not to solve the entire mystery without me, dear boy!"

Perry chuckled. *I don't think that's very likely!*

37

LATER, TUESDAY 5 OCTOBER

Bea slipped into the dimly lit auditorium, choosing a seat in the back row of the first set of stalls. Before her, the stage lights created a golden halo around the performers, who were deep in rehearsal, unaware of her arrival.

Perry stood centre stage, his blond hair catching the light as he delivered his lines with perfect timing. He looked utterly transformed—not Perry, her best friend who hated to run, but Algernon Moncrieff, Victorian gentleman and professional Bunburyist. She was so proud of him.

She sighed. *Should I tell him about Tom and Peter Tappin?*

As she pondered the question, a figure popped up in front of the stage and adjusted a stage light. Bea squinted. *Is that Colin?* Although surprised to see him up and about so soon, she was pleased that he had fully recovered after his accident. He disappeared up the stage steps and into the wings.

On the stage with Perry was Gabe Rossi. Tall with an athletic build, his olive skin and tousled dark waves gave him a rugged appeal that somehow worked perfectly for his character. As he spoke, Bea found herself leaning forward a little.

"Good heavens, what are you doing here?" he asked.

"Dear brother, I have come down from town to tell you how very sorry I am for all the trouble I have caused you. I intend to lead a better life from now on," Perry replied, his face a study of contrived contrition.

As the scene continued, Kurt and Gina flanked them, trading witty barbs while petite Millie chimed in with perfect comic timing.

Hold on. Kurt had just referred to Gina as Miss Prism? *Wasn't Millie supposed to be playing that part? So why was Millie playing Cecily, Gina's old part? I'll have to ask Perry what's happened.*

Bea sat back as the dialogue sparkled, and the blocking flowed seamlessly. Pride swelled in her chest. *Perry's found his place*, she thought. *He belongs here. Simon will be so proud when he sees the final performance.*

Her eyes flicked to the wings and narrowed. Tom Hatlee skulked behind the curtain, his gaze laser-focused on Perry. Bea's skin prickled. *That look is pure venom.* She shifted uneasily. Maybe Perry's paranoia wasn't so far-fetched, after all...

Could Tom be the killer? Tom and Noel had been at school together. Had something happened then that had made Tom kill him all these years later? If the way he'd been looking at Perry a few minutes ago was anything to go by, he definitely had the capacity to feel the sort of hatred Bea imagined one needed to kill someone. Her heart flickered. Was that someone Perry? Had Tom got Noel and Colin by mistake? *No*—she mentally shrugged it off—*surely not. But,* she thought, staring at Tom, *I will tell Perry about Tom and Peter Tappin. Just so he can be careful around him until we figure this all out.*

As if sensing her attention, Tom's eyes flicked to her for a moment before he disappeared behind the curtain.

She checked her watch. Still twenty minutes before Mike would arrive to interview Tom about Noel.

"That's a wrap for this scene," Liv called out, clapping her hands twice. "Take ten everyone."

As Kurt, who had been playing Canon Chasuble, shuffled off the stage, adjusting his glasses as they slipped down his nose, Bea considered their other suspect. He had a chemistry background and no alibi for either Noel's murder or the attempted murder of Colin. And that was all. What could his motive be? *Unless, of course, he was Noel's dealer?*

Perry, who had been talking to Gabe, turned to walk offstage. Bea raised her hand and waved, trying to catch his attention. He squinted into the darkened auditorium. She waved more enthusiastically, and he finally raised one hand to his eyes, peering out like a sailor searching for land. As recognition dawned, his face broke out into a huge grin. "Bea!" he cried, hurrying down the stage steps. His blue eyes sparkled with excitement as he reached her. He leaned in and hugged her, then threw himself down in the seat next to her. "What are you doing here?"

She lowered her voice. "I'm meeting Mike to re-interview Tom about his relationship with Noel."

"That's handy because Ralph told me something interesting earlier. He saw Kurt driving past him the afternoon Colin was almost killed."

"When?"

"When he was on his way to the theatre."

Really? But hadn't he—

"But didn't he tell you that he was at home?" Perry asked.

"Indeed." Bea glanced towards the wings where Kurt had disappeared. "So he lied to us." *That's promising...*

Perry leaned in and whispered, "Do you think he's our man?"

"He could be. Although of course, it could all be an innocent mistake—he simply popped out for milk and forgot to mention it. But Mike will definitely want to interview him again." Bea pulled out her phone and quickly typed a text to Mike.

Perry gestured at the stage, where Gabe was reviewing his script. "So what do you think of our new Jack?"

"I see what you mean about him," Bea replied. "He's gorgeous *and* incredibly talented."

"Yes. It's very unfair," Perry said, pouting.

"Oh, by the way, I thought Millie was playing Miss Prism and Gina was Cecily. Did I get them the wrong way around?"

Perry shook his head. "No. They did a swap. Gina's trying to organise her wedding next month, and her head's not in the play, and Millie's desperate to get a more substantial part on her CV." He shrugged. "So they've done a swap."

"Well, it seems to be working if what I've just seen is anything to go by."

Perry nodded. "They're both much happier. In fact, it turns out that's why Millie was here early on the evening Noel died. She and Gina had already spoken about swapping roles the night before. They wanted to run it by Em to get her advice on how to approach Liv to suggest the swap. Millie volunteered to be the one to come in early and talk to Em. She didn't know Em was directing until she arrived."

Ah, so that makes sense…

"Perry! Tom! Places, please!" Liv called from the stage, startling Bea.

Perry sprang up, and blowing Bea a kiss, he jogged back up the stairs.

Rats! Bea mentally slapped her forehead. *I forgot to tell him about Tom. I'll tell him as soon as he's next offstage...*

The scene began with Gabe and Perry as Jack and Algernon sparring verbally.

"You're a scoundrel, Algy!" Gabe declared, his eyes flashing. "I won't have any Bunburying around here!"

Tom sauntered onstage, a cigarette case in hand. "I've put Mr Ernest's things in the room next door to you, sir."

As he spoke, Tom crossed to Perry and handed him the case.

"His things?" Gabe cried in horror.

"I'm afraid I can only stay a week this time," Perry said, a sly smile on his face.

"Order the dogcart, Merriman. Mr Ernest has been called back to town," Gabe said in an exasperated tone.

"Very good, sir," Tom replied with a slight bow before exiting with a flourish that seemed a touch over-the-top for the restrained character of a butler.

Perry opened the cigarette case, extracting one as he turned to Gabe. "What a frightful liar you are, Jack," he said. "I've not been called back anywhere."

He offered the case to Gabe, who waved it away. "Yes, you have!"

Setting down the case, Perry kept the cigarette between his fingers. He reached for a prop lighter, flipping it open. As he brought the cigarette to his lips, his nose wrinkled in obvious distaste. Bea stifled a giggle. *Oh, Perry!* He was so transparent.

Perry barely touched the cigarette to his lips before jerking it away with a grimace he couldn't hide. "I haven't heard anyone calling me." He raised his other hand to his ear, his voice a touch strained.

"It's your duty as a gentleman that's calling you," Gabe responded.

"My duty as a gentleman has never…" He trailed off, wiping his forehead with the back of his hand.

A prickle of unease ran through Bea. Something wasn't right. Perry looked… off somehow. Like he was struggling to focus. Her stomach clenched. What was happening? Icy fear trickled down her spine as Perry swayed on his feet.

Bea shot up from her seat. A strange fizzing filled her ribs. "Perry!" Her voice cracked with panic. *This can't be happening.* She had to get to him, had to do something—

"I can't—" Perry gasped, tugging at his collar. "Can't breathe—"

As she raced down the aisle, the cigarette slipped from Perry's fingers, and he crumpled to the stage in a boneless heap.

Horror flooded through Bea as she stumbled to a halt at the edge of the stage, fumbling for her phone. Her fingers shook as she dialled, every second feeling like an eternity.

"Emergency services, what—"

The operator's voice was drowned out by the roaring in Bea's ears. "I need an ambulance at Windstanton theatre, now! My friend, he's collapsed. I don't know what's wrong!" The words tumbled out as she tried to keep her voice steady while giving the operator the details.

Inside, she was screaming.

She dropped to her knees beside Perry's still form. Nausea pooled in her stomach.

His face was chalk-white, his breathing ragged and laboured. *Oh God, what if he…*

No! She couldn't think like that. She reached out with a trembling hand, smoothing sweat-damp hair back from his clammy forehead. "Perry? Perry, can you hear me?" Bea's voice cracked on his name. *Should I be doing something?* Her brain seemed to have stopped working. "Please hold on. Help is coming, I promise. You're going to be okay." Her heart was exploding in her chest. She was suddenly breathless. Perry looked so frail, so lifeless. What if the ambulance didn't make it in time?

Tears blurred Bea's vision as she clung to Perry's limp hand. *Keep breathing, Perry! Stay with me!* Around her, the theatre erupted into chaos, voices raised in alarm. But Bea barely heard them. All she could focus on was Perry and the terrifying possibility that this might be the last time she ever saw him alive.

38

AN HOUR LATER, TUESDAY 5 OCTOBER

At the hospital in King's Town, Bea stared into the murky depths of her coffee, the words on the mug blurring before her eyes. 'A wise doctor once wrote' it proclaimed in a flourishing script, followed by an indecipherable scrawl. It was, of course, meant to be a joke about how bad a doctor's handwriting was, but it was wasted on Bea right now.

Memories of the frantic ambulance ride with Perry came flooding back. His face had been obscured by an oxygen mask as the paramedics had worked over him with urgent efficiency. Wires had snaked out from under his shirt, connecting him to monitors that had blipped and buzzed in a staccato rhythm. An IV line had dripped steadily into his arm while she'd wondered if any of it would be enough to save her best friend…

One of the medics had kept sneaking glances her way, his eyes widening with recognition. Of course she should have realised she would be recognised. She'd given him a weak smile. Not that it had mattered. The only thing that had mattered right then had been Perry.

But now, in this private waiting room, a disturbing question was circling her brain like a persistent mosquito: had the killer targeted Perry all along? Had they been chasing the wrong scent? Following trails of red herrings while the real prey had been right under their noses? Bea squeezed her eyes shut against the thought. *No, I can't go there.*

Possible nicotine poisoning—that was what she'd told them. Perry's reaction to the cigarette had been so similar to how Noel's response had been described to her in the early days of the investigation. It seemed possible that the killer had used the same method...

Was that killer Tom? She shivered. Her brain was too fogged up to contemplate it further. *Just please let Liv have secured that cigarette,* she prayed silently. Had the director heard Bea's shout as she'd followed Perry onto the gurney to not let anyone touch it? It could be their only clue. She pictured Mike arriving at the scene, his quiet authority taking charge. He would know what to do, how to handle this. She had to believe that.

She took a sip of the acrid instant coffee and grimaced. All she could do now was wait and hope. Perry had to pull through. *He has to.*

Clutching the mug in her hands, she relived their arrival at King's Town General Hospital fifteen minutes ago. The ambulance had screeched to a halt, jolting Bea from her spiralling despair. A wave of relief had washed over her as the hospital doors had flown open and a flurry of activity had erupted around Perry's stretcher. She'd scrambled out after him, desperate to follow, but a firm hand had stopped her.

"I'm sorry, miss, but you can't go any further."

Bea had stared at the 'Restricted Area' sign, her middle clenching. She'd stood there mutely, watching as Perry had disappeared behind those ominous double doors. Alone in the sterile corridor, the weight of the situation had crashed down on her. *Where are Rich and Simon?*

She'd remembered calling Rich as they'd loaded Perry into the ambulance, her words a jumbled mess of panic and pleas. What had she even said? It didn't matter. Rich would know what to do. *He always does.*

A prickling sensation had crept up her spine, and Bea had become acutely aware of the sudden stillness. She'd glanced around, catching a huddle of nurses whispering and casting furtive looks her way. *Why are they staring at me and not helping Perry?* Self-consciousness had slammed into her. *God, what must I look like?* She'd tried to straighten out her dishevelled hair and had wiped her tear-streaked face. She'd felt exposed and vulnerable. *Rich, where are you?*

Just then, a senior nurse had approached, her expression a mix of concern and barely concealed curiosity. "Lady Beatrice?" Bea had nodded. "Why don't you come with me, my lady? We'll get you settled in a quiet room while you wait for news of your friend." Bea had followed numbly as the nurse had ushered her inside a stark white room with two leather sofas facing each other. Her stomach had dropped even further. *Isn't this the same as the rooms on TV where they deliver bad news to someone's loved ones?*

"I'll bring you a cup of coffee, shall I?" the nurse had asked. Bea had thanked her. "The doctor will be in shortly to update you on your friend's condition," the woman had said as she'd left.

Friend? The word now echoed hollowly in Bea's mind as she remembered the nurse's words. *Perry is so much more than that.* He was her rock, her champion, her confidant, the little brother she'd never had. What would she do without him? *No! You can't think like that. He* will *be alright. He has to be alright.*

Shortly after, the nurse had returned, pressing a steaming mug into Bea's hands. A man in a crisp blue suit had entered behind her. The nurse had introduced him as Mr Harris, the senior consultant on duty. Bea had rapidly searched his face for clues, but his expression had remained professionally neutral.

"Mr Juke is stable, my lady," he'd said. A flicker of hope had ignited in her chest. *Stable is good, isn't it?* "We've administered treatments to counteract the toxin, including activated charcoal and supportive measures. He's currently undergoing further evaluations to ensure all toxins have been effectively neutralised."

Bea had absorbed his words in silence, the medical jargon washing over her. Only one thing had mattered. "Will he be alright?"

The doctor had hesitated, and Bea's heart had squeezed tight. "It's too early to say for certain, but we're doing everything we can. His vital signs are encouraging, and we'll continue to monitor him closely." The doctor's tone had softened. "Your suggestion that it was nicotine poisoning likely saved his life. If we hadn't known…" He trailed off, shaking his head. "Let's simply say every second counted."

Bea hadn't been able to meet his gaze. His praise had felt hollow, undeserved. She should've protected Perry from the start. She should have seen this coming. Some best friend she was.

"I'll be back with updates as soon as I can, my lady." With a nod to the nurse, he'd left, the door swinging shut behind him.

The head nurse had turned to Bea, her face etched with sympathy. "Is there anything I can get you, my lady? Anything at all?"

Bea had swallowed past the lump in her throat. "My

fiancé, Richard Fitzwilliam, and Perry's husband, Simon Lattimore, should be here any minute. Could you…?"

"Of course." The nurse had smiled kindly. "I'll let the main reception know to expect them, and I'll bring them straight here when they arrive."

Bea slumped back on the sofa, her limbs heavy as lead. That had been five minutes ago. *Where are they?*

As if summoned by her desperate plea, the door burst open, jolting Bea upright. Rich and Simon stumbled in, their faces pale and drawn. Bea flew into Rich's arms, burying her face in his chest. For a moment, enveloped in his warmth, she could almost believe everything would be alright.

Almost.

She pulled back, turning to Simon. "He's stable," she said, her voice wobbling. "The doctor says his vital signs are good."

Simon collapsed into a chair, his head in his hands. Bea joined him on the sofa and squeezed his shoulder, knowing there was nothing more she could say at this time to comfort him.

The nursing manager reappeared, a tray laden with more coffee and biscuits in hand. "The doctor will be back as soon as there's news," she said gently, setting the tray down.

Bea poured Simon a coffee, then joined Rich on the other sofa. She reached out and took his hand. All they could do now was wait. Wait and pray that Perry would pull through. *Because the alternative… well, that isn't an option.*

39

LATER THAT EVENING, TUESDAY 5 OCTOBER

B ea sank into the plush sofa in the drawing room of The Dower House, her mind reeling. Daisy jumped up to join her while Rich paced by the ornate fireplace, and Detective Inspector Mike Ainsley leaned against the mahogany mantelpiece.

"We've sent the fake cigarette for testing," Mike said. "But I'm fairly confident it will contain a lethal dose of nicotine, the same as the one that killed Noel."

Bea's stomach churned. Thank God Perry had barely touched the wretched thing, let alone inhaled it like poor Noel had. Mr Harris had been clear when he'd come to see them shortly after Simon and Rich had arrived at the hospital. He'd said that had Perry inhaled the nicotine, they'd be having a very different conversation.

Rich stopped pacing. "It's pretty ballsy of the killer to try the same method twice, don't you think?"

Mike shrugged. "It worked the first time. And their attempt using the lighting rig failed, so they went back to what they knew was effective."

In a twisted way, Bea had to admit it made sense.

Her mouth felt dry as she glanced down at the phone she was clutching in her hand. Nothing from Simon. What was going on at the hospital? *I should be there with Simon!* Daisy nudged her hand, and Bea ruffled the wiry fur on her little terrier's head.

The blasted press again! She hadn't wanted to leave the hospital, but once word had got around that she and Rich were there, it had turned into a circus. The hospital administrator had assured them they were coping with the press intrusion, but it had been clear that it had been causing in an inordinate amount of trouble as reporters had hovered around the main entrance, trying to get quotes and opinions from anyone who would talk to them. As the number of press had grown, the police had been called, and they'd set up a cordon to contain them.

At that point, Bea had realised that their presence was making life difficult for both staff and patients to gain swift access to the facilities, and she'd felt compelled to leave.

If anything happens to Perry and I'm not there, I will never forgive them…

"My lady," Mike said, interrupting her thoughts. "I'm afraid we need to consider the possibility that Perry was the intended target all along."

It was what she'd been thinking, and she and Rich had discussed it on the way home, but hearing Mike say it made it seem real. But would Tom really want to harm her fabulous, larger-than-life best friend, who lit up every room he entered? She ran her hand through her hair. *The notion that someone wanted to snuff out his bright light…*

She glanced up at Rich, wondering if his mind was racing down the same dark paths as hers. His tense jaw and faraway eyes suggested it was.

"Was it Tom?" she asked. "Or is there someone else who

would want to…?" She trailed off, the unfinished question hanging heavy in the air between them.

Mike inhaled and exhaled slowly, his shoulders sagging slightly. "That's what we need to find out," he said grimly.

"Is Kurt your other suspect?" Rich asked.

Mike nodded. "They were both there for the cigarette poisonings, and neither has an alibi for when someone attacked Colin."

A memory sparked in Bea's mind. "Wait," she said, leaning forward. "I've remembered something Perry told me —Ralph saw Kurt drive past him when he was on his way to meet Perry at the theatre, just before Colin was almost killed."

Mike's eyebrows shot up. "Okay, well, that's new information. I'm interviewing both men down at the station later today, so I'll be sure to ask Kurt about that."

"Maybe someone can check any CCTV footage to see if Kurt's car was parked near the theatre?" Rich suggested.

As he and Mike continued to discuss the investigation, something was nagging in Bea's brain. A puzzle piece that didn't quite fit. *How is that possible?* "If Perry was the target, how did the killer intend to kill him with the lighting rig? Perry and Ralph weren't due to be there until much later."

Mike exchanged a glance with Rich before answering, "We've worked out that the rig landed where Perry would've been standing when rehearsals began."

The image of Perry being crushed in front of the entire cast flashed through Bea's mind, making her stomach lurch. She shook her head, trying to dispel the horrific thought. "Why did I not know this?" She looked at Mike, then at Rich.

The two men shared another loaded glance, and Bea's suspicion grew. "What's going on?" she demanded.

Mike hesitated, his eyes flicking to Rich once more. Bea

tapped her foot. "Out with it," she commanded in her best royal voice.

Mike held up a placating hand. "I didn't want to alarm you, Simon, or Perry."

Bea's mind reeled. "Why did you do nothing to protect him?" She felt sick. "This could have been avoided…"

Her eyes met Mike's, and she saw the regret there. He rubbed his forehead. "I'm so sorry, my lady, but we've uncovered nothing concrete to support the theory that Perry was the target. Even the background checks we've done on him—there are no links whatsoever to any of the cast until Fitzwilliam here found out about his link to Tom. But before I had time to question him, well, you know…" He looked down at his hands.

Rich coughed, and she looked at him. "Bea. What we need to do now is find out who tried to kill Perry. So let's go over what we know, shall we?"

She nodded slowly.

"Tom has a motive, and he was there for both the cigarette poisonings and the attack on Colin—I mean, Perry," Rich continued. "We also have Kurt who lied about where he was when Colin was hit by the rig. He also had opportunity for the poisoning of Noel."

"Exactly," Mike said, glancing at his watch. "I'll have a lot to discuss with both Kurt and Tom when I see them shortly. I'll let you know how I get on."

As Mike left, Bea hoped they were on the cusp of a break-through. The thought of Perry being the intended target all along sent a chill down her spine, but at least now they had a solid lead to pursue…

Ring! Bea's stomach flipped as she looked down at her phone and saw Simon's name. *Oh my goodness, please let this be good news…*

40

EARLY MORNING THE NEXT DAY.
WEDNESDAY 6 OCTOBER

T*he Daily Post* online article:

Theatre Production Plagued by 'Curse' as Lady Beatrice's Business Partner is Poisoned; Arrest Made for Attempted Murder

It's all going down in Fenshire: The Windstanton Royal Theatre's latest production has been thrust into turmoil following the hospitalisation of Perry Juke, who collapsed onstage during rehearsals because of suspected poisoning. Juke, husband of renowned crime novelist Simon Lattimore and business partner to Lady Beatrice, the Countess of Rossex, is out of intensive care and in a serious but stable condition.

. . .

Fenshire police have confirmed they have arrested a man late last night on suspicion of attempted murder in connection with the incident. The suspect's identity has not been released, but sources indicate he is affiliated with the production.

This incident is the latest in a series of misfortunes plaguing the production of The Importance of Being Earnest, *including the death of one of the lead players, prompting many to label it as 'cursed'. The turmoil has sparked a debate about whether the show should continue under such ominous circumstances.*

The Windstanton Theatre Players have yet to release an official statement regarding the future of the production. Fans and theatre-goers are left in suspense, wondering if the recent plague of bad luck will bring the curtain down on this ill-fated play.

41

MID-MORNING, WEDNESDAY 6 OCTOBER

"The doctors are confident he can come home tomorrow. They're optimistic, citing Perry's quick response to the activated charcoal and his overall good health, that he'll make a full recovery and there will be no permanent damage."

Bea let out a deep sigh as she fell back onto the worn leather sofa by the window in the Morning Room of The Dower House. Her limbs were heavy. Her lack of sleep was catching up with her. She looked at Daisy, who was curled up beside her. *Perhaps I should have a nap too*... Now that she knew Perry was out of danger, she might convince her brain to shut down and let her rest.

She glanced over at Simon, who was still pacing by the window. His forehead creased as he continued, "They say all he needs is some proper rest over the next few days."

"That's great," Rich replied from the armchair next to her. "You should go home now, mate, and get some sleep."

"Oh, it's okay. I got a little shut-eye in the chair in Perry's room. What I really need to do is go home and write."

Really? Bea was amazed that Simon could write

anything under the circumstances. She didn't feel like she could string a sentence together right now, let alone write a book.

She started as Rich's phone rang. "It's Mike," he said, hitting the speaker. "Morning, Ainsley. You're on speaker. I'm here with Bea and Simon."

"That's handy because I have news for you all." Detective Inspector Ainsley's gravelly voice filled the room. "Tom Hatlee's fingerprints are on the cigarette Perry used, and we found an empty vial and some gloves in his bag that were in the dressing room. Both have traces of nicotine."

Bea's stomach churned.

"Well, that sounds... pretty damning," Rich said.

"It does," Mike agreed with a sigh. He sounded weary. *He's probably not had much sleep either.*

Bea's thoughts drifted back to Mike's call to her and Rich late the previous night, after he'd interviewed Kurt and Tom.

Kurt, he'd said, had claimed he'd gone out to the petrol station for some chocolate and it had slipped his mind. Mike had told them they were looking to see if they could verify it with CCTV footage from the garage. He'd added, "He seemed genuinely upset about Perry and kept going on about someone trying to sabotage the show. He said he wasn't continuing until we caught the culprit."

It had sounded like Kurt wasn't the killer, but Mike had pointed out that they needed to prove his alibi before they could completely rule him out.

Then, his voice tinged with disbelief, he'd told them about his interview with Tom. "He doesn't seem the least bit upset about Perry's close call. In fact, he seemed almost... hopeful… He said something about Liv finally giving him the part he deserves." Mike had continued, "Tom didn't even bother to hide his feelings. He called Perry the confident, show-off-y type who sails through life getting exactly what they want."

Bea had never wanted someone to be revealed as the killer more than she had right then.

Mike had told them that Tom had then admitted that his friend Peter, who he'd lodged with when he'd first come to live in the area, had been hurt when a man had stolen someone Peter had feelings for. Tom claimed that at the time, he hadn't known who Peter was referring to. But when Tom complained to Peter about this upstart who had taken his role, Peter had told him it was the same man. Of course, Tom had denied killing Noel and attempting to kill Perry when Mike had suggested it, and last night, Mike ended the call by telling then that as much as he disliked the man, it had seemed like he'd been brutally honest. But about an hour later Bea had received a text message.

Mike: *CCTV confirms Kurt was there when he said he was. We've let him go. Tom has been arrested.*

"Now with the fingerprints and the nicotine," Mike said, dragging Bea back to the present, "I'm confident we'll have enough to charge Tom. I'm waiting to see if Forensics comes up with any more evidence before I go ahead."

"And does he still deny it all?" Rich asked.

"I interviewed him again this morning," Mike replied. "He claims he's never touched the cigarette, at least not that he can remember. And he's insisting the gloves aren't his, and he's never seen the vial before."

Bea let out a deep sigh. *On the one hand, I would expect him to say that even if he was guilty. But on the other...* Out of everyone she'd seen being interviewed, Tom had been the only one who had seemed to be telling the truth and not hiding anything. Maybe he was a much better actor than everyone else made out. *Or it could be that he's not lying…*

"Oh, and I asked him about being at school with Noel, like you suggested, Fitzwilliam," Mike added. "He said he didn't really know Noel back then. They were in different classes, and it was a large school. It feels like a dead end, to be honest."

"Thanks, Mike. Please keep us posted," Rich said, ending the call.

"That's it, I guess," Simon said. "I'm going to go home and try to get some writing done before I visit Perry in hospital later this afternoon."

Bea and Rich rose. Bea hugged Simon. "Thanks for coming over and giving us an update."

As Simon closed the door behind him, Rich turned to Bea. "What's on your mind, love? I can practically hear the cogs turning."

Bea smiled. He knew her so well. She raked a hand through her hair. "I don't know. It doesn't feel right. Tom being the killer, I mean."

"Is your famous woman's intuition trying to tell you something?" he teased gently.

She shot him a look. "Very funny. But seriously, Rich. Something's off here, but I can't put my finger on what."

Rich nodded, his expression turning thoughtful. "Okay. Why don't you mull it over while I'm out? I'm meeting Fred to take the newly appointed Three Lakes CEO for lunch in Fenswich." He hesitated, "But if you need me to stay—"

She waved him off. "No, no. You go. I'll be fine." She mustered a smile. "I might have a nap. It might jog something loose in this brain of mine."

"Alright, if you're sure." He pressed a quick kiss to her temple. "Ring me if you need anything, okay?"

"Will do."

After Rich left, Bea flopped back on the sofa with a sigh. Daisy leapt up to join her. As the little dog got comfy, Bea stared up at the ceiling as if the answers might be written there in the swirls of plaster. She closed her eyes. Tom's fingerprints on the cigarette, the vial and the gloves with nicotine traces in his bag... It was all damning evidence. But something in her gut insisted it was too neat, too easy.

Her phone pinged with an incoming text. She opened her eyes, and shifting Daisy, she fished her phone out of her pocket.

Perry: *SOS. No croissants, coffee is awful. Spring me from this hellhole? Pretty please?*

42

EARLY AFTERNOON, WEDNESDAY 6 OCTOBER

The afternoon sun streamed through the windows of the Garden Room, highlighting Perry's pale face as he reclined on a chaise in the middle of the room. Bea perched on the edge of an armchair, watching Mrs Fraser fuss over her friend like a mother hen.

"Are you quite sure you shouldn't still be in hospital, Mr Perry?" the housekeeper cum cook clucked, shooing Daisy out of the way as she adjusted a pillow behind Perry's back. "Does Mr Simon know you're here?"

Perry waved off her concern with a weak hand gesture. "I spoke to him briefly and told him not to worry and to get back to writing, Mrs F. Besides, with you looking after me, I'll recover far more quickly here than in that dreadful hospital." He flashed her a charming grin.

"What can I get you?" she asked, placing a blanket across his knees.

He paused dramatically. "I think perhaps a bacon sandwich would aid my speedy recovery."

Bea tried to stifle a grin. She'd been warned by the doctor

who'd discharged Perry that he might feel a little sick for the next twelve hours or so. *It would appear not!*

Mrs Fraser nodded knowingly. "I'll get one whipped up straight away," she said and bustled out of the room.

As soon as she'd gone, Daisy crept out from under the chaise and jumped onto Perry's lap. She tugged at the blanket to make it into a neat pile, then curled up and closed her eyes.

Bea eyed her best friend. He looked tired and a bit shaky but seemed to be in good spirits. *Is he simply putting on a brave face?* "How are you *really* feeling, Perry?"

He rubbed at his temples, his pep deflating slightly. "Honestly? I'm gutted. Ralph texted earlier—rehearsals are on hold indefinitely because half the cast thinks the production is cursed."

Bea huffed. "That's not what I meant, and you know it." She narrowed her eyes. "But just in case you need me to spell it out. How do you feel knowing someone tried to kill you?"

Perry's gaze held hers for a second, then he looked down at his hands. He was quiet for a moment, picking imaginary lint off the blanket. "Honestly? After the initial panic subsided... I felt strangely calm about it all." His gaze met her's again, a shadow of vulnerability in his blue eyes. "I knew you were there with me in the ambulance, Bea. It was a real comfort having you by my side, you know?"

Bea wiped the corner of her eye with a finger. It felt a tad wet.

"And I wanted to tell you," he paused, "but that mask was on my face, so I couldn't—"

Tell me what?

"—that if I didn't make it to donate my shoe collection to the V&A."

What? Bea saw the hint of a twinkle return to his eyes. She huffed. "You and your stupid shoes. I'll tell you now, if you ever dare to die on us, Simon and I will chuck the whole lot on a bonfire simply out of spite."

Perry gasped and slapped a hand to his chest. "You wouldn't!"

She narrowed her eyes. "Oh, yes, I would!"

He snorted, causing Daisy to stir. Bea rolled her eyes.

At that moment, Mrs Fraser reappeared with a fat bacon sandwich, and Perry's face lit up like a child on Christmas morning. She pulled up a small side table and put the plate down before grabbing Daisy and placing her on the floor. "No bacon for you, Daisy. Go and sit in your bed." She pointed to a large dog bed by the window, and Daisy slunk off with a huff as Mrs Fraser left again.

A few minutes later, as Perry was swallowing a mouthful of bacon and bread, his expression turned serious. "You know, Bea, I didn't really believe I was the target at first. But now…" He dropped his gaze to the floor. "Well, it appears I was. And I feel awful about poor Noel and Colin getting caught in the crossfire." He wiped his mouth with a napkin Mrs Fraser had placed on the side of his plate. "What I don't understand is—if Tom wanted me dead so badly, why not corner me in an alley and be done with it? Why go to all this elaborate trouble with the fake cigarette and falling lights?"

He has a point. There are less complicated ways to kill someone.

"And the falling rig thing?" he continued, holding the other half of his sandwich. "I don't get it."

"What do you mean?" Bea asked, her brow creasing.

Perry took a bite of the sandwich, then put the rest down. "Mike told me they worked out that the lighting rig was set to fall right on my mark—exactly where I should've been standing during rehearsals later that evening." Perry shivered and pulled the blanket up to his waist with his free hand. "But here's the thing—you know me, I'm always moving about and waving my arms around. I'm rarely precisely on my mark at any given moment. And Tom would know that after all our rehearsals. It seems like an awfully risky move knowing that, doesn't it?"

Bea had to agree. The more she considered it, the more the pieces refused to fit.

"And here's the other thing," he continued. "If I was the intended victim all along, why not wait until that scene in Act Two where I'm the only character who smokes?"

"You mean like yesterday?"

"Precisely. Noel got caught in the Act One attempt because we both light up. Again, that seems terribly risky if I was supposed to be the target."

Bea's thoughts were spinning like a washing machine cycle. This wasn't adding up. *If someone has framed Tom, then they are still out there and could be ready to strike again.*

But why choose Tom? An uncomfortable thought occurred to her. What if the killer knew about Tom's animosity towards Perry? Or perhaps they already knew that the police had narrowed their suspect list down to two?

The door swung open, and Mrs Fraser bustled in again, this time balancing a tray with a huge mug on it, with pink and white mini marshmallows poking over the rim. "Here we are, Mr Perry. A nice hot chocolate, just as you like it."

Bea put her hand over her mouth to disguise her grin. *This is ridiculous!*

"Mrs F, you're an angel in sensible shoes," Perry proclaimed as he made space on the side table next to him.

"I don't know about that," she chuckled, a slight blush appearing on her cheeks. "Now finish your food, drink this up, and then you must rest."

As the door closed behind her, Bea's gaze snapped back to Perry. "You know how by yesterday afternoon, we'd fairly much ruled out Em and Stella as suspects, so we only had Kurt and Tom left?"

Perry paused mid-bite, a strip of bacon dangling from his mouth. "Mmph?"

"Did you tell anyone when you were at rehearsals later?"

Perry chewed thoughtfully. "I discussed it with Ralph." His eyes slowly widened. "But surely you're not suggesting Ralph's involved? I know he can be cutting sometimes, but he wouldn't hurt a fly."

Bea leaned forward. "Could anyone have overheard you?"

"Well," Perry paused, taking a sip of hot chocolate. "Gabe and Gina were onstage with Liv. I don't think they could've heard us from there. Colin was testing lights in the auditorium. Tom and Kurt were skulking about in the wings, as per usual."

"But did you actually see Tom or Kurt?"

Perry's hand, which was holding his mug halfway to his mouth, froze. "I… I can't remember. Why is that important?"

The fog in her brain was retreating, and a hazy picture was forming. "Because if someone knew there were only two suspects left, the obvious move would be to frame one of them."

43

MEANWHILE, WEDNESDAY 6 OCTOBER

Simon stared at the blinking cursor, his mind as blank as the page before him. The garden office felt stuffy, the air thick with his own frustration.

"Come on, Pike," he muttered to his fictional detective. "What's your next move?"

But Detective Inspector Billy Pike remained stubbornly silent, frozen in the wasteland of Simon's imagination.

He read over the last paragraph again, hoping for a spark of inspiration.

Detective Inspector Billy Pike stood amidst the desolate expanse of the industrial estate, the icy wind cutting through his coat as he surveyed the abandoned car before him. The vehicle, a battered red Ford Mondeo, sat incongruously beneath the dim glow of a solitary streetlamp, its presence a stark reminder of the city's underbelly. Inside the trunk lay the lifeless body of a woman, her identity yet to be confirmed, but the scene bore the unmistakable marks of a calculated execution.

Simon sighed, rubbing his beard. "Great. Now what?" Where to go from here? His head felt stuffed with wool, his thoughts scattered and refusing to cooperate. He glanced out the window at Rose Cottage's autumnal garden. Crimson leaves fluttered from the Japanese maple, blanketing the lawn. But even nature's beauty couldn't penetrate the fog in his brain. He pressed his palms against his eyes. Normally, the view would inspire him, but today, his thoughts kept circling back to Perry.

Is he resting well enough at Bea's? He's probably eating... He'd complained about the hospital food when Simon had talked to him earlier. *I don't mind.* A complaining Perry was infinitely preferable to a dead one.

"Focus, Lattimore," he chided himself. "You're a crime writer. You write about death all the time."

But never when the love of his life had so recently brushed against it.

Simon pushed back from the desk, his stocky frame protesting after hours of inactivity. He paced the small office, five steps one way, turn, five steps back. *Coffee.* He needed coffee. And maybe, just maybe, the caffeine would jumpstart his brain, and the words would finally flow.

Ten minutes later, he was back at his desk, a mug in his hand but his head still not in the writing game. His mind drifted back to that horrifying phone call from Rich, his steady voice telling him that Perry was on his way to the hospital with suspected nicotine poisoning. "Are you kidding me?" Simon had blurted out, his brain having refused to process Rich's words.

Of course, he hadn't been kidding. Who would joke about something like that? He'd hardly registered Rich's instructions to wait outside as he would be there to pick him up in a minute. Numb, Simon had grabbed his keys, fumbling with the cottage's lock as Bea's Bentley had screeched to a halt outside.

Rich had leapt out before the car had fully stopped. "Get in," he'd ordered, snatching the keys from Simon's hands and locking up for him.

The drive had been a blur. Simon vaguely recalled Rich's reassurance that Perry was breathing on his own. Small mercies. Later, word had come that Bea and Perry had reached A&E, and Perry was being assessed.

When they'd finally arrived at the hospital, Fraser had held the car door open as Rich had bundled Simon out. "I hope Mr Perry will be alright, sir," Fraser had said to him.

"He'd better be, or I'll kill him myself." The words had tumbled out, earning a startled look from Fraser, who'd been unsure whether to be amused or appalled.

Simon took a sip from his mug and grimaced. Lukewarm coffee. Had it all really only happened last night? He checked his watch. A couple more hours, then he'd head to Bea's.

He thought back to the conversation he had with his husband a short while ago when Perry had rung to tell him he was at The Dower House.

"I'm feeling so much better," Perry had said when Simon had asked him why he'd left when he was supposed to be resting in hospital. "And I was sooooo bored there. The staff were lovely, but the food? Just awful."

"Really?" Simon couldn't help the smile that had tugged at the corners of his mouth. If Perry was thinking about food then he must be feeling better.

"And don't get me started on the noise... Anyway, I didn't want to disturb you, I know you're writing, so I sent a distress signal to Bea, and she busted me out."

Simon had shaken his head as his smile had widened. *Of course she had!* "So, you didn't want to disturb me, heh?"

"Well, you're busy. You've got a deadline..."

"And I would have told you to stay put!"

"Yes, well, there's that too," he'd replied slightly sheepishly. "Anyway, I'm here, and I'm resting, I promise. Please don't worry. Get your writing done, and I'll see you later."

Simon had been torn between relief at hearing his husband sounding so alive and frustration that Perry had discharged himself from the hospital, no doubt against doctor's orders. At least he was safely with Bea at The Dower House. And knowing Mrs Fraser, she was probably making a right fuss of him.

He turned back to his laptop, determined to untangle this fictional mystery. But his eyes kept straying to the garden, to the riot of autumn colours—gold, orange, red. Normally, he'd be itching to describe it all. Now he could barely string two words together. All he could see was Perry, still and pale against stark hospital sheets, hooked up to beeping machines. Simon wasn't a praying man, but he'd sent up a silent plea to whoever might have been listening. *Save him. Please save the man I love more than life.*

And someone had listened. *Thank goodness!*

He leaned back in his chair, his mind churning. "It doesn't add up," he muttered, drumming his fingers on the desk. Something about Tom being the killer didn't sit right.

Sure, the man had been miffed when Perry had snagged the coveted role of Algernon. And it was possible that he felt Perry had stolen Simon from Peter Tappin. He snorted, remembering Peter's misguided attempts at flirtation. *As if I'd ever—*

He cut himself off, feeling a pang of guilt. Simon's mind drifted back to those early days at Rose Cottage, when he'd been fresh from his divorce and a career change. He'd been friendly to everyone, desperate for connections. *Surely, I didn't lead Peter on, did I?* He scrubbed a hand over his beard. Was this whole mess his fault? *No. No, that way leads to madness.*

But the evidence against Tom... Simon's brows drew together slowly. *Why so careless?* To go from meticulous— undetected through Noel's murder and Colin's attack—to leaving glaring clues in his attempt to kill Perry? Fingerprints on the cigarette, an empty vial, gloves thick with nicotine... Simon muttered, "It's like he wanted to get caught."

A chill ran down his spine as a new possibility emerged. "Or like someone wanted him to get caught."

But who? And why?

Was Perry even the real target, after all?

A sudden thought for his book jabbed at Simon, sharp as a stiletto. What if the dead woman in DI Pike's case was connected to the detective's ex-girlfriend in the previous book? The one who'd wormed her way into his life, all to get the heads up on what was happening in her uncle's case? Pike had sent her packing, but what if her family was out for payback?

Simon turned around at his desk and started typing. He had to get this down, had to untangle it now. Only then could he focus on the possibility that in his real life, the police had the wrong killer. Or even the wrong victim.

For fifteen minutes, Simon's fingers flew across the keyboard as his thoughts took shape. Finally, he exhaled slowly, the tension easing from his shoulders. His writer's block had crumbled, but the nagging doubts about Tom's guilt now demanded his attention.

He glanced at the back of his phone, on the edge of his desk, turned over to stop him from being distracted. *Who can I talk to about my doubts?* He didn't want to speak to Mike yet—he needed to know his thoughts were not merely delusional hopes to relieve his fear that someone wanted to kill his husband.

Perry? No, he was supposed to be resting. The last thing Simon wanted was to upset him and set his recovery back.

Bea? She'd been shaken to her core by the attempt on Perry's life. Was she ready to rehash the details? *Probably not. And Perry would no doubt ask her what's going on.*

Rich? Simon could always count on his level-headed advice. *Yes, I'll talk to Rich.*

He reached over and grabbed his phone. Opening the text app, he typed a text to his beloved.

Simon: *You'd better have your feet up right now. I'm just finishing up here, and then I'll come and get you. Rest!!*

He hit send, then scrolled through his favourites and selected Rich's number from the list. He'd discuss his thoughts with Rich, and together, they could decide the next steps.

44

BACK AT THE DOWER HOUSE, WEDNESDAY 6 OCTOBER

B ea absently traced the edge of her teacup with her finger, her thoughts churning as she stared out of the window at The Dower House. The china clinked as Mrs Fraser cleared away Perry's mug and refilled Daisy's water bowl.

"Anything else I can get for you, Mr Perry?" the housekeeper asked.

"No thanks, Mrs F, I'm all set." Perry flashed her a charming smile. She bustled out, leaving them alone once more.

Perry's phone beeped, and he glanced down at it. He smiled as he read the message, then turned to Bea, his brows raised. "Alright, out with it. What are you thinking, Miss Marple?"

Bea bit her lip. "I'm wondering... what if we had it right the first time? What if Noel was the intended target all along?"

"But the attack on me—" Perry began.

"Was a setup. To frame Tom," Bea cut in. "Think about it —if Tom 'accidentally' killed Noel while actually trying to get you, it paints a clear picture. Which is exactly the story the police have adopted."

Perry's eyes widened. "Blimey. So you reckon if Tom was framed…"

"Then Noel was always the real victim all along," Bea finished grimly. "And his killer is still out there."

Perry rubbed his jaw. "Right. But if Noel was the victim, then who did him in? Before Tom's arrest, we were down to two suspects—him and Kurt. But if Tom's been framed and Kurt's got an alibi for when the lighting rig was sabotaged, then there's no one else left."

Bea shook her head slowly, the cogs in her head still turning. There had to be an angle they were missing, a link they hadn't found. Her eyes fell on Daisy, who was curled content at her feet. *Maybe I should sleep on it too…* She sighed. "I don't know, Perry. But I have a feeling if we can find that missing piece, this whole awful mess will finally start making sense. We need to look at it from another direction."

Bea's eyes suddenly lit up. "Hold on. Let's go back. Before Colin was attacked, we had another suspect in our sights. Remember?"

Perry frowned as he seemed to mentally rewind the events of the past few days. Then it clicked. "Well, yes… it was Colin himself, wasn't it? But then he got framed too with the pills."

"But what if that was intentional?" Bea leaned forward, excitement building. "What if it was all a diversion to take the heat off himself so he'd slip under the radar?"

Perry's eyes narrowed. "Hang on. But someone tried to kill him!"

Bea fixed him with a probing stare. "Did they? How do you know?"

"Because I saw it!" Perry sputtered.

"What did you actually see?" Bea pressed.

Perry exhaled and closed his eyes. "Okay. So Colin was on the stage. He said hello to me and Ralph. Then the rig above moved, and I yelled at him to scarper. He dived out of the way just as I grabbed Ralph." Perry shuddered at the memory. "The whole thing came crashing down right where he'd been standing. A bit of the metal guard from a spotlight clipped him as he rolled clear."

"But you said someone was above the stage up in the rigging, didn't you?"

Perry nodded.

A thrum of energy danced under her skin. "So how did you know? Did you see them?" She held her breath. Her entire theory depended on his answer.

Perry opened his mouth to reply, then paused. His eyes widened. "Oh. Because... because Colin told me he heard footsteps up there. Oh my giddy aunt!"

Bea let her breath out in a *whoosh*. "Exactly." She sat back, a satisfied gleam in her eye.

Perry gaped at her. "So you're suggesting… Colin staged the whole thing?"

Bea nodded grimly. "I think it's possible. It would have been risky, mind you. He did get hit by some of the debris. If he hadn't dived out of the way fast enough…" She let the thought hang.

"You really think he'd go that far? Risk his own neck like that?"

"If he was desperate enough. If he thought the police were looking at him as an actual suspect." Bea turned her palms up. "Think about it—he could've planted his tools at the top, then undone the rope that held up the rigging. He would only have had to wait until the first cast members arrived. Then as they approached, he could let go. Instant witnesses to confirm the supposed attempt on his life."

Perry let out a low whistle. "I hate to say it, but it fits." He glanced sharply at Bea. "So we reckon Colin was Noel's dealer then?"

Bea shrugged. "If he orchestrated this whole thing, then yes. I say he planted the drugs on himself to make it look like he'd been framed. It would also give him a way out of being charged for drug dealing."

Perry shook his head in disbelief. "I think you're onto something, Bea." Then he paused. "But why come after me then? If this was all simply a ploy to get himself off the hook for Noel's murder, what was the point of trying to get rid of me?"

Bea chewed her lip thoughtfully. The same question had niggled at her too. "I think he saw an opportunity and seized it—to put an end to the investigation once and for all by framing Tom." She leaned towards him. "Remember, you said Colin was in the auditorium fiddling with the lights when you and Ralph were talking?"

Perry dipped his chin slowly. "Yeah, he was behind us at the lighting desk. I suppose he could've overheard us from there." A wry smile touched his lips. "Ralph's not exactly known for his inside voice."

"Exactly!" Bea snapped her fingers. "He heard the police thought it was Tom or Kurt."

"And Ralph actually said if it had been me who'd been killed, he would've thought Tom had done it because of the looks he'd been giving me."

"See?" Bea raised an eyebrow. "The perfect opportunity to change the narrative *and* the intended victim."

"Oh, oh." Perry tapped Bea on her arm. "Wait till you hear this. Not long after Ralph and I were talking, Colin went onstage and said something to Liv. Then he disappeared for an hour or so. Liv had to ask Em to take over the lights because Colin had to pop home."

Bea's eyes widened. "You think he went to grab the nicotine?"

"It would explain the identical method," Perry agreed.

"No time to plan anything else. He had to move fast so he could direct the suspicion to fall on Tom," Bea said, excitement thrumming through her veins.

Perry shook his head, half-smiling. "It was risky, but it worked. Tom's been arrested, and the police think they have their man."

"It all fits, don't you think?" A shiver went down Bea's back as the pieces slotted neatly into place.

Perry grinned at her, his eyes sparkling with shared triumph. "So what's our next move? Confront Colin direct?"

Bea shook her head, already reaching for her phone. "That's too risky. We need backup."

Perry pouted, but she remained resolute. She'd promised Rich last year that she would not act alone when confronting potential killers.

She dialled Mike's number.

45

MEANWHILE, WEDNESDAY 6 OCTOBER

As the Range Rover zoomed along the Fenshire country roads, Rich drummed his fingers on the steering wheel, a satisfied smile tugging at his lips. The lunch meeting at Fenswich had gone great—the new CEO totally got Fred's vision for Three Lakes, probably because he was ex-military himself and had seen service in Afghanistan. He would start next month and would get everything ready for their first clients early in the new year.

Rich shook his head, still in awe at how much more fulfilling this volunteer work felt compared to the organisational drudgery he'd been slogging through since his promotion. Helping places like Three Lakes, making a real difference in people's lives—now that gave him a buzz like nothing else. Spreadsheets, policies, and internal politics certainly didn't.

His mind drifted to Bea's mother's suggestion of taking a six-month sabbatical to try out an official royal role. The irony wasn't lost on him—going from protecting the royals to potentially being one of them.

But how would his bosses react? They'd been pushing

him to be a poster boy for City Police since he'd announced his engagement to Bea. Would they be willing to lose the good publicity so soon? But then, as Fred had pointed out, this request came with the backing of the king. Would they dare refuse?

It's definitely worth a shot. In fact, it was a no brainer for him. But what about Bea?

Her hesitation to make a decision worried him, and she hadn't been very forthcoming yet about exactly what her concerns were. Every time they'd discussed it, she'd thrown up barriers, asking him if he was aware of the strain the media circus would put on him and his family. She'd pointed out that he'd worked so hard on his career; could he risk jeopardising it for something that he might not enjoy, she'd queried. How would he feel about being in her shadow, she'd questioned, pointing out that the press would more than likely give her more coverage than him. And, she'd wondered aloud, would the press continue to stir things up with Rich's estranged father?

Along with her worries for him, she'd also expressed her unease about how being thrust into the public eye may impact Sam as he approached the stage in his life when he would have to make important life choices?

There was a different concern each time.

He agreed they were all valid considerations, and they would need a strategy to deal with them, but underneath it all, he sensed he and Sam were being used as an excuse. That somewhere deep down, there was a reluctance on her part that she wasn't vocalising, but he guessed it was about her age-old relationship with the press.

When Bea had made the decision to leave Perry at the hospital yesterday so that the staff and patients could be rid of the chaos the press attention was causing, she'd been furious that because of them she'd had to abandon her best friend's sick bed, not knowing if he would survive the next few hours or not. Rich had felt it was an overreaction on her part. The head administrator had assured them that the hospital had it all in hand, and the police had acted swiftly to remove the press from the building and set up a cordon around them outside, but Bea's instinctive reaction had been to take responsibility for their presence and, subsequently, to provide the solution too.

He sighed. Would she ever be happy if she accepted a role that would require her to deal with situations like that more frequently?

They definitely needed to have a heart-to-heart about it all. He'd been putting it off while they had been involved in the investigation into Noel Ashworth's death, but now that that was all resolved... well, it was time to be brave and tell her how he felt.

Only it didn't feel resolved to him. Something wasn't adding up.

As he turned off the main road and onto the narrower country lanes, he tried to sort out what was bothering him about the case. For a start, they'd had no solid evidence from the previous two incidents, and now suddenly, they had gloves, a vial, and fingerprints practically handed to them gift-wrapped? It felt all too convenient.

Rich mentally reviewed the other two crimes, searching for the missing link. If Perry was the proper target, then how had Noel ended up with the poisoned cigarette? A killer with any sense of precision would have made sure the tainted prop went to the intended victim. So why not poison his coffee or something else?

Rich's thoughts raced ahead to the falling rig 'accident'. Again, if Perry was the target, why trigger the rig's collapse prematurely, when Perry hadn't even been in position? It defied logic. None of it made a lick of sense. Unless...

Suddenly, the gears in Rich's mind whirred to life, clicking into place.

What if...

But then...

His pulse quickened as the implications hit him. *Oh, so that would explain...*

But then that would mean...

The shrill ring of his mobile yanked Rich out of his preoccupation. Simon's name flashed on the screen of his car. *Perfect timing!* Rich needed to bounce his theory off someone. He jabbed at the steering wheel button to accept the call.

"Fitzwilliam, I think Tom was framed," Simon blurted out, his voice tight with urgency.

At the same instant, Rich declared, "I think Colin is our killer."

46

MEANWHILE BACK AT THE DOWER HOUSE, WEDNESDAY 6 OCTOBER

B ea paced the sitting room at The Dower House, her phone pressed to her ear as she listened to Mike Ainsley's voicemail for the third time. She left a message, then cut the call with a huff. "Still no answer."

Perry looked up from his own phone, his brow furrowed. "I can't reach Simon either. He's not picking up. It's going to voicemail."

"I'll try Rich." Bea punched in the number, but after several rings, it went to voicemail too. *Rats!* She really didn't want to have to do this alone. With Perry supposed to be resting, she could hardly take him with her. *But...* She threw up her hands. "That's it. I'll have to tackle this myself."

"Yay! Let's go," Perry said, pulling the blanket off himself and springing up. Daisy, who had returned to the end of the chaise after Mrs Fraser had left, gave an excited *yap* as she jumped down.

Oh, no, you don't... "Whoa there, James Bond," Bea said, holding up her hand to Perry. "Where do you think you're going?"

"To talk to Colin, aren't we?"

"No, *we're* not going anywhere. *I* am going to talk to Colin while *you* stay here under Mrs Fraser's watchful eye and rest. You should still be in hospital right now, remember?"

Perry shook his head. "Oh, no, I don't think so. Not after what happened in Portugal this summer. I'm not being left behind again!" He put his hands on his hips and stared her down.

Bea suppressed a huff. Perry had still not forgiven her for having gone off without him while going after the suspected killer of an American film producer.

"For goodness sake, Perry. How many times do I have to tell you? I didn't leave you behind. I didn't know that—"

"Ah, ah." He raised his hand, palm up. "Did you or did you not confront a potential murderer without me being there?"

It wasn't that simple... "Well, yes, but—"

"No 'but', my lady. You promised never to do that without me again."

I don't think I did... "Er, no... I didn't really say—"

"Bea!" he cried abruptly. "I'm not debating this. I have a right to confront my almost-killer, so I'm coming. End of!"

Bea stared at Perry. Determination was radiating off his body.

He has a point...

She gave a barely-there nod. "Alright. Hopefully, we won't actually have to do anything other than watch the police take him away. I've left a message for Mike, so he's bound to get back to us soon. But we may as well get a head start." She paused. "Oh, but go where exactly?"

Perry tapped his chin thoughtfully. "Let me think... Er, the theatre is closed today, so Colin is probably at home."

"And that would be where?"

"Er, no idea." He rubbed his chin, then a grin spread over his face. "But I know a man who probably does."

"Ralph?"

"Ralph!"

"Great, you ring the grande dame, and I'll get the car brought around. I'll meet you out front in five minutes."

Perry was already scrolling through his contacts. "On it."

Bea strode out of the room, her boots clicking decisively against the hardwood floor. Daisy trotted along at her heels, her tail wagging.

Time to get some answers, with or without the others.

———

Twenty minutes later, Bea, Perry, and Daisy were settled in the back of the Bentley as it purred into Windstanton, with Fraser at the wheel. Bea had just finished filling him in on their impromptu mission.

"Pardon me for saying so, my lady, but perhaps it would be prudent to wait for the authorities? Or at least for Mister Richard?" Fraser glanced at her in the rearview mirror, his tone respectful but firm.

Bea blew out a breath. "I've left multiple messages for DI Ainsley. And I can't reach Rich—his mobile is still going straight to voicemail. Simon's too."

Fraser gave a low *humph*, then reverted his eyes to the road ahead.

Perry fidgeted nervously beside her as he peered out the window. "It's down here, I think."

Fraser slowed the Bentley as they approached a rather large bungalow with a red door. On the spacious drive, a blue BMW M5 was parked. *Nice car...* Behind that was a double garage with its door partly open. Inside, Bea could make out a figure moving about.

She nudged Perry and pointed. "Is that Colin?"

Just then, Perry's phone rang. He glanced at the screen and mouthed, "Simon," to her before answering.

Fraser pulled up outside the house.

"Er, no, not exactly. I'm with Bea." Beside her, Perry nervously stroked Daisy. "Where? Oh... um..."

Bea shrunk back into the leather seat. *Is Simon going to be mad at me for bringing Perry to confront a killer?*

Perry looked at Bea and pulled a face that said he was in trouble. "Er, no, not at The Dower House, we're—"

After giving him a sympathetic look, she glanced out of the window. As she did, Colin peered around the garage door and spotted them. He darted inside, and a few seconds later, the door rolled shut.

Did he see it's us? At least he'd shut himself inside the garage, so they knew where he was.

"But, love, what's important right now is that we don't think I *was* the victim. We—"

Should I go and talk to him now?

"Yes. We think that too! In fact, we're at his house now, and—"

She'd leave Perry in the car, and Fraser was here too. She could hardly be in any danger...

"But I'm not going to! We're just—"

"I'm going to talk to him," Bea said, reaching for the door handle.

Perry grabbed her arm. "Wait! Simon and Rich are on their way. We should sit tight until they get here."

Bea hesitated, then nodded tersely. She hated waiting, but they had a point. Best not to spook Colin into doing something rash. At that moment, her phone lit up. *Mike!* She punched the call accept button.

———

"We'll wait here then," Bea told Mike, having brought him up-to-date with their thinking. Mike had told her that after having interviewed Tom earlier, he himself had been unconvinced that Tom was guilty. A further interview had revealed that Colin had asked Tom to hold a piece of glass from a light he'd said he was mending about an hour before Perry's collapse. The police were now thinking that maybe that was how Colin had got Tom's fingerprints so he could transfer them to the fake cigarette. *Clever!*

Just then, Colin emerged from the garage. "Hold on, Mike. Colin is coming out." As he rolled the garage door up, Bea leaned against the window to watch him. She caught a fleeting glimpse inside the dimly lit space. There was a large exhaust fan mounted near the ceiling. *That's odd…* Up against the wall, several propane tanks were lined up. *What is he up to in there?* "Er, Mike. There is something strange going on in Colin's garage." As she told him what she could see, Colin looked around. He stared at the car. Bea instinctively jerked away from the window, but it was too late. Colin spun on his heels and dashed inside the house. "Rats! I think he's seen us, Mike."

"Stay where you are. I'm on my way, and a local unit will be there in ten minutes."

She agreed and cut the call.

Next to her, Perry was still on the phone to Simon. "So he's this minute gone into his house."

The words had barely left his mouth when Colin emerged again, a duffel bag in one hand and car keys in the other. He cast one last harried look at the Bentley before sprinting towards the BMW.

Bea's heart sank as the engine roared to life. *Oh no! He's going to get away.* Colin sped out of the drive and onto the road ahead of them.

Bea nudged Perry urgently. "He's making a run for it!"

"Colin's in his car. He's taking off!" Perry hurriedly relayed to Simon and Rich.

Bea leaned forward. "Fraser, follow him!" she cried as she snatched up her mobile and called Mike's number again.

As Fraser deftly manoeuvred the Bentley in pursuit of the BMW, Bea filled Mike in on their location.

Perry did the same for Simon and Rich.

Next to Bea, Daisy let out an excited *yip*, her paws on Bea's knees and her dog seat belt straining, as she watched the chase unfold.

Ahead, Colin's car accelerated, weaving through the light traffic.

"Fraser, don't lose him!" Bea urged, her pulse quickening.

"Don't worry, my lady," Fraser replied, unruffled. "I did a spot of evasive driver training when I first started chauffeuring you and the late Mister James. I know what to do." With a calm determination, he floored the accelerator, and the Bentley surged forward.

Bea and Perry exchanged a look.

"Hold on tight, my lady, Mr Juke," Fraser called back as he hurled the Bentley around a small roundabout, hot on the heels of the blue car.

Bea suggested to Perry that they both put their phones on speaker so they could update Mike, Simon, and Rich all at the same time.

A few miles later, the BMW turned off the main road, onto a smaller country lane. Bea called out the new direction as Fraser deftly navigated the winding roads in pursuit of the BMW.

They were speeding up. Butterflies filled Bea's tummy as they hared around a sharp bend. She grabbed Daisy, whose was still sitting on her lap, her little pink tongue lolling out, and held her tight.

"We're going to turn off to the right at the next junction so we can come in from the opposite direction," Rich informed them.

In the front seat, Fraser shouted out, "Good idea, Mister Richard. That will leave him with nowhere to go."

"That's the plan, Fraser. Keep on his tail."

"Will do, sir."

"Hold on, I think I can see you behind us, Mike," Simon shouted.

"Yes, we have you in our sights now," Mike confirmed. "We'll follow you!"

A high-pitched screech of tyres came from the other end of Perry's phone, and Bea's heart stuttered. "Are you alright, Rich?" she cried out.

"Yes, sorry. Took it a bit fast. We're all good!" he replied, sounding a little out of breath.

Bea's heartbeat continued at its frantic pace. *I don't like this…*

"It's like actually being inside a movie car chase," Perry said to her excitedly as he grabbed her arm. "I love it!"

Ahead, Colin took a sharp right, his tyres squealing as he barely made the turn.

Bea's stomach lurched. *At this speed, one wrong move will spell disaster.* "He's going to get himself killed," she said, gripping the edge of her seat with her free hand as Fraser deftly whipped the Bentley into the turn.

"We should have sight of you both soon," Rich shouted

through the speaker. "Fraser, be prepared to slow down and block his exit."

"Yes, sir," Fraser shouted back.

"Oh my goodness," Bea murmured, chewing her lip. The last thing they needed was a head-on collision.

As if on cue, a familiar Range Rover came into view up ahead, flashing blue lights visible behind it.

Rich! Bea's chest felt lighter. It was almost over…

Colin's brake lights flared red as he stomped on the pedal.

As Colin came to a halt, Fraser decelerated quickly but smoothly. Beside her, Perry let out a noisy breath. "We've got him!" he announced triumphantly.

Suddenly, the BMW's white reverse lights came on, and the blue car accelerated backwards.

What's he doing? Bea's stomach clenched. *Can't he see we're here?*

As the rear of the car came hurtling at them, Fraser shouted, "Hold on, my lady!" as he cranked the wheel hard to the right, sending the Bentley fishtailing towards the grassy verge.

Bea instinctively wrapped her arms around Daisy, her insides turning to liquid as the car slewed sideways in an ear-splitting screech of rubber on asphalt.

47

A FEW SECONDS LATER,
WEDNESDAY 6 OCTOBER

The Bentley skidded to a halt, Bea still clutching Daisy to her chest as she stared out of her side window in horror. Colin's car was barrelling straight in their direction.

We need to get out!

Bea unbuckled Daisy's car restraint.

"My phone!" Perry cried, scrabbling around on the floor beside her.

"We need to get out now," Fraser said firmly. His calm demeanour belied the urgency as he climbed out of the front and flung open the door next to Perry.

Bea reached over Perry, who was still bent over with his head in the footwell, and thrust Daisy into Fraser's arms.

Colin's car engine roared. It was far too close.

"Forget your phone. We're about to be killed!" she shouted as she grabbed Perry's arm and yanked him upwards. She pushed him across the seat as Fraser hauled him out the other side with his free arm.

Bea's hands felt clammy as she grabbed the headrest and dragged herself along the back seat. There was a squeal of brakes as Bea threw herself out of the door.

Crunch! The screech of metal on metal didn't sound as loud as Bea had expected as she scrambled to her feet. As she stood up, she saw why. The BMW hadn't hit the Bentley; instead, it had veered sharply right, crashing through a gate into the adjacent field.

A black saloon car, presumably Mike's, and two police cars screeched to a stop around them, along with Rich's Range Rover. Bea watched, stunned, as Colin leapt from his smashed-up vehicle and took off running across the field.

Daisy let out an excited *yap* and wriggled free from Fraser's arms, bounding after him.

"Daisy, no!" Bea cried. She turned to Perry in alarm.

He folded his arms. "Don't look at me. I can't run—I'm a sick man, remember!"

Bea started forward, her legs like jelly, but Simon called out, "Don't worry, Bea, we've got her!"

Bea watched open-mouthed as Simon, two uniformed officers, Mike, and Rich all sprinted across the field in pursuit of Colin and Daisy.

From beside her, Perry snorted. "It's like watching the Keystone Cops."

"More like Benny Hill if you ask me, sir," Fraser replied dryly.

Bea couldn't help but grin at the absurdity of it all, her racing heart beginning to calm. *Where does Colin think he can go?*

I can't miss this... "I want to see what happens," she said to Perry, then jogged off after them.

"I'm going to watch it all from here," Perry said happily behind her.

Rich surged ahead of the pack, his powerful legs carrying him swiftly across the field. With a flying leap, he tackled

Colin to the ground in a move that would have made any rugby coach proud. They landed with a resounding thud.

Bea grinned. *My hero!*

Simon snatched up a yapping Daisy while the police officers ran around him and hauled Colin to his feet. They cuffed him as Simon reached out his free hand and helped Rich up.

Mike, slightly winded, stopped in front of the subdued suspect. "Colin Myatt," he said, his voice carrying across the field, "I'm arresting you on suspicion of the murder of Noel Ashworth, the attempted murder of Perry Juke, and the possession of a Class B drug with intent to supply."

———

Rich walked over to join Bea. "Hey, you," he said as he encircled her shoulders with his arms and pulled her close. He leaned down and kissed her on the forehead. She leaned into him and smiled, letting out a heavy breath. *It's all over now...*

They turned around, and arms entwined, they followed Simon as he headed back to the Bentley, with Daisy still in his arms. As he arrived, he passed the wriggling pup to Fraser before pulling Perry into a tight hug. "I don't think the doctor would class this as rest, do you?" he said as he leaned back and looked into his husband's face.

Perry gave him a sheepish grin. "At least I didn't run this time."

Simon laughed.

Bea grinned as she and Rich passed them. "That was some driving, Fraser," Rich said, clapping the older man on the shoulder when they reached him.

"Thank you, Mister Richard. I quite enjoyed it." He handed Daisy back to Bea, then said, "But perhaps we could keep this quiet from Mrs Fraser. You know how she tends to fuss."

"Of course," Rich and Bea replied together, smiling.

Two police officers marched a subdued Colin past them. He kept his head bowed, refusing to meet their eyes. Mike trailed behind, pausing to address them.

"Thanks for your help, everyone. I'll speak to you later." With a brisk nod, he set off after his men.

Rich turned to Fraser. "Would you mind taking Perry and Simon to Rose Cottage, Fraser? I'll drive Bea and Daisy back to Francis Court."

"Of course, sir," Fraser agreed readily.

"Come over this evening," Bea said to Perry and Simon as they headed to the Bentley. "I think we could all do with a drink after all this excitement."

———

"Well, that was fun!" Rich said as he started the Land Rover.

Bea rolled her eyes but couldn't suppress a grin. "Oh, indeed. Nothing says 'relaxing afternoon' quite like a car chase and the arrest of a murderer."

He laughed out loud as he pulled off smoothly and fell in behind the Bentley.

A comfortable silence fell over them, only interrupted by the occasional gentle snoring coming from Daisy, who was curled up in the back in her car seat.

Bea relaxed back into the soft leather of the passenger seat. *This is nice, just the two of us...*

They hadn't had that much time together recently, and she realised now how much she'd missed it. Rich's job had taken him up to London frequently over these last few months, and they'd all been busy with the Three Lakes project. It had been good this last week or so working on this case together, discussing their thoughts and theories, working towards the same goal. Like it had been before.

Her belly fluttered.

Is this what it would be like if we accept the offer to become working royals?

She mentally slapped her forehead. She couldn't believe she hadn't considered that aspect of it until now. She and Rich would be doing it together—as a team.

She looked over at Rich, his handsome profile so familiar to her now. Her pulse quickened. Was she so focussed on the negative aspects of the change, she'd not properly taken into account all the advantages?

She licked her lips. She knew they needed to make some decisions about their future. She'd been putting it off, paralysed with fear about the changes it would bring to their lives, but suddenly, she could imagine those changes being exciting, coming with an opportunity not simply to find a purpose but to combine it with doing it with the man she loved by her side.

Is this the right time to bring it up? There was only one way to find out…

She cleared her throat. "Er, Rich. Can we talk?"

48

THAT EVENING, WEDNESDAY 6 OCTOBER

B ea nursed her Tia Maria, watching the ice cubes dance as she swirled her glass. The Dower House's drawing room felt cozy, the standard lamps casting a gleam over the assembled group. Rich and Simon were sitting in armchairs next to each other, debating the merits of some new Scandinavian crime show while Perry, sprawled elegantly on the sofa beside her, was softly reciting his lines to an enthralled Daisy.

Bea settled back, drink in hand. It was over. They had their killer.

They were still waiting for Mike to give them all the details, but a call from CID Steve to Simon two hours ago had confirmed that the vial Daisy had found in the alleyway behind the theatre had Colin's fingerprints on it. The police's theory, according to Steve, was that Colin had thrown it out of the men's toilets window on the night of Noel's death, having planned to retrieve it when the coast was clear, but it had ended up buried under the fast food bag that Daisy had uncovered, so he'd been unable to find it.

Steve had also reported to Simon that this key piece of

evidence might prompt Colin to talk as so far, he had been fairly uncooperative and wasn't saying much.

Just as Bea wondered if, indeed, the evidence had prompted Colin to change his approach, the door slowly opened, and Fraser entered. "Detective Inspector Mike Ainsley, my lady."

They all rose as Mike strode in, looking less haggard than earlier that day. The lines of exhaustion around his eyes had smoothed out, and there was a new bounce in his step.

"Ainsley!" Rich greeted him with a handshake. "Can we get you a drink?"

Mike grimaced. "Unfortunately, I'm driving. But a coffee wouldn't go amiss."

"Right away, sir," Fraser gave a short bow, then glided out of the room.

Bea smiled. "Do sit down, Mike."

She gestured at a third armchair opposite the sofa where Daisy was sitting upright, her tail wagging furiously. "Hello there, little girl." Mike laughed, ruffling her ears before sinking into his seat with a grateful sigh.

The others returned to their seats just as Fraser came in with a pot of coffee. He poured the inspector's drink, then handed it to him, and made to leave.

"Fraser," Rich called after him.

Fraser stopped and turned. "Yes, Mister Richard"

"I think you should stay and hear what the inspector has to say. After all" —he lowered his voice— "you were instrumental in catching the killer."

Fraser glanced at the door, then dipped his head. "Thank you, sir. I would like that." He walked over to the wall, put his hands behind his back, and looked at the inspector expectantly.

"First off," Mike said, blowing on his cup. "I wanted to

thank you all. We wouldn't have cracked this case nearly as quickly without your help."

Perry preened a touch, and Bea suppressed a smile.

"Not only did you work out who the real killer was," Mike continued, "but you also prevented Colin from doing a runner." He dipped his head towards Fraser, who gave a curt nod. "When we brought Mr Myatt to the station, he had his passport and a one-way ticket to Thailand in his bag. He was planning to scarper tonight."

"Thank goodness you got him when you did then," Simon said.

Mike grimaced. "Oh, yes. He'd even sent a message to Ms Belmont claiming he had to dash off abroad for a family emergency."

Clever…

Mike took a gulp of coffee before continuing, "When we searched his garage, we found he had a full drug lab set up, complete with storage space above. It turns out that's where he was manufacturing his products, mainly speed."

Bea's eyes widened. So Colin was some sort of low-level drug kingpin?

"He was actually dismantling the operation when you and Mr Juke showed up, my lady," Mike said, nodding at Bea. "If you'd been even an hour later, a lot of crucial evidence would've been destroyed. We found pills matching the ones in Noel's possession and the ones Colin had planted on himself, along with vials like the one discovered in the alley and in Tom Hatlee's bag." He took another sip of his coffee. "Not to mention a large stock of liquid nicotine. He had quite the enterprise going."

"I can't believe it," Perry murmured, looking stunned. "I mean, before all this happened, when I first met him, he would've been the last person I'd have labelled as a drug dealer and killer."

"Turns out he was supplying uppers to fairly much all of the local student population, along with teenagers at the sixth form college, and club-goers both here and in Fawstead."

Simon let out a low whistle. "That's some local business."

"So he's admitted it all, has he?" Rich asked hopefully.

Mike's face stayed neutral as he answered, "Not all of it. Well, not at first. He admitted to supplying drugs. He really had no option. His garage was a bit of a giveaway." Mike chuckled as he took another gulp of coffee, then he put down his cup and rested his hands on his knees. "That's all he would hold his hands up to initially. When we questioned him about Noel's death, he clammed up and asked to see a lawyer."

"So you can't charge him with Noel's death?" Perry asked, sounding confused.

Bea shifted forward on the sofa. *But you have the finger-print evidence…*

Mike gave a slow smile. "All in good time, Perry."

Next to her, Perry slumped back and crossed his arms. Daisy shuffled sideways and rested her head on his knee.

Bea looked at Rich. He winked.

"But of course, we have Colin's fingerprints on the vial that you found Perry," Mike said.

Perry ruffled Daisy's head. "I can't take full credit. It was Daisy's desire for a takeaway that really led us to the discovery."

While they all laughed, Daisy wagged her tail.

Mike continued, "Well, thanks to Daisy, that critical evidence linked him directly to Noel's murder, which was a game changer when we finally got to interview him this afternoon. By that time, Forensics had also matched the pills found in the garage to those found on Colin when he was taken to hospital. And we'd also found in a bin in the store-room at the theatre some discarded adhesive tape with both Colin's and Tom's fingerprints on. The bit of glass Colin had given Tom was also in there, again with both their finger-prints on it. And finally, in Colin's house, we found notes Colin had made, calculating how to set up the lighting rig so he would have time to get out of the way when it fell. When we presented all this evidence to Colin and his lawyer, not surprisingly, Colin decided to confess to secure a shorter minimum term before parole."

Phew! For one awful moment, Bea had been worried that Colin would refuse to co-operate, and the case would drag on. That would've been bad for Perry and for the Windstanton Players.

"From what Colin said in his interview, Noel was one of his best customers. He made pills to meet Noel's specific needs. But recently, Noel was taking too much speed, and Colin was worried he would kill himself, so he cut him off. Noel didn't take kindly to that. He threatened to expose Colin and his drugs enter-prise if he didn't keep supplying him the drugs. Colin knew that if that got out, his life would be ruined." Mike leaned forward in his seat. "And on top of that, Noel then demanded them for free."

"Cheeky," Perry whispered to Bea.

"So Colin carried on supplying him for a while. But as most of the cast noticed, Noel's behaviour was getting more erratic, and Colin thought it was only a matter of time before Noel said something to someone and blew the whistle on his entire operation anyway."

"So he killed Noel to keep him quiet?" Rich said.

Mike nodded.

Perry shifted on the sofa next to Bea, and resting his hand on Daisy's head, he leaned forward, his head tilted to one side. "But why didn't he leave it there? He probably would've got away with it if he hadn't tried to cover it all up."

Mike nodded again. "He said he was sure we'd put two and two together once we knew about his background. He wanted to be certain he was off the suspect list for good."

"So he staged the so-called accident?" Simon said.

"Right. He rigged it up using the pulleys that were already there. His plan was to let go of the rope as soon as the first cast member arrived that afternoon, giving himself time to dive out of the way while the pulley system slowed the release."

"So it was simply bad luck that he got hit by the debris," Rich commented, slowly shaking his head.

"And it could've been anyone who walked in and witnessed it. It just happened to be me and Ralph…" Perry trailed off, then sighed.

"Colin's intention was to leave it at that, then as soon as the play was wrapped, he planned to go abroad and start afresh," Mike continued.

Rich frowned, scratching his chin. "So why go after Perry then? Seems like overkill to me." He quickly looked at Perry. "No pun intended."

Mike gave a wry smile. "Colin admitted that when he overheard Perry and Ralph saying there were only two suspects left, he couldn't resist the opportunity. Frame Tom for attempted murder, shift the focus away from Noel, and buy himself some security."

Bea's stomach turned. *So cold and calculated.* He'd been playing with Perry's life. Silence settled over the room as they all absorbed the details and the true scope of Colin's machinations.

Bea reached over and squeezed Perry's hand, overwhelmed with gratitude that he was still here with them. "And thanks to you, that turned out to be his downfall," she whispered.

Perry squeezed back, a somewhat smug smile on his face.

"So what happens now?" Rich asked, voicing the question on everyone's mind.

Mike stood, straightening his jacket. "Hopefully, he pleads guilty. He's confessed, so I don't have any doubt that's what his lawyer will advise him to do. In the meantime, Tom's been released without charge."

Bea snapped her head around and looked at Perry, her mouth wide open. "Oh my goodness, I'd forgotten about Tom."

Perry addressed Mike, grinning. "No chance you can keep him a little longer, is there, Mike?"

They all laughed, then rose to say goodbye to the inspector.

Mike offered them a warm smile. "Once again, thanks for your help. And Mr Juke, my wife and I are very much looking forward to seeing you at the theatre. We have tickets for the Friday night." With a final nod, he followed Fraser out.

As they settled down again and discussed Colin's confession, Perry's phone chimed, breaking up the conversation. He glanced at the screen, a slow grin creeping across his face. "It's Liv," he said. "Rehearsals start again tomorrow." His smile faltered a fraction. "But she says I'm to wait until I'm well enough."

Bea studied her friend, noting the exhaustion that seemed

to have settled on him over the last hour. "And how are you feeling?"

Perry stifled a yawn. "Tired. Glad it's over." His eyes sparkled with a hint of their usual mischief. "And looking forward to getting back to the play."

"When you're fully rested," Simon interjected, his tone firm but laced with affection.

Perry rolled his eyes good-naturedly. "Yes, dear."

49

FINAL DRESS REHEARSAL. MONDAY
25 OCTOBER

The final curtain fell with a heavy thud, echoing through the near-empty auditorium. Bea winced, hoping it wasn't an omen for tomorrow's preview night.

Perry came rocketing down the aisle, still looking incredibly stylish in his tweed suit and brown brogues. He threw himself dramatically into the seat beside Bea, letting out a groan.

"That was a complete disaster!" he moaned, burying his head in his hands. "It's going to be the worst performance of *The Importance of Being Earnest* in the history of theatre. I'll be a laughing stock!"

Bea bit back a smile at his over-the-top reaction. She waited patiently for him to finish his moment of woe before patting his arm reassuringly. "It wasn't that bad," she soothed, although privately, she had to admit it had been a bit of a mess. An unusual number of the cast had fluffed their lines, Perry included, which had surprised her this late in the day.

As if reading her mind, Perry lifted his head and fixed her with a baleful stare. "Did you not see me stumble through that exchange with Gabe and Ralph towards the end? I might as well have been speaking Swahili for all the sense it made."

"I'm sure the audience won't even notice. They'll be too captivated by your devilishly charming portrayal of Algernon," Bea replied, patting his arm.

Perry snorted. "Devilishly charming? More like a bumbling idiot who can't remember his lines to save his life." Perry fanned himself dramatically with a prop handkerchief he still had in his hand. "The critics will rip us to pieces. My theatrical career will be over before it's begun!"

"Your theatrical career so far only consists of this one production."

"Exactly! And now it's ruined!"

Just then, Liv's voice boomed out from the stage. "Alright everyone, I know that felt a bit rough, but I promise you, the final dress rehearsal is always all over the place. Don't lose heart!"

"See," Bea said to him, hoping Liv was right for Perry's sake. He'd worked so hard, putting his heart and soul into this role. In fact, he'd nearly died for it. Literally! She couldn't bear to see it all fall apart now.

Ralph came bounding up to them, still in his Lady Bracknell's costume. He leaned over their seats with a conspiratorial grin. "So, my darlings," he said, his moustache twitching. "That was a bit of a jumble, but don't despair. I've been treading these boards since before you were in short trousers, young Perry. Take it from me—it'll be alright on the night."

Bea patted his arm consolingly. "Indeed. You'll be brilliant tomorrow, Perry. You were born to play Algernon."

"More like born to embarrass myself in front of the entire town," Perry muttered.

Ralph clucked his tongue. "Now, now, dear boy. You'll be

dazzling, and we'll give them a show they won't soon forget!" He winked broadly before sashaying away in a swirl of petticoats.

Perry groaned again. "We'll certainly give them something they won't forget, like a bad nightmare!"

"Right, enough of his defeatist talk," Bea said firmly. "Let's go and join the others at SaltAir. Food will make you feel better." She rose and hauled Perry to his feet.

He shrugged, then gave a wry smile. "I don't suppose it can do any harm, can it?"

———

As they stepped out into the warm evening air, they made their way along the promenade in the direction of SaltAir. The restaurant was closed to the public tonight, but Ryan had insisted on cooking a meal for his local friends to celebrate some good news.

"I can't believe Ryan sold his stake in his London restaurant," Bea mused as they walked, the salty sea breeze ruffling her long red hair. "He and Faye must really love it up here."

"I think they were ready to move on," Perry said as he wrapped his jacket around himself. "And with Ryan having signed a deal for the next three series of *Bake Off Wars*, all being filmed at Francis Court, it makes life so much easier for him to be this close by."

"And they must be thrilled to have SaltAir all to themselves now."

"They are," Perry agreed. "Although, I'm glad they've asked Simon to stay on purely as a business partner. It's the best of both worlds for him, really. He can focus on his writing and that extensive book tour next year but still have a hand in the restaurant."

"And are you looking forward to going with him on the tour?"

Perry nodded, but a flicker of hesitation crossed his face. "I am, yes. But I really want to see the Three Lakes project through to completion first. It's been such a rewarding venture, and I know it's going to be marvellous."

A pang of guilt twisted in Bea's stomach. She bit her lip. "Perry, about that. Are you sure you can manage on your own? Now that Rich and I are... you know?"

"Taking on royal duties?" Perry finished, waving her away with his hand. "Bea, my dear, I'll be fine. And anyway, you'll still be around some of the time, won't you?"

"Of course. We're only going to be doing it part-time initially."

"Well, then, we'll be absolutely fine," he said, hooking his arm through hers. "And you and Rich will make a worthy royal couple."

I hope so! As they continued along the promenade in companionable silence, Bea recalled her fateful conversation with Rich on their way home from Colin's arrest three weeks ago. She'd been so worried about him taking a break from his career, but he'd been adamant that it was a risk worth taking. She'd told him about her concerns around the press. He'd told her he accepted that the attention came with the territory but had pointed out that once the press was focused on reporting on their work rather than their love life, it would be easier.

She'd seen in his face how excited he was about all the possibilities, and he'd told her that he and Fred had already had some thoughts about some causes they would like to get behind together. She'd teased him that it felt like he and Fred were actually going to be a royal couple rather than her and him, and they'd laughed about how the press would love that.

Rich had, however, reassured her what he was most

looking forward to was them working as a team. They'd then talked about things that were close to their hearts, and by the time they'd got home, they'd already had a long list of charities and organisations they could champion together.

Bea had never seen Rich so passionate about their future, and when Sam had responded to their news a few days later with, "Does that mean we'll be able to watch the rugby in the royal box?" and had been told, "Yes," then they'd known he, too, was okay with their plans.

Rich's bosses had been surprisingly accommodating about his sabbatical, and Fred, Summer, and her mother had, as expected, been over the moon. She and Rich had still both been a little daunted when they'd finally gone to the palace last week to give her uncle, the king, their decision, but her mother must have already prepped him as her cousin, Robert, The Prince of Wales, had been there too, and father and son had greeted their news with grateful thanks before they'd discussed the draft announcement that had already been prepared.

On the way home from Surrey, Bea had felt a renewed surge of excitement for the future. Yes, it would be a big adjustment, but with Rich by her side and their friends and family cheering them on, she knew they could face any challenge that lay ahead.

As they approached the entrance to SaltAir, Perry suddenly stopped short, rubbing his face. "Bea, what if I completely botch it tomorrow night? I don't think I could bear to see disappointment in Simon's eyes."

Bea turned to face him, her hands coming to rest on his shoulders. "Perry, listen to me. You're an incredible actor, and more importantly, you have a passion for this role that shines through in every line you deliver. Trust in that and trust in yourself."

Perry's blue eyes searched her face, seeking reassurance. "But the critics…"

"Forget the critics! You're not doing this for them. You're doing it for you, for Simon, and for everyone who loves and believes in you. And that, my dear, is a far more important audience."

A slow smile spread across Perry's face, his posture straightening as if a weight had been lifted from his shoulders. "You're absolutely right. What would I do without you, Bea?"

"Probably overdose on croissants and coffee," she teased, linking her arm with his once more as they opened the door to the restaurant. "Luckily for you, I'll always be here."

As they stepped inside, the warm aroma of Ryan's cooking enveloped them, mingling with the happy chatter of their friends. Bea's heart swelled with affection as she took in the sight of Simon, Rich, Faye, Ryan, Summer, Fred, and even Daisy, all gathered around the table.

This is what it's all about, she thought as she moved to join them. *These precious moments of love, laughter, and togetherness.*

And with this new chapter beginning in her life, there would be no more murders. *Hopefully….*

50

TWO DAYS LATER. WEDNESDAY 27 OCTOBER

T*he Windstanton Echo* online article:

The Importance of Being Earnest *Shines at Windstanton's Theatre Royal*

Theatre goers gathered in anticipation at the historic Theatre Royal for the official opening night of Oscar Wilde's classic The Importance of Being Earnest *last night. The production staged by the Windstanton Players far exceeded expectations, delivering a performance that was both captivating and memorable.*

Gabe Rossi's portrayal of Jack Worthing was nothing short of masterful. His nuanced performance captured the essence of Wilde's wit and the complexity of his character, earning him resounding applause. Opposite him, Perry Juke embodied the mischievous Algernon Moncrieff with flair and charisma, bringing a fresh energy to the role that delighted the audience. Ralph Harvey, a dame of the theatre, took on the iconic role of Lady Bracknell. His performance was a tour de force, blending authoritative presence with impec-

cable comedic timing, reminding us why he remains a stalwart of the stage. Credit must be given to Olivia Belmont for her meticulous adaptation of Wilde's script. Her vision preserved the play's original charm while infusing it with contemporary relevance. The direction was seamless, guiding the ensemble cast to deliver a cohesive and dynamic performance that resonated with both seasoned theatre-goers and newcomers alike.

As well as the celebrated crime writer Simon Lattimore, husband of Perry Juke, in attendance was a large royal contingent comprising of: Lady Beatrice, the Countess of Rossex, accompanied by her fiancé, Richard Fitzwilliam, and her son, Samuel; Lord Frederick Astley and his soon-to-be bride, Summer York; and Lady Sarah Rosdale, her husband, John Rosdale, and their two children, Robbie and Charlotte.

The journey to opening night was not without its challenges. The untimely death of lead actor Noel Ashworth during rehearsals four weeks prior cast a sombre shadow over the production. However, the company's resilience and dedication transformed this adversity into a testament of their commitment to the arts, culminating in a performance that honoured Ashworth's memory. Colin Myatt, a member of the backstage team of the Windstanton Players, recently pleaded guilty to the murder of Mr Ashworth and the attempted murder of Perry Juke. He will be sentenced next month.

In royal news, it has been confirmed that Richard Fitzwilliam will be taking a sabbatical from his role as Superintendent in the City Police. This decision comes as he and Lady Beatrice prepare to undertake official royal duties to support both the King and the Prince of Wales. Furthermore, the much-anticipated wedding of the couple has been announced as Saturday, 15th April. The forthcoming union has been met with widespread enthusiasm and well-wishes from the public.

———

I hope you enjoyed *Murder Most Wilde*. If you did then please consider writing a review on Amazon or Goodreads, or even both. It helps me a lot if you let people know that you recommend it.

Want to know how Bea and Perry solved their first crime together without knowing it? Then join my readers' club and receive a FREE novella, *A Toast To Trouble* at https://www.subscribepage.com/helengoldenauthor_bmatttrm or if you'd prefer you can buy the ebook or paperback in the Amazon store.

For other books by me, take a look at the back pages.

If you want to find out more about what I'm up to you can find me on Facebook at *helengoldenauthor* or on Instagram at *helengolden_author*.

Be the first to know when my next book is available. Follow Helen Golden on Amazon, BookBub, and Goodreads to get alerts whenever I have a new release, preorder, or a discount on any of my books.

CHARACTERS IN ORDER OF APPEARANCE

MURDER MOST WILDE

Perry Juke — Lady Beatrice's business partner and BFF. Married to Simon Lattimore. Plays Algernon, Windstanton Players.

Emily 'Em' Shaw — Stage Manager, Windstanton Players.

Noel Ashworth — Originally plays Jack, Windstanton Players.

Olivia 'Liv' Belmont — Manager of the Theatre Royal and director of the Windstanton Players.

Kurt Grant — plays Lane, the butler; Canon Chasuble; and understudies for Jack, Windstanton Players.

Tom Hatlee — plays Merriman, the butler, and understudies for Algernon, Windstanton Players.

Stella Vance — plays Gwendolen, Windstanton Players.

Ralph 'Rafe' Harvey — plays Lady Bracknell, Windstanton Players.

Gina Travers — plays Cecily, Windstanton Players.

Amelia 'Millie' Trent — plays Miss Prism, Windstanton Players.

Lady Beatrice — The Countess of Rossex. Seventeenth in line to the British throne. Daughter of Charles Astley, the Duke of Arnwall and Her Royal Highness Princess Helen. Niece of the current king.

Simon Lattimore — Perry Juke's husband. Bestselling crime writer. Ex-Fenshire CID. Winner of cooking competition *Celebrity Elitechef.* Joint owner of SaltAir with Ryan Hawley.

Lord Frederick (Fred) Astley — Earl of Tilling. Lady Beatrice's elder brother and twin of Lady Sarah Rosdale. Ex-Intelligence Army Officer. Future Duke of Arnwall. Secret Special Observer (SO) MI6.

Charles Astley — Duke of Arnwall. Lady Beatrice's father.

HRH Princess Helen — Duchess of Arnwall. Mother of Lady Beatrice. Sister of the current king.

Summer York — comedian and TV presenter. One of presenting duo on *Bake Off Wars.* Lord Fred's future wife.

Sam Wiltshire — son of Lady Beatrice and the late James Wiltshire, the Earl of Rossex. Future Earl of Durrland.

James Wiltshire — The Earl of Rossex. Lady Beatrice's late husband killed in a car accident fourteen years ago. Sam's dad.

Ryan Hawley — Executive chef at *Nonnina* in Knightsbridge, judge on *Bake Off Wars,* and joint owner of SaltAir with Simon Lattimore.

Characters In Order Of Appearance

Isla Scott — Simon Lattimore's daughter.

Richard Fitzwilliam — Former Detective Chief Inspector at *PaIRS (Protection and Investigation (Royal) Service)* an organisation that provides protection and security to the royal family and who investigate any threats against them. Now a Superintendent at *City Police*, a police organisation based in the capital, London, heading up the Capital Security Liaison team.

Archie Tellis - Sam's best friend from school.

Colin Myatt — stagehand and lighting technician. Windstanton Players

Mike Ainsley — Detective Inspector at Fenshire CID (Police).

Daisy — Lady Beatrice's adorable West Highland Terrier.

Fay Mayer — Ryan Hawley's girlfriend and food journalist.

Dawn Fitzwilliam — Richard's mother.

Elise Boyce — Richard Fitzwilliam's sister

King James and Queen Olivia — King of England and his wife. Bea's uncle and aunt.

Lady Sarah Rosdale — Lady Beatrice's elder sister. Twin of Fred Astley. Manages events at Francis Court.

Detective Inspector Steve Cox/CID Steve — ex-colleague of Simon Lattimore at Fenshire CID.

Roisin — Simon Lattimore's friend and ex-flatmate who works in Forensics at Fenshire Police.

Gabe Rossi — new lead playing Jack, Windstanton Players.

Marco Rossi — Fenshire food critic and wine expert. Liv Belmont's partner.

Fraser (William) — driver/butler/handyman at The Dower House.

Mrs Fraser (Maggie) — cook/housekeeper at The Dower House.

Robert, Prince of Wales — Heir to the British throne. Bea's cousin.

Anika, Princess of Wales — Robert's soon-to-be ex-wife.

Peter Tappin — owner of Tappin's Teas in Francis-next-the-Sea.

John Rosdale — Lady Sarah's husband.

Robbie & Charlotte Rosdale — Lady Sarah's children.

A BIG THANK YOU TO…

To my editor Marina Grout. Thank you for your insight, patience, and the perfect balance of encouragement and honesty.

To Ann, Ray, Lissie, and Carolyn for being my beta readers and/or additional set of eyes before I push the final button. I really appreciate your help in making my books the best version of themselves.

To my ARC Team. You are fantastic! I really appreciate your feedback and your constant support.

To my fellow authors in the Cozy Mystery Writers' Clubhouse Group. Thank you for being a haven of advice, cheerleading, and therapy.

To you, my readers. Thank you for your loyalty, your enthusiasm, and your wonderfully suspicious minds. I'd like to thank one reader in particular - Helen Harvey who won a competition to name a character in this book. Thank you for taking part, and I hope you enjoy seeing your name in print.

As always, I may have taken a little dramatic license when it comes to police procedures, so any mistakes or misinterpretations, unintentional or otherwise, are my own.

ALSO BY HELEN GOLDEN

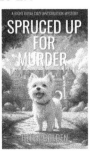

A novella lenght prequal in the series A Right Royal Cozy investiation series. With Perry and Bea working against each other, can they still save the party—or will it be ruined beyond repair along with Francis Court's reputation as a gold-standard venue?

A short prequal in the series A Right Royal Cozy Investigation. Can Perry Juke and Simon Lattimore work together to solve the mystery of the missing clock before the thief disappears? FREE novelette when you sign up to my readers' club. See end of final chapter for details. Ebook only.

First book in the A Right Royal Cozy Investigation series. Amateur sleuth, Lady Beatrice, must pit her wits against Detective Chief Inspector Richard Fitzwilliam to prove her sister innocent of murder. With the help of her clever dog, her flamboyant co-interior designer and his ex-police partner, can she find the killer before him, or will she make a fool of herself?

Second book in the A Right Royal Cozy Investigation series. Amateur sleuth, Lady Beatrice, must once again go up against DCI Fitzwilliam to find a killer. With the help of Daisy, her clever companion, and her two best friends, Perry and Simon, can she catch the culprit before her childhood friend's wedding is ruined? Also in Audio format.

The third book in the A Right Royal Cozy Investigation series. When DCI Richard Fitzwilliam gets it into his head that Lady Beatrice's new beau Seb is guilty of murder, can the amateur sleuth, along with the help of Daisy, her clever westie, and her best friends Perry and Simon, find the real killer before Fitzwilliam goes ahead and arrests Seb? Also in Audio format.

ALSO BY HELEN GOLDEN

A Prequel in the A Right Royal Cozy Investigation series.
When Lady Beatrice's husband James Wiltshire dies in a car crash along with the wife of a member of staff, there are questions to be answered. Why haven't the occupants of two cars seen in the accident area come forward? And what is the secret James had been keeping from her?

When the dead body of the event's planner is found at the staff ball that Lady Beatrice is hosting at Francis Court, the amateur sleuth, with help from her clever dog Daisy and best friend Perry, must catch the killer before the partygoers find out and New Year's Eve is ruined.

Snow descends on Drew Castle in Scotland cutting the castle off and forcing Lady Beatrice along with Daisy her clever dog, and her best friends Perry and Simon to cooperate with boorish DCI Fitzwilliam to catch a killer before they strike again.

A murder at Gollingham Palace sparks a hunt to find the killer. For once, Lady Beatrice is happy to let DCI Richard Fitzwilliam get on with it. But when information comes to light that indicates it could be linked to her husband's car accident fifteen years ago, she is compelled to get involved. Will she finally find out the truth behind James's tragic death?

An unforgettable bachelor weekend for Perry filled with luxury, laughter, and an unexpected death.
Can Bea, Perry, and his hen's catch the killer before the weekend is over?

ALSO BY HELEN GOLDEN

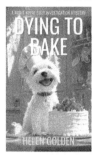  

Bake Off Wars is being filmed on site at Francis Court and everyone is buzzing. But when much-loved pastry chef and judge, Vera Bolt, is found dead on set, can Bea, with the help of her best friend Perry, his husband Simon, and her cute little terrier, Daisy, expose the killer before the show is over?

Even in a charming seaside town, secrets don't stay buried for long as Bea and Perry discover when they uncover the remains of a chef who disappeared 3 years ago. As they unravel a web of professional rivalries and buried grudges, they must race against time to solve the murder before the grand opening of Simon's new restaurant.

Lady Beatrice's peaceful holiday in Portugal is shattered when a Hollywood star's husband is found dead. What appears to be an accident soon reveals itself as murder. Tasked with clearing an innocent woman's name, Bea and Rich must untangle a web of lies to uncover the truth before it's too late.

An introductory novella in the new The Duchess of Stortford Mysteries series set in the 1890s and featuring Alice, The Duchess of Stortford.
When an heir to an earldom goes missing Alice is asked to investigate, but with the clock ticking and the gossip swirling, can Alice find the missing heir before it's too late?

It's Alice's father's 60th birthday and all of London high society has descended on Francis Court for the celebrations. But when Alice's husband is found in a heap at the bottom of the stairs, and the police declare it an accident, Alice believes it's murder. Helped by her maid and footman, can she find out what happened before the guests disburse and a killer goes free.

PAPERBACKS AVAILABLE FROM WHEREVER YOU BUY YOUR BOOKS.

www.ingramcontent.com/pod-product-compliance
Lightning Source LLC
La Vergne TN
LVHW090143300625
815006LV00007B/49